PRAISE FOR PERILOUS TRUST - OFF THE GRID: FBI SERIES #1

#1 NEW YORK TIMES BESTSELLING AUTHOR BARBARA FREETHY

"Perilous Trust is a non-stop thriller that seamlessly melds jaw-dropping suspense with sizzling romance, and I was riveted from the first page to the last...Readers will be breathless in anticipation as this fast-paced and enthralling love story evolves and goes in unforeseeable directions."

— *USA Today HEA Blog*

"Barbara Freethy's first book in her OFF THE GRID series is an emotional, action packed, crime drama that keeps you on the edge of your seat...I'm exhausted after reading this but in a good way. 5 Stars!"

— *Booklovers Anonymous*

"Getting tangled up with Perilous Trust is a rush. Barbara Freethy sets the adrenaline level so high that it takes a while to come back down to solid ground. A tortured love affair sets off a chain of events that are explosive and deadly. The suspense is killer, the danger is intense and the electricity generated between Sophie and Damon is off the charts. All come together to a create a lethally seductive thriller."

— *I Love Romance Blog*

"The adventure that Barbara Freethy takes us on in PERILOUS TRUST is full of twists and turns. It is a perfect suspense that will keep you guessing until the very last moment. This book definitely deserves 5 stars."

— *Reading Escape Reviews*

"Perilous Trust was an action packed romantic suspense novel that from the first page you are bang in the middle of the story. I liked Barbara' Freethy's writing, the story was told in duel POVs which definitely made for a good read to see both perspectives of the case developing. I also liked the side characters woven into the story. I am looking forward to seeing more of them in the series."

— *Reading Away the Days Blog*

"This book had a great plot, full of action and suspense. There are some great secondary characters who I can't wait to have their stories told. The plot twists are pretty awesome and even better, I couldn't figure out who the actual bad guy was. I can't wait to read the next book in this series."

— *Nice Ladies Naughty Books Blog*

"Perilous Trust is such a thrill ride! I love the mystery and the intense action of the characters and plot."

— *Cuz I'm a Nerd Blog*

"It's been a while since I have had the fun of reading a brilliant romantic suspense book – Perilous Trust gets me back into this genre with a bang!"

— *For the Love of Fictional Worlds*

"A uniquely seductive, gripping and exhilarating romantic suspense that is fast paced and action packed...Barbara Freethy is the ultimate seducer. She hooked me and slowly and keenly reeled me in. I was left in a trance. I just cannot wait for the next book."

— *MammieBabbie.com*

"This was my first time reading Barbara Freethy and I loved this story from start to finish. Right from the start the tension sets in, goodness, my heart was starting to beat a little fast by the end of the prologue! I found myself staying up late finishing this book, and that is something I don't normally do."

— *My Book Filled Life Blog*

"The suspense and action continued throughout the whole novel really keeping the pacing going strong and the reader engaged. I flew through this story as Sophie and Damon went from escaping one danger into having to fend off another. I'd definitely recommend this novel to anyone who like suspense romance or even contemporary romance. Its fast paced, entertaining and filled with sexually tense moments that would appeal to any romance lover!"

— *PopCrunchBoomBooks.com*

"This was just a well-written story with lots of twists and turns. Who's bad? Who's good? Who killed Sophie's father? There's also lots of hot and steamy romance! I'm looking forward to the next installment! 5 Sexy Stars!

— *Knottygirlreview.com*

Also By Barbara Freethy

RECKLESS WHISPER

Off The Grid: FBI Series

BARBARA FREETHY

HYDE
STREET
—PRESS—

HYDE STREET PRESS
Published by Hyde Street Press
1325 Howard Avenue, #321, Burlingame, California 94010

Printed in the United States of America

Cover design by Damonza.com

ISBN: 978-1-944417-36-9

One

—⟫✖⟪—

*Y*ou'll be sorry."

The hoarse, whispered words shook her out of sleep. Special Agent Bree Adams sat up in bed, holding her phone closer to her ear. "Who is this?"

Silence followed, but she could hear breathing.

"If you want to threaten me, don't you want me to know who you are?" she challenged.

The call disconnected.

She drew in a breath and let it out, looking around her shadowy bedroom. Through the curtains, she could see the New York City lights, and hear the loud noises from the garbage trucks making their way through the back alley behind her apartment building. The clock on the bedside table told her it was just past dawn.

Getting out of bed, she threw on a robe and shivered as she walked into the hallway of her one-bedroom apartment to turn on the heat. It was early October, and it definitely felt like winter was coming. The cold mornings were actually a welcome change from the long, hot summer, a summer where so many things had changed. There had been a massive shakeup at the FBI New York field office in June, the fallout of which was still rippling through the building.

As she entered her kitchen and turned on the coffeemaker, she looked around her apartment. Everything appeared to be normal. Nothing was out of place. But she felt unsettled, which was obviously what the caller had been going for.

How had he gotten her number? As a federal agent, she used every precaution to protect her personal life. She'd ask one of the techs to see if they could trace the call, but it was doubtful that would be successful. Prepaid burner phones that could be dumped after every call made tracing criminals through their phones extremely difficult.

The male voice had also been deliberately altered, which meant that whoever was calling her had been smart enough to mask his voice. *Was that because she knew him?*

Since joining the FBI five years ago, she'd spent most of her career working child abductions and had become a member of the CARD program seven months earlier, making her part of one of several Critical Action Response Detail teams who sprang into action to help local law enforcement find an endangered child within the first critical hours after an abduction.

It was a job filled with highs and lows—sometimes frustrating, discouraging, terrifying and occasionally jubilant. But she loved it. Being able to put a family back together always made her feel a bit more whole.

Her phone rang again, and her nerves tightened.

Walking quickly back into the bedroom, she picked up the phone from the bed, steeling herself to hear the same creepy, cryptic voice.

But it was her team leader, Special Agent Dan Fagan, and she knew what that meant.

"What happened?" she asked.

"Ten-year-old disappeared from the backstage area of a school concert last night just after eight p.m. A broken white rose was found near the back door."

Her body tightened. This would be the fourth time in six months that a child had disappeared from a school event. The eleven-year-old girl in Newark had been found dead seven days later, the twelve-year-old girl from Albany had also been killed a week after her disappearance, and the twelve-year-old girl from Philadelphia had been found alive in an abandoned building, probably only one day before she would have met the same sad ending. While they'd been thrilled to save that child's life, the kidnapper was still in the wind.

Had he struck again?

Was the creepy phone call she'd just received somehow connected to this incident?

She'd been the one to track down the girl in Philadelphia. She'd been the face on the news. She'd been the one to promise that they would do everything they could to find the White Rose Kidnapper, as the press had dubbed him.

"Where did it happen?" she asked.

"Chicago. He's apparently moving west."

Her heart jumped into her throat, and the phone slipped out of her hand, the crash bringing her back to reality.

She picked it up, seeing a crack on the screen, which felt prophetic. She'd left Chicago a long time ago and vowed to never go back.

"Is the Midwest team on it?" She could barely manage to get the words out through her tight lips.

"Yes. But they want you to consult. You've been working up a profile on this guy for months. How fast can you get to the airport?"

"I'll be there within the hour. But you should know—I just got a threatening call, altered male voice. He said I'd be sorry."

"That was it?"

"That was it," she confirmed.

"I'll get Oscar to look into it," Dan said, referring to one of their techs. "You get yourself to Chicago and be careful."

She set the phone down and drew in several deep breaths. She would go to Chicago because it was her job, and a child's life was on the line.

But just because she was going back to Chicago didn't mean she was going home.

After landing in Chicago just after nine a.m. on Wednesday morning, Bree received a thorough briefing at the Chicago FBI field office, led by Assistant Special Agent in Charge (ASAIC) Warren Hobbs. Warren was a stern-looking man in his mid-forties with black hair and dark eyes, and from what Bree knew of Hobbs, he was a smart, aggressive investigator, but he clearly had no patience for slow thinkers.

His briefing had been on point, from the AMBER alert, to the crime scene investigation, witness and family interviews, neighborhood searches, and media coverage. When it was over, Hobbs called on her to read the agency in on the details of the previous abductions linked to the White Rose Kidnapper and the behavioral profile they'd built so far.

Just like the three other girls, Hayley had vanished from her school, a place where she should have been safe. Bree had worked up several theories on why the school setting appealed to the kidnapper, why a white rose was left at the scene, and the fact that all three previously abducted children had been kept alive for seven days before they were either discovered or killed. If the timing held true, they had less than one week to find Hayley alive.

They had few details regarding the identity of the kidnapper, other than that he was male, around six feet tall, with a muscular build and brown hair. The surviving victim had been blindfolded through most of her ordeal, and on the few occasions the blindfold had been removed, the kidnapper had worn a ski mask to obscure his features. The victim had stated that the kidnapper's voice was deep and low and always menacing. He'd said very little, but he'd referred to her as his pretty little girl and occasionally had quoted a phrase from the Bible about redemption or revenge.

Bree thought that the seven-day timeframe might possibly be tied into the biblical idea that God had created the world in seven days, and that the kidnapper might be creating his own world in that amount of time. Whatever the reason, every minute counted if they were going to find the latest victim, Hayley Jansen, alive.

When the briefing ended just before eleven, she took a cab across town to meet with Hayley's parents. While she'd be retracing steps already taken by the Chicago special agents and the local police, it was important for her to make her own assessment, and also determine whether this could be a copycat event.

The Philadelphia case had hit the national news, and someone in Chicago might have decided to make their own play, ride someone else's coattails toward their own fame.

There were a few small differences in the abduction scenarios. The other three girls had all been blonde with brown eyes while Hayley had brown hair and brown eyes. The white rose found near the back door of Hayley's abduction had been a hybrid tea rose while the other three roses had been floribundas. They were small details and might mean nothing, or they might mean a lot.

--->>><<<---

The Jansens lived in Lincoln Park, an upscale neighborhood on the north side of Chicago. Their two-story, three-bedroom home was on a beautiful tree-lined street, not far from the Lincoln Park Zoo, Lake Shore Drive and Lake Michigan.

This neighborhood was a far cry from the city streets she had roamed as a child, which was both reassuring and disturbing. As a kid, she'd always believed that children who lived in houses like these had everything they needed, that they were safe and protected. Of course, now she knew better, but it still felt wrong when she went into a community where residents weren't used to being exposed to the dark side of humanity.

As she got out of the cab, a blast of cold wind almost knocked her off her feet. The Windy City was living up to its reputation, but she was okay with that. Maybe the cold would freeze her heart and keep the memories away.

She made her way across the street, through the crowd of reporters getting ready to file their stories for the noon news. After flashing her badge, the local police officer waved her inside.

Stepping into the entry, her practiced eye swept the interior, noting quick details. The home was nicely decorated with paintings on the walls, sleek hardwood floors and furniture that looked comfortable and remarkably clean, considering there were apparently three children living in the house. Hayley had a younger brother who was six and a sister who was four.

The children seemed confused and out of sorts, the little girl crying, as she and her brother were taken into the kitchen by their grandparents. Other assorted family members and close family friends made themselves scarce as she sat down with Hayley's parents, Mark and Lindsay Jansen, in the living room.

She knew quite a bit about the Jansens already. They were an attractive, fit couple, in their early forties. They had met in college and married shortly thereafter, celebrating their twentieth wedding anniversary three weeks earlier. Mark was the chief financial officer for Buckner Investments. Lindsay was a former teacher, now a stay-at-home mom.

Hayley was their oldest child. She had been adopted after the Jansens experienced eight years of infertility and two years on adoption waiting lists. To their shock and amazement, when Hayley was four years old, they'd conceived their son Connor, and two years later, their daughter Morgan.

Hayley's adoption had been closed, and while the Jansens knew nothing about the biological parents, a local judge had unsealed the records shortly after Hayley's disappearance. The biological mother, Samantha Harkness, had been a sixteen-year-old teenager living in Hammond, Illinois, a poverty and crime-ridden suburb of Chicago. She'd died of an overdose, six months after Hayley's birth. The biological father was unknown. While the police couldn't completely rule out the possibility that someone from the bio family was involved, it didn't seem likely, especially not with the white rose connection.

Mark took Lindsay's hand as they settled on the couch. He had the look of a runner, long, lean, and thin. He wore gray slacks and a light-blue, button-down shirt. Lindsay had on black yoga pants and a form-fitting zip-up jacket. Neither looked like they had slept. They were pale, with shadows under their eyes and desperation written across the lines of their faces.

"What can we tell you to help us get our daughter back?" Mark asked quickly. "The other FBI agent said you're some kind of expert?"

"I've investigated similar cases. I know you've already told your story several times, and I promise this won't take long, but I need you to tell me again when you realized Hayley was missing."

"All right. Whatever it takes to bring my baby home." He drew in a breath. "Hayley was supposed to perform a ballet number at the fall concert last night," he said, his voice thick with pain. "When the curtain came up for her group, she wasn't on stage." He swallowed hard. "We went into the back to find out what was wrong. We thought she had gotten stage fright. She can be shy at times. The teacher said she'd seen her go into the bathroom with Grace before their group performed."

"But Hayley wasn't there," Lindsay continued. "I went into the restroom, and there was no one inside. I looked all around for her. You can't imagine the terror that ran through my mind. It was her school, a safe place. Everyone backstage knew her." Her voice broke as a tear ran down her face.

"The back door to the stage was open," Mark said, when his wife faltered in the story. "We ran into the staff parking lot. Hayley wasn't there, but one of the other kids said she saw Hayley leave with someone. That's when the police were called."

"That child would be Grace Roberts?"

"Yes. She's a year younger than Hayley, but they have been taking ballet together for the last two years, and they've become good friends," Lindsay put in. "Grace said she thought Hayley had just gotten scared and decided not to perform." Lindsay took an anguished breath. "You have to find my daughter, Agent Adams. She must be so scared. I can't imagine what she's thinking." More tears ran down Lindsay's face, and Mark pulled his wife into a tight embrace.

"Please," he said, heartbreak in his voice, as he looked back at her. "Find her. She's our baby girl. I've already told the detective I'll take a polygraph. I'll do whatever needs to be done, as will Lindsay and anyone else in the family. I know the father is always the first suspect. Do what you have to do to cross me off the suspect list, so we can figure out who took her."

She nodded, seeing sincerity and candor in Mark's eyes. "Is there anyone who has a problem with you or your wife? Any incidents with neighbors, friends, coworkers? A road rage incident you might have forgotten about? Any small problem that you don't think is connected but might be?"

"No," he said. "We've thought and thought all night long. We don't have problems with people. Our lives have been drama free until now. We can't imagine anyone who would want to hurt us or Hayley. She's just a sweetheart."

"And no one has contacted you?" she pressed, hating to put them through this, but finding Hayley was all that mattered. "There hasn't been any request for money? No one has told you not to tell the police or work with the FBI?"

"No," Mark said, shaking his head again. "I wish someone had contacted me. I'd sell everything we own to get Hayley back."

Mark and Lindsay were saying everything she would have expected them to say, and their behavior was absolutely consistent with what they were going through, but she wanted to split up the husband and wife team for at least a few moments.

"Mrs. Jansen—can I see Hayley's bedroom? I want to know as much about her as I can, and it helps to see where she sleeps," she said, getting to her feet.

Lindsay stood up, wiping the tears off her wet cheeks. "Of course. I'll show you."

Bree was happy that Mark chose not to accompany them upstairs. He seemed to have the bigger, strong personality, and she wanted to know what Lindsay would say on her own, if her husband wasn't in the room.

As Bree stepped into Hayley's bedroom, she felt like she was walking into a childhood dream. Everything was white and pink and purple. There were pillows and stuffed animals on the bed, shelves filled with books, an overflowing toy box, and a big bay window that overlooked the front street.

She couldn't imagine what it would feel like to grow up in a room so special, so safe, so comforting and then to be ripped out of it.

Hayley Jansen was not a tough, street kid; she was a pampered princess, just as she should be, and they needed to find her fast.

Walking across the room, she paused in front of a family photo. It had been taken before Hayley's siblings had been born, and the brown-haired little girl was about two years old. She looked happy and well loved.

"That's one of my favorite pictures. I like to have photos of each one of my kids on their own," Lindsay said.

"I understand Hayley was adopted."

"Yes. She's our miracle. We tried for ten years to have a child or to adopt, and we'd almost given up hope when Hayley came along. She was the prettiest baby I'd ever seen, even though she was bald as could be, with only about three strands of hair on her head." Lindsay gave her a sad smile. "She smiled at me, and I knew she was mine. She was home. She was where she was supposed to be."

Lindsay's heartfelt words tugged at her heart. Interviewing the parents was always tough, and it took all she had to keep it together and focus on the job.

"I understand your other two kids are your biological children?"

"Yes. It was crazy. All those years of trying and nothing. Then Hayley turns four, and I find out I'm pregnant with Connor. Morgan came two years later. I love them all so much. I don't love Hayley less because I didn't give birth to her. She's my child—one hundred percent."

"I believe you," she said, feeling as if Lindsay needed some sort of reassurance.

"The police asked me about her biological parents, but we never knew anything about them. The mother wanted a closed adoption, and we did, too. We wanted to be Hayley's parents. We didn't want anyone else in the mix. Maybe that sounds selfish, but it felt like it would be too complicated any other way."

"Does Hayley know she's adopted?"

"No. We're going to tell her when she's older."

"You're not afraid someone in the family will say something to her?"

"My parents know, and they feel the same way we do— that Hayley isn't ready to deal with it. Mark's parents are deceased."

"What about friends, cousins, neighbors?"

"There are a few other people who know, but they would never say anything." Lindsay paused, giving Bree a questioning look. "Do you know anything about the biological parents? I asked the detectives, and they wouldn't say. Are they involved in this?"

"I honestly don't know. But we're going to run down every lead as fast as we can. I can promise you that."

"The waiting is torture."

"I know. Now, tell me what Hayley is like."

"She's shy, but she can be funny when she's with her friends, when she feels comfortable. She's very caring. She loves animals, especially bunnies," she said with a watery laugh as she tipped her head toward the pile of animals. "Unfortunately, my son Connor is allergic, so we haven't been able to bring a pet into the home. It's crazy now that there are dogs searching for her. The detectives took some of her things, so the dogs could pick up her scent." Lindsay's mouth shook again. "I want them to find her alive. I can't bear the thought that they won't."

"Try to stay positive."

"You've worked on cases like this before? Something to do with the white rose?"

"Yes."

"What happened to those other children?"

"The last one was found alive. She's going to be okay." Bree hoped that piece of news would give Lindsay a little hope.

But Lindsay focused in on three words. "The last one? What about the others?"

"We don't know if Hayley's case is tied to the other abductions."

"But it sounds like it might be."

"We're going to do everything we can to find your daughter. You have a huge team looking for Hayley."

"I know. Mark and I are so grateful. We just want to bring her home, take her in our arms and never let her go."

"I hope that happens really soon," she said, as they headed downstairs.

When they reached the entry, Mark came out of the living room and pulled his wife into an embrace. She left the two of them in their anguish as she walked out of the house, pushing her way past reporters who asked her if she had anything new to report. She made no comment. She was definitely not the official spokesperson for this case.

As she reached the end of the block, she pulled out her phone to check on the other address she'd been given. She wanted to check in with their only eyewitness—Grace Roberts. She lived just three blocks away. While Grace had also been interviewed extensively, Bree wanted to ask a few of her own questions. Now that some time had passed since Hayley's abduction the night before, Grace might remember more than she had previously.

She was almost to Grace's house when her phone vibrated.

Pulling it out of the pocket of her navy-blue slacks, she saw an unidentified number. Her pulse sped up. "Agent Adams," she said crisply.

"So formal," the altered voice said. "You and I are going to get very close…Bree."

"Then maybe I should know who you are."

"That would take the fun away."

"What do you want?"

"What you want—a worthy competitor."

"I'm not competing with you."

"Aren't you?" He paused. "I like it better when you wear your hair down." At the end of his statement, the call disconnected.

Her gut tightened as she looked around the neighborhood. *Was he watching her?*

She thought she saw a curtain flutter in a window across the street, but that could be anyone, or just her imagination.

"You want to compete," she muttered. "You better be ready to lose."

She slid her phone into her pocket, wondering what the game was, and if Hayley was also an unwilling player.

Two

➤➤◄◄

"Do the police have any leads?" Nathan Bishop asked, as he slid onto the stool at his sister's kitchen island and watched her fix lunch for her daughter Grace, who would normally be at school. But since Grace's friend, Hayley Jansen, had disappeared from the concert last night, Josie had kept Grace at home. His sister and niece were both shaken and terrified about what had happened to Hayley, and he couldn't blame them. He was just happy to see that Josie had calmed down since the night before.

"Not that I know of," Josie replied, pausing from making tuna fish sandwiches to pull her dark-brown hair into a ponytail.

His sister looked exhausted and anxious, taking him back in time to the life they'd lived as kids, when sleeplessness, hunger, and anxiety had plagued their every step. He hated to see her back in that state of mind. She'd been doing so well the last several years, and Grace needed her mom to be whole. He was going to do everything he could to make sure she stayed that way.

"The police keep sending people over to talk to Grace, and I really wish they'd stop," Josie added. "She has told them all she knows, and it upsets her to think about what has happened to Hayley."

"Where is Grace?" The house seemed unusually quiet.

Grace was a high-energy, talkative kid, and when she was around, she was always noticeable.

"She's in my bed, watching a movie. I really wanted Kyle to stay home with us today, but he couldn't. It's always work, work, work with him. Even after the night we had, he still puts his clients ahead of us."

He really didn't want to ask about her marriage. He'd never been a super fan of her husband Kyle, but he tried to keep that opinion away from his sister. He told himself that as long as Kyle took care of Josie and Grace, he could deal with Kyle's over-the-top arrogance.

Josie suddenly squealed as she accidentally stabbed herself with the knife. "Damn, damn, damn." She moved to the sink to run water over her finger.

"You need to take a breath, Josie."

She grabbed a paper towel and wrapped it around her finger. "How the hell am I supposed to do that when Hayley is God knows where with God knows who? It could have been Grace, Nathan. She was right there. She went into the bathroom with Hayley. If she had stayed there with Hayley…"

He saw Josie's bottom lip start to tremble, and he slid off the stool and walked around the counter, putting his hands on her shoulders the way he'd always done when she was a little girl and the world was getting too scary. "It's going to be all right. They'll find Hayley."

"You don't know that. She could be—"

"Stop. Don't think the worst."

"But the worst happens." She gazed into his eyes. "We both know that."

He couldn't argue with that statement. "Well, I hope it doesn't happen this time. Can I help you finish the sandwiches?"

"I've got it." She slipped away to grab a Band-Aid out of the drawer. As she put it on, she said, "Let's talk about something else."

He was immensely relieved by the suggestion. "Go for

it."

"What's happening with you and Adrienne?"

He inwardly groaned as he grabbed a bottled water from the fridge. "How about a different subject?"

"We can't talk about your girlfriend?"

"She's not my girlfriend. We've just been hanging out."

"For two months," she said pointedly. "In which time, I've only seen her once. I want to get to know her better. Why don't you bring her around?"

"I will."

"When?"

"Sometime."

"I can keep secrets, you know."

He frowned at her comment. "I'm not worried about that."

"Good. Because you've moved beyond your past, Nathan. You're a completely different person."

"Exactly, so no reason to talk about it."

"But who you used to be—where we come from—it's part of you. You're going to have to share it with someone at some point."

"Why would I do that?" he challenged, taking a swig of water.

"Because it won't be a real relationship until you're completely honest."

"Who said anything about having a real relationship?"

She made a face at him. "Don't you want what I have? A family? The kind of family we always wanted?"

"I have you and Grace for that." As he finished speaking, the doorbell rang. "Are you expecting someone?"

"No, and the police promised me that they'd keep Grace's name out of the news, but I'm worried a reporter will find us."

"I'll get it. I'll send whoever it is away."

"Thanks," she said with relief. "Once they're gone, we'll have lunch."

He walked down the hall and opened the front door, prepared to get rid of whoever was there. But the woman on the porch stole the breath out of his chest... her light-brown hair, her compelling green eyes, the hot, sexy mouth that he'd spent too many nights dreaming about.

Damn!

He hadn't seen her in over ten years, but the time in between suddenly vanished, and he felt like he was once again standing on the edge of a ledge with a woman who could save him or push him off.

Her jaw dropped as the same kind of wonder filled her gaze.

"Nathan?"

Her sweet voice socked him in the gut.

"Bree? What the hell are you doing here?" The question came out more aggressive than it probably should have, but he wasn't ready to see her again.

"I was going to ask you the same question." She licked her lips. "I'm looking for Grace Roberts."

"Are you a reporter now?"

"No." She pulled open her navy-blue blazer, revealing navy-blue slacks and a white shirt, but it was the shiny piece of metal at her waist that shocked him for the second time in the last sixty seconds. "I'm an FBI special agent."

"No way!"

"It's true."

"You? You became a fed? How did they let *you* in?"

She frowned at his attacking words. "They let me in, because I'm good at the job. Who is Grace to you?"

"She's my niece."

Now it was Bree's turn to be surprised. "Seriously? Grace is Josie's daughter? Josie is okay? Last time I saw her, I wasn't sure..."

"She's been okay for a while," he said shortly. "Up until last night when one of her daughter's best friends was abducted. Now she's a mess, terrified for Grace and for Hayley."

"That's why I'm here. I need to speak to Grace about what happened. Let me in, Nathan."

He suddenly realized he was blocking the door. He took a step back and waved her into the house, which felt like the absolutely wrong thing to do.

Letting her into Josie's house, into his life—was he crazy?

But this wasn't about the past; it was about Hayley.

"I'll get my sister. Wait here." He walked down the hall and into the kitchen, still having trouble taking in a full breath.

"Who was it?" Josie asked. "A reporter?"

"No." He closed the kitchen door behind him. "It's an FBI agent. She wants to talk to Grace."

Josie frowned. "But Grace already spoke to the police—several different detectives. It's just going to upset her all over again. Can't you get rid of her?"

"Believe me, I want to," he said tersely. "But she's not going anywhere."

"Then I'll talk to her. I'll tell her Grace isn't up to it."

"Wait." He grabbed her arm as she came around the counter.

"What?" Josie asked, a question in her eyes.

"It's Bree."

She blinked in confusion, and then that confusion turned to shock. "Bree? No."

"Yes."

"She's an FBI agent? How—how is that possible?"

"No idea. But she showed me her badge. She's working on Hayley's disappearance."

Josie stared back at him. "I didn't think she'd ever come back to Chicago."

"I didn't, either."

"I don't know exactly what happened between—"

"And it's not important," he said, cutting her off. "Just don't say anything personal about you or me or what we're doing now."

"What are you worried about, Nathan?"

"Everything," he muttered, letting go of his sister's arm.

As Josie left the room, he drew in a deep breath. He needed a minute to get his head together.

Bree—he'd never thought he'd see her again.

The years had been good to her. In fact, she looked better now than she had the last time he'd seen her. Then she'd been pale, scared, and a little broken. Now, she was sharp, clear-eyed, confident, and…strikingly pretty.

She'd clearly gotten her life together.

Well, so had he, and he wasn't going to let her drag him backward.

Bree paced restlessly around the living room, her nerves on edge, her stomach churning with nausea, her head aching with tension. She'd told herself that coming back to Chicago did not mean going back in time, but that's exactly where Nathan Bishop had taken her.

Nathan! How could he be here? How could the only eyewitness be connected to him?

It was improbable and yet it was true.

The last time she'd seen him had been at the bus station. She'd been eighteen; he'd been nineteen—skinny and long-haired and…angry. He didn't want to be there, but she'd called in an old debt, and he'd paid up.

Apparently, his anger at her hadn't diminished over the years. He had definitely not looked happy to see her.

But he had looked good. He'd become a man—a muscled, fit, handsome man. He still had the thick brown hair that always looked windblown, a shadow of beard on his jaw, and light-brown eyes that could be kind and friendly but also piercing and judgmental.

When they were kids, she'd mostly seen the friendly side of Nathan, but as they got older, as they moved into their late teens, that had changed.

A woman entered the living room, and the butterfly tattoo on her neck told her it was Josie, Nathan's little sister.

Josie's hair was darker than she remembered. Her skin was healthy, her eyes worried, but she looked far more alert now than she had as a drug-addicted teenager.

She'd actually gone with Josie when she'd gotten the tattoo against the wishes of her big brother. Josie had wanted a symbol of freedom, something to strive for, something to believe in, and Bree had wanted that for her, too.

In return, Josie had not treated her very well.

Her relationship with both Bishops had certainly been fraught with problems.

Josie shook her head in bemusement. "Nathan said it was you, but I can't believe it—Bree Larson."

"Actually, it's Bree Adams now."

"You got married?" Josie asked.

"No, I just changed my last name."

"To become an FBI agent?"

"I had a lot of reasons. But, yes, I am an agent. I'm part of a critical action team that assists with child abductions, and I need to speak to Grace." If she could keep this all business, it would be better for all of them.

Josie stiffened, the bewildered look in her eyes turning into protective maternal fierceness. "Grace has already told the police everything she knows, and it upsets her to talk about it. She and Hayley are very close."

"I understand," she said gently. "I know she's scared—as are you, because Grace was so close to Hayley when this happened."

Josie's eyes watered. "It could have been her."

"But it wasn't. Grace is safe, and I promise I will do everything I can not to upset her, but I need to speak to her now."

Josie stared back at her. "You were always so strong. I admired that for a long time. But then you changed into someone else."

"Look, I don't want to cut you off, Josie, but time is important right now. And I'm not here to talk about the past. We need to find Hayley, and we need Grace's help to do that."

"I'll get her. But be careful, Bree. I may not have ever stood up for myself, but I will stand up for Grace."

"The last thing I would want to do is hurt your child."

As Josie left the living room, Bree let out a breath of relief, but her calm was short-lived as Nathan returned to the room.

He'd always been tall, six foot one or two, but he had a much stronger presence now, or maybe she was just very aware of his angry wariness. His eyes were shooting sparks at her, and she didn't know if the emotion was coming from the past or from right now.

But she couldn't find the words to ask. There was too much to say and too little time.

Thankfully, Josie came back into the room with a little girl wearing leggings and a big pink sweater, her long, dark-brown hair loose around her shoulders.

Grace was the spitting image of Josie as a little girl. "She looks just like you," she murmured, the words slipping out before she could stop them. She wanted to keep this professional, not personal, but already she'd stumbled.

Grace blinked and looked at her mom. "She knew you when you were my age, Mommy?"

"Yes," Josie said. "Bree is a—friend—from a long time ago. And like I said, she has a couple of questions to ask you."

"Why don't we all sit down?" Bree suggested, taking a seat on the couch.

Grace and Josie sat down on the sofa facing her, while Nathan took up a protective position by the entryway, his arms folded across his chest.

"I heard you're a really good ballet dancer," she said to Grace, giving the little girl a warm smile. "I always wanted to take ballet, but I never had the chance."

"I'm not as good as Hayley," Grace said solemnly. "Do you know where she is?"

"No. But I'm looking for her. You told the police that you

saw Hayley leave through the stage door with someone."

Grace nodded and looked at her mom.

"Just tell her what you remember." Josie put her arm around Grace's shoulder.

"You went to the bathroom with Hayley," Bree encouraged. "What happened after that?"

"Hayley was taking too long. She was really nervous. The bathroom smelled bad, so I left. I went over to our group. Our teacher, Miss Delancey, told us to stay close, because it was almost our turn. When it was time to go on, Hayley wasn't there. I was at the back of the line, so I went to find her, and I saw her going through the door. I thought she decided not to dance. She was scared about forgetting the steps. Then Miss Delancey called me, and I went on the stage. I didn't know someone took her until after our dance."

Grace was a smart, articulate girl. Now, if she could just get her to remember a few more details. "You said the person was wearing a puffy black coat and a blue beanie, is that right?"

Grace nodded.

"You couldn't see their hair?"

The little girl shook her head.

"Do you remember if there were any words on their clothes? Like for a sports team or something?"

"I didn't see any."

"And you couldn't tell if it was a man or a woman?"

"I think it was a man, because he was so tall, but I don't know for sure."

"Do you remember what kind of shoes he was wearing? Tennis shoes? Boots? Work shoes?"

Grace thought for a moment, then shook her head. "I don't know."

"Was he holding Hayley's hand?"

"No, he had his arm around her. Is Hayley going to be all right?"

"I hope so. You're doing really good, Grace. You're being very helpful."

"Hayley is scared of the dark. Do you think she's in the dark?" Grace asked, fear in her eyes.

Bree could hear the terror in the little girl's voice, and she wanted to reassure her, but she also didn't want to lie to her. "Is there anything else you remember, Grace? Did you see a car through the open stage door?"

"There were lights outside. They were bright. I think they came from a car."

"Was Hayley yelling or kicking her feet or trying to pull away from the person?"

Grace's mouth turned down in a frown, and then she slowly shook her head. "She wasn't doing anything."

Was that because Hayley knew the person who had come into the backstage area of a school concert? Was the kidnapper someone who was familiar to people at the school so that they wouldn't be questioned?

The police were already looking into the janitorial staff and everyone else at the school, but it wouldn't hurt to keep what Grace had just told her in mind. "Did Hayley ever talk about anyone bothering her? Was she mad or upset with anyone?"

"She said her dad was mad at her for not cleaning up her room, and she might not be able to go to the park with me this weekend."

"Anyone else?"

"Carter told her she was clumsy, and she was going to fall during our show," Grace added. "I told him not to be mean and that Hayley wasn't going to fall."

"Who is Carter?"

"He's a boy in our class. He always says rude things."

She didn't think this Carter had anything to do with Hayley's disappearance, but the more Grace talked, the more she might remember.

"I want Hayley to come home," Grace said, her bottom lip starting to waver.

"I think that's enough," Josie interrupted, obviously disturbed by her daughter's distress.

"You did good, Grace," she told the little girl.

Grace sniffed. "I should have run after Hayley. I should have saved her."

"No. That wouldn't have helped. And you're doing exactly what you're supposed to be doing now. You're telling us what you remember."

"Why don't you go upstairs and finish watching your show?" Josie said. "I'll bring up lunch in a few minutes."

Grace slid off the couch, then paused, something odd in her eyes as she looked back at them. "There was something shiny on the man's hand. The hand that was on Hayley's back. Like Daddy's big ring."

"Your daddy's wedding ring?" she probed.

"No, the baseball ring."

"My husband has a ring from the Chicago Cubs when they won the World Series," Josie put in.

"Really? What does he do for the Cubs?"

"He doesn't work directly for the team. He's a real-estate developer, and he has been working with the organization to buy up some of the properties adjacent to the ballfield for additional expansion of outfield seating. You know how small Wrigley Field is, how close the apartment buildings are."

"Part of its charm," she muttered.

"At any rate, since the team hadn't won a world series since 1908, they gave out 1908 rings to staff and employees," Josie continued. "Basically, anyone who had anything to do with the team got one. They're not as nice as what the players got, of course."

Was there defensiveness in Josie's voice? Had Josie just picked up on the fact that her daughter had identified the kidnapper as having a ring similar to the one her father wore?

"Was your husband with you at the concert last night?" she asked.

"No, he had to work late. Are we done here?"

She could see that Josie was finished talking, and she'd

probably gotten all she could from Grace. "That's all for now."

"Go on upstairs, honey," Josie told Grace.

Grace paused by her uncle on her way out of the room. "Do you want to watch a movie with me, Uncle Nathan?"

"I'll be up in a bit," he told her, giving her a smile.

As Bree saw Nathan's lips curve up in kindness and affection, she was reminded of a much younger Nathan—the kid who'd once been her friend, who'd given her the last bite of a shared candy bar, who'd dreamed with her about a better life, a pretty house by the sea.

But that kid had disappeared long before she'd left Chicago.

Josie stood up. "I need to get Grace her lunch."

"Thanks for letting me speak with her," she said, getting to her feet.

"I really hope you can find Hayley. She's a sweet little girl who doesn't deserve this," Josie said.

"I'm going to do my best."

As Josie left the room, Nathan moved from his post by the entry to block her way.

"What are you thinking?" he challenged.

She shrugged. "I don't know. Just taking it all in."

"Really? You're not wondering if Kyle had something to do with this, because Grace thought the person was wearing a ring like her father's?"

"As Josie said, a lot of people have that ring."

"Exactly."

"What is Josie's husband like?"

"He's…fine."

The slight hesitation told her a lot. Nathan didn't like his brother-in-law. But then Nathan had always been protective of Josie. Maybe no man would be good enough for his sister.

"Kyle takes care of Josie and Grace. He provides well for them," Nathan continued. "He works for a large real-estate development company. He makes a good living. Josie gets to live in this nice house, and Grace gets to go to a good school.

That's what's important."

"Sounds like you're trying to convince yourself."

"Kyle had nothing to do with this, Bree."

"I didn't say he did. And I don't jump to conclusions."

He raised an eyebrow. "Seriously? You don't jump to conclusions?"

She hesitated for a split second. "Not anymore."

"I still can't believe you're a fed. Do they know all the shit you were involved in? Do they know about Johnny?"

She stared back at him. "Why are you so angry, Nathan? Weren't we friends once?"

Her direct question seemed to take him aback. "Now you remember that we were friends? Because it seemed like you forgot that a long time ago. You got on a bus and never looked back. But even before that, you changed."

"So did you," she reminded him.

"I don't like you being back here," he muttered. "My life is different now. I don't need a reminder of how things used to be. I don't need to get back in that mud pit."

"Believe it or not, I feel exactly the same way. My life is different now, too. And I'm not thrilled to be back in Chicago, but it's only until we find Hayley. Then I'll return to New York, where I live."

"New York, huh?"

"Yes."

His tension seemed to ease with the reminder that she was only in town temporarily.

"When did you get to New York?" he asked.

"Last year."

"And before that?"

"Lots of places," she said vaguely. "What about you, Nathan? I thought you wanted to leave this city."

"I did, but Josie met Kyle and got pregnant..." He shrugged. "My family is here. I had to stay."

"What do you do for a living?"

"I'm a contractor."

His words made her smile. "You always wanted to tear

down the bad buildings and build new ones. And now you're doing it. That's cool. You and your brother-in-law must have a lot in common, if he's a real-estate developer."

"Actually, we're usually on opposite sides when it comes to development. He's in it purely for the money. The bigger the project, the better—never mind how many neighborhoods get displaced or ripped apart in the process."

"I knew you didn't like him, Nathan."

"I never said that."

"You didn't have to. I can hear it in your voice."

"Look, he's a blowhard, and he's greedy, but he's harmless." Nathan cleared his throat. "Do you think Hayley was kidnapped for money? I know Mark has a very good job."

"You know Mark Jansen?"

"We run together. We did a triathlon last year. I can't imagine what he's going through. He adores Hayley and his other kids. He's a real family man."

"You still run," she mused, thinking of the times Nathan had tried to convince her to go on a run with him, but she had almost always refused.

"My go-to sport," he acknowledged.

"If you run fast enough, the pain, the sadness, and the fear can't catch you," she said softly, remembering the words he'd spoken to her on more than one occasion.

His gaze darkened. "Still holds true—most of the time."

"I—I need to get back to work," she said, realizing she was getting lost in the past.

Nathan stepped aside but dogged her heels on the way to the front door. Then he barred her way once again. "I don't want Josie's life messed up again, Bree. She's good now, and Grace needs her mom to be good, if you know what I mean."

She knew exactly what he meant. Josie had had issues with drugs when she was a young girl. "I only wish Josie the best."

"If that's true, don't go after her husband."

"I'm going to follow every lead, Nathan, no matter where

it goes. Hayley deserves that."

"I get that. I want you to find Hayley. I just don't want you to hurt Josie in the process. Kyle can't be a suspect. He's not that kind of guy."

"Right now, everyone is a suspect. Are you going to let me out?"

He opened the door for her, then said, "Bree..."

She stepped onto the porch and looked back at him. "What?"

He seemed to have some debate going on in his head and then he said, "I'm glad you made it."

She was surprised by his words and felt a wave of unexpected emotion. "I'm glad you made it, too."

"Let's try not to mess up each other's lives."

"That's the last thing I want to do." She walked away, feeling Nathan's gaze on her back until she turned the corner.

Nathan Bishop was an unexpected complication, but she'd handled it.

Hopefully, that would be her one and only encounter with the past.

Three

"Is Bree gone?" Josie asked, as he entered the kitchen.

"Yes."

His sister let out a sigh. "Good. Because you've got that look in your eyes again, Nathan. And you should not go there."

"I'm not going anywhere."

"You always had a thing for Bree—even when she was with Johnny."

He would have liked to deny his sister's words, but it would be pointless. "We don't need to talk about her."

"Of course we need to talk about her. She's back. She's in our lives."

"Not for long. As soon as Hayley is found, she'll return to New York."

"I hope so, because I like seeing you happy, and you were rarely happy when we were younger."

"That wasn't because of Bree."

"Sometimes it was. I may have been out of my mind a few of those years, but I didn't miss everything. You did things you wouldn't have normally done, and I've always thought they had something to do with Bree. It's like she's your kryptonite."

He shook his head at the worry in her eyes. "Bree is not *my* anything. She never has been, and she never will be."

"If you say so," Josie said, as she wiped down the counter.

"I do." He took a breath, knowing his next question was going to get her worked up even more, but he had to ask. "How could Kyle miss the concert? Grace was so excited about performing. He really couldn't get away?"

"No, he couldn't," she snapped. "He was supposed to be there, but something came up. It happens. I wasn't thrilled, and I know Grace was disappointed, not that she's had much time to think about that. But what can I say? Kyle works hard to support us. Complaining is being ungrateful."

"Is that what he tells you?"

"He doesn't have to tell me. After the way we grew up, Nathan, I appreciate everything Kyle does for us. He is a great provider, and I get to stay home with my daughter. I have everything I ever wanted. Don't try to poke holes in my happiness."

"I'm not doing that. I'm just concerned."

"About what?"

"About where Kyle was last night when Hayley disappeared. When did he show up? Did he come to the school? To the police station?"

"I called him when the police arrived at the school. They wouldn't let anyone leave until they had searched the area. It took him a little time to get my message. He ended up meeting us at the police station."

"Was he working with a group last night? Was he on his own?"

"I don't know. Why are you asking me all these questions?"

"Because Grace said she saw a ring similar to the one her dad wears on the kidnapper's hand, and Bree asked me about Kyle after you left."

"What did you say?"

"That he had nothing to do with this."

"Of course, he didn't. I mean, my God, how could anyone think he would kidnap a child—and Grace's best friend at that?" Angry tears spilled out of her eyes. "He's a good man. He works too much, but that's his only fault."

He didn't think that was Kyle's only fault by a long shot, but he kept that thought to himself. "It's going to be okay, Josie. Don't cry. I'll talk to Kyle. I'll let him know that Bree might be heading his way."

"I didn't say where he worked."

"She's FBI. She can probably find him in less than two seconds."

"And she probably still has a grudge against me for what I did to her. Maybe I was wrong to tell you to stay away from her. Maybe she needs to see us as friends again."

"No. You were right. We should both stay away from her. Hopefully, Hayley will be found soon, and Bree will be gone from our lives."

"And we'll get back to normal," Josie said, meeting his gaze.

"Normal," he agreed, not even sure what that was.

Bree felt even more tightly wound after seeing Nathan and Josie again. She'd thought she wouldn't run into anyone from her past if she stayed away from the old neighborhoods, but that had been a foolish idea. No one stayed in one place. She'd moved on, and so had they.

Josie was married to a successful man. She had a beautiful home, a sweet daughter, and a brother who still watched out for her. Nathan had also made himself into the man he'd always wanted to be. And she'd turned her life around, too.

It was all good, so why did it feel like everything was about to crash?

Shaking her head, she called for a car and while she was waiting for her ride, she punched in Dan's number.

"Fagan," he said crisply.

"It's me."

"How's it going in Chicago?"

"The usual full-court press—all-hands-on deck. I may have discovered a small clue. The young witness thought she saw a replica of the Cubs World Series ring on the kidnapper's hand."

"That might be more than a little clue."

"Apparently over a thousand rings were handed out, but it's something. I'll get the team looking for those rings as soon as I get into the office."

"The girl in Philly said the man didn't wear any rings. That's different."

"I know. And I'm also thinking that anyone wearing a Cubs ring would probably be from Chicago. The other three kidnappings were states away. I feel like something is off, Dan."

"He's on the move. He's changing up the game."

"Yes. I got another threatening call, too."

"What was said this time?"

"He told me he and I were going to get close, that he wanted a worthy competitor. He added that he likes it better when I wear my hair down, implying that he had eyes on me. Did Oscar ever turn up anything on the first call to my phone?"

"Unfortunately, no. Whoever is calling you knows what he's doing."

"It's weird that he hasn't mentioned Hayley specifically. Why wait? If he's ready to play the game, why not let me know the stakes—remind me that a little girl's life is in jeopardy?"

"Good questions. I wish I had some answers."

"So do I."

"Have you read the Chicago team in on the calls?"

"I mentioned the first one when I got in this morning. I haven't been back to the office since the second call came in."

"They definitely need the information, Bree."

"And I intend to share it, but I have to say, Dan, that while I know ASAIC Hobbs asked for my help, the rest of the team has been polite, but they don't seem excited to have me around. And there's one woman on the team that I went to Quantico with, who is definitely not a fan of mine."

"Who's that?"

"Agent Tracy Cox."

"I don't know her. Why doesn't she like you?"

"She was an outsider at the academy. She didn't like that I got closer to people than she could. I don't think working with her now is going to be a picnic. She barely said hello to me when I arrived, and I could feel her sharp, irritated glance on me throughout my report."

"Well, do your best. The team may be territorial, but they still want to find that kid."

"I know. I just don't have patience for politics and territories in situations like this. Anyway, I'm going to keep doing what I do, and hopefully we'll get a break."

"Keep me posted, and I'll have Oscar check your phone again, see if we get lucky tracing the second call."

"It's going to take more than luck."

—➤◄—

On her way downtown, Bree looked up information on Kyle Roberts. His employer, Skye Developments, took up the entire thirty-ninth floor of a downtown skyscraper that the company had built ten years earlier and was one of Chicago's most impressive buildings.

Kyle was vice president of sales, only a few rungs down on the corporate ladder from Donovan Skye, who had founded the company forty years earlier and his sons, Lawrence and James Skye. The Skyes were one of Chicago's most prominent and wealthiest families.

At age thirty-eight, Kyle Roberts had a bright future ahead of him, and kidnapping his nine-year-old daughter's friend seemed about as farfetched an idea as any she could possibly have. But she still needed to talk to him. She'd been at her job long enough to know not to discount anyone as a suspect.

She wondered where Josie had met Kyle, how the street junkie kid had ended up with a graduate of Yale and a now very successful businessman. Kyle was also ten years older than Josie, and Grace was nine. She frowned, doing the math in her head. Josie was a year younger than her, making her twenty-eight now, so she must have been nineteen when she had Grace. Kyle would have been twenty-nine at the time. She couldn't imagine that he and Josie had run in the same circles then, unless Kyle had a past, too.

Did that change anything? Probably not. She needed to rein in her speculation and focus on the facts. With that thought in mind, she got out of her cab, and headed upstairs.

Kyle had an administrative assistant guarding his door, a red-haired woman dressed in a black sheath dress. She promptly told Bree that Mr. Roberts was on a call and couldn't be disturbed.

At the flash of Bree's badge, and the mention that a missing child's life was at stake, the admin reluctantly interrupted her boss and then waved her inside.

When she entered the room, she was impressed with the opulent furnishings, the luxuriously thick carpet under her feet, and the jaw-dropping view from Kyle's floor-to-ceiling windows that looked out over Lake Michigan.

Kyle Roberts was just as impressive as his office. He was a handsome man, with dark-blond hair and blue eyes dressed in an expensive gray suit and navy-blue patterned silk tie. He didn't look like a man who ever got his hands dirty, which also made him less likely to be the man who had kidnapped Hayley Jansen the night before. The only ring he wore was a narrow gold wedding band.

Kyle gave her a wary, polite smile. "My assistant said you're here about Hayley Jansen's disappearance. I'm not sure what I can tell you." He motioned for her to take the chair in front of his massive desk. "But, of course, I'm happy to help."

"I just spoke with Grace and your wife. Josie mentioned that you weren't able to attend the concert last night."

"No, I had a lot of work to do. I couldn't get away."

"You were working here in your office?"

"Yes."

"Was anyone else here?"

"There were other people in the company working late. Is this about my ring? Josie said that Grace remembered the kidnapper wearing a ring like the replica World Series Cubs ring that I received."

"I did want to talk to you about that. Do you have the ring?"

"It's at home, in my dresser. I can assure you that I did not kidnap Hayley Jansen."

Kyle had barely finished speaking when the door to his office flew open, and Nathan strode in, followed by the admin, who gave Kyle an apologetic look.

"I told him you were tied up," the admin said.

"It's fine. Shut the door on your way out," Kyle replied, frowning at his brother-in-law. "What are you doing here, Nathan?"

"Don't tell her anything, Kyle." Nathan shot her a dark look.

She was surprised that Nathan was treating her with such hostility, but she wasn't going to back down from doing her job just because he was worried she might shake up his sister's perfect life.

"I have nothing to hide," Kyle said.

"I still don't think you should be talking to the FBI unless you have a lawyer present," Nathan said.

"Does he need a lawyer?" Bree cut in.

"I don't." Kyle sent Nathan an irritated look before he turned his gaze back to her. "There are thousands of people who have the same ring I do, or a variation of it. I'm glad that Grace remembered such an important detail. I hope it will provide you with a good lead, but you're not going to get anywhere focusing on me."

Despite Kyle's attempt to be polite and firm, there was something in his tone that gave her pause. "Is there anyone who can corroborate your whereabouts between eight and eight thirty last night?"

"I don't know. My assistant left around seven. I wasn't aware of what was going on outside my office." He pressed his fingers together, giving her a speculative look. "When Josie called me, she also warned me that you might have a personal grudge against her. She said she took some jewelry of yours when you were kids."

"This is not about that, and I don't have a personal grudge against your wife."

"But you did have a problem with her."

"We were teenagers. It was a long time ago. I'm happy that Josie is doing so well now."

"Are you?" Kyle murmured, looking from Nathan to her, obviously sensing the discord between them as well. "What do you think, Nathan?"

"I think you should stop talking," he said.

"Well, perhaps I'll follow my brother-in-law's advice," Kyle said, getting to his feet. "I have a meeting, so if you'll excuse me…"

She stood up, knowing this interview was over. "Thank you for your time, Mr. Roberts."

"I hope you bring Hayley home very soon."

When she left the office, she couldn't help noticing that Kyle's admin was now nowhere to be seen. *Was that deliberate? Had she not wanted to be questioned?* Maybe she hadn't left the office at seven. Maybe she knew something about what her boss had been doing the night before.

Of course, she had absolutely nothing to base that thought on, but there had just been something very evasive in Kyle's tone.

Nathan caught up to her at the elevator. "You shouldn't have come here."

"No. You shouldn't have come here. This is FBI business. And if your brother-in-law has nothing to hide, he shouldn't be bothered by a few questions. The fact that you felt it necessary to run down here and warn him also doesn't put you or him in a good light. Why do you think he needs protection?"

"Because law enforcement sometimes spins the facts. It's not like you and I didn't see that happen when we were teens, Bree."

His pointed comment was impossible to deny. "Well, I wouldn't do that."

"You did it before—you spun a story for Johnny to save his ass."

"That's not even close to being true. You don't know what happened back then."

"I know a lot."

"I'm not talking about that with you." She punched the elevator button several more times, wishing it would arrive, so she could get away from Nathan.

"Leave my family alone, Bree. They don't have anything to do with Hayley's disappearance."

"I'm just following the facts. And you know I forgave Josie for stealing from me all those years ago. She was a drug-addicted mess at the time."

"She had a lot of good reasons for needing to escape from reality."

"I know that, Nathan," she said, softening when she saw the pain in his eyes. "That's why I let it go. For you and Josie to suggest I would come after her husband because of that is ridiculous. You're both overreacting."

"Maybe we just know how fast good can turn to bad."

She knew a little about that, too. "Okay. Fine. I get it. And it's done." She was relieved when the elevator finally arrived.

"Is it done?" he asked, getting into the elevator with her. "You're going to leave Kyle alone?"

"I'm going to follow up on all the rings that were distributed by the organization. That's the best I can give you."

"Why did they call you in from New York? Aren't there enough agents in Chicago to work this case?"

"Hayley's abduction might be linked to other cases I've been investigating. You need to stay out of this, Nathan. You're dangerously close to impeding a federal investigation."

"Is that a fact?"

"Yes, it is. I know that protecting Josie is deeply ingrained in you. But you have to back off. Bringing home Hayley is all that matters."

"I want that, too."

"Then focus on that."

She stepped out of the elevator, hoping they were finished, but he remained right behind her until they reached the sidewalk. Then he put a heavy hand on her shoulder.

She turned around, feeling an odd jolt at the personal touch, the familiar gesture. She'd tried to walk away from Nathan a lot of times before, but he'd always made the same move.

His gaze darkened as she looked back at him, and she couldn't help wondering if he was thinking the same thing.

He pulled his hand away. "Sorry," he muttered. "Look. I won't get in your way again, but I'd like to help if I can."

"So you can help me focus on someone besides your brother-in-law?"

"Do you really believe Kyle went into the auditorium and kidnapped his daughter's best friend without anyone recognizing him?"

"I don't know," she said honestly. "Kyle could have easily explained his presence backstage if anyone questioned him."

Nathan did not look happy with her answer. "Seriously, Bree?"

"He was hiding something, Nathan."

"If he was, it wasn't that."

"Well, if you really want to protect Josie, and Kyle has a secret, maybe you should try to find out what it is."

"I don't think Kyle is going to tell me. We're related by marriage, but we are not the best of friends."

"I can see why. He is not the kind of man you would respect."

He raised an eyebrow at her comment. "Really? A lot of people respect Kyle. He's very well-connected in this city."

"He's slick and cocky and very impressed with himself."

"You got all that in your short conversation?"

"I got all that in the first minute, and I didn't need FBI training to figure it out."

"You're better at reading people than you used to be."

"And you're a lot worse at the not-so-subtle digs."

"Then I'll stop being subtle. You were a sucker once upon a time."

"I was a desperate, lonely girl once upon a time. And one of my friends stopped being my friend, and that hurt."

His lips tightened. "You didn't want to be my friend. You had Johnny."

"I don't want to talk about Johnny." She groaned. "Why are we even having this conversation?"

"Because you came back to Chicago."

"It wasn't by choice."

"When you got on that bus, and you told me you'd let me know where you settled, I thought I'd see you again before more than ten years had passed. But you vanished."

"You knew why I had to disappear."

"I knew why you had to leave Johnny, not why you couldn't have any contact with me."

"Talking to you…talking to anyone from the old neighborhood was too risky. I couldn't chance it." She paused, her heart beating hard against her chest. "Did you ever tell anyone?"

"Not a soul. Just like I promised. You called in my debt to you, and I paid up." The anger returned to his voice. "Although my silence put me in the hospital for a few days."

"What?" she asked in surprise. "What are you talking about?"

"Johnny came after me. He wanted to know where you were. He tried his hardest to get me to talk, but I didn't tell him a thing."

"He beat you up?"

"Him and two of his friends."

She shook her head. "I had no idea. I'm so sorry, Nathan." She felt an enormous wave of guilt. "I didn't think Johnny would find out you'd helped me."

"He was desperate to get you back. I'd never seen him like that." Nathan drew in a breath. "You made the right decision when you left. But you made the wrong decision to come back now. Johnny still lives here. If he hears you're in town, he'll come looking for you."

"I can't imagine how he would hear I'm in town, unless you're going to tell him?"

"I haven't seen him since that day he beat me up. I left the neighborhood as soon as I got out of the hospital. I took Josie as far across the city as I could get. And I have never been back there."

"Well, I'm going to be in and out of this city, a couple of days, maybe a week at most. And even if he did find out, I can protect myself now. I'm not that scared girl anymore. I'm a trained federal agent. I don't run from bad guys; I take them down."

A reluctant smile crossed his lips. "Well, I must say this is a new side of you."

"I grew up, Nathan. So did you. Can we move forward?"

"I'd like to say yes, but I just have this sick feeling in my gut."

"I've had the same sick feeling since I found out I was needed in Chicago. But I am here to do a job. That's it. So, what's it going to be, Nathan? Are we going to be friends? Enemies? People who once knew each other but really don't want to have anything to do with each other now?" She paused, waiting for him to immediately choose the last choice, but he dug his hands into his pockets, his gaze running across her face, down her body, and the air between them seemed ridiculously tense. "Well?" she prodded.

"When I figure it out, I'll let you know." He turned and

walked away.

As she watched him leave, she was filled with mixed emotions. But one thing was very clear. Nathan was a complication she didn't need. A very sexy, attractive complication, her brain couldn't help pointing out.

She frowned. Maybe she'd had a teeny, tiny little crush on Nathan a hundred years ago, when they were young teens, when they were friends. But then they didn't see each other for a few years and when they reconnected in the last two years of high school, Nathan had become harder, moodier, angrier. He'd been so critical of all her choices that they'd ended up closer to enemies.

What they were now was anyone's guess. But hopefully, she wouldn't be staying in Chicago long enough to find out.

Four

Bree returned to the FBI office a little past three, determined to put Nathan out of her mind.

After briefing her fellow agents on her interviews with Grace and Kyle Roberts, as well as the disturbing phone calls she'd received, she grabbed a salad from the on-site cafeteria and sat down at an empty desk. As she ate, she got onto her computer, reading through the reports being posted by the numerous teams working on the case.

They had agents and analysts tracking down locally known child predators, surfing the dark web for chatter about a kidnapping for ransom or any other motivation, running computer patterns to compare Hayley's case with the three other known child abductions involving a white rose, coordinating with volunteer and police-led neighborhood searches, and continuing to interview and re-interview everyone who had been at the concert the night before. There were also numerous personnel dedicated to tracking down every lead that came in from the public, no matter how incredible it might appear.

Despite the massive manpower at work, they were unfortunately no closer to finding Hayley now than they had been the night before, and everyone was acutely aware that in cases like these, every minute counted.

After finishing her salad, she typed up her own notes,

thinking again about her conversations with the Jansens, Grace Roberts, and Kyle Roberts. Aside from the ring, she hadn't gained a lot of new information, but the ring could still be significant. One of the Chicago team members had already volunteered to contact the Cubs and get a list of those lucky people who had received rings. It was a long list and a long-shot lead, but it was something and right now all they had to go on.

Thinking about the Cubs reminded her of the baseball chat forum she and her tight-knit group of friends from Quantico had set up during their training in order to coordinate assignments. Later, it had become a place to ask for help outside the usual professional channels, a place that was all theirs.

They'd adopted monikers from the 1986 World Series Mets, which had been Jamie Rowland's favorite team. Jamie had been their leader until he had died in a tragic accident during a training mission. She still missed his smiling face. They'd dated for a few weeks during their time at Quantico. He was the first man in a long time she'd been able to trust. She didn't know if she would have loved him forever, but his death had torn away another piece of her heart.

It would be five years tomorrow that he'd died. Jamie's father Vincent and sister Cassie had invited her to attend a small gathering at their house to celebrate Jamie's life, and she'd planned to attend, but now she doubted she'd make it back to New York by then. She'd been looking forward to it and hoping to catch up with at least one or two of her friends. It had been too long.

On impulse, she pulled out her phone and opened up the forum. It had gone unused since June when Damon and Wyatt had been running for their lives and had needed her help.

It was a good thing that no one had needed a lifeline since then, but she missed her buddies. They were spread out all over the world and most of the time she had no idea where anyone was, but she still felt connected to them. They had saved each other's lives. They had gone through tragedy together. And when there was no one else to trust, they knew they could trust each other. In her world, trust was a rare commodity, proven even more rare this past summer when they'd found a traitor among them.

Pushing that thought out of her mind, she started a new thread, speaking in the baseball code they used. *Looks like Cubs are on their way to another pennant. Can't make tomorrow's celebration. Anyone close enough to catch a game with me?*

She signed off with her moniker Knight, in honor of Ray Knight, a third baseman for the Mets the year they won the World Series. She'd picked his name because she fancied herself a knight. And since there weren't any females on the team, she and Parisa had been stuck with male names. Parisa had chosen Dwight Gooden, because she liked what a star he was and how much money he made.

Smiling to herself, she clicked out of the forum. She'd check it later to see if anyone responded. She wouldn't mind seeing a friendly face. The Chicago team had their own way of working, and while they were polite and professional, she'd felt a distinct tension when she'd told them about the ring on the kidnapper's finger.

No one, especially Tracy Cox, had liked that she'd broken the only lead. They also hadn't reacted well to her mention of the threatening phone calls, questioning whether they were really about this case. Tracy seemed to feel she was trying to make the case about her, which was ridiculous; she just wanted to find Hayley and catch the kidnapper and put him away for good.

Speaking of Tracy, she inwardly sighed as the assertive and critical agent in her late twenties sat down in the chair adjacent to her desk. Tracy had short blonde hair that was straight and angled and steel-blue eyes. Despite her attractive face, there was a hardness and a coldness to Tracy. She was smart, but she was also sharp, prickly, easily angered, and obsessed with protocol and policy.

"You should have called me regarding the information on Mr. Roberts before you went to his office," Tracy said. "We could have interviewed him together."

She could have done that, maybe *should* have done that, but she was used to tracking down leads on her own. And she and Tracy had never worked well together. "I wanted to catch him before his wife gave him the heads-up," she said. They hadn't talked about their past relationship, and she was hoping to avoid that by sticking to the case.

"But that didn't happen."

"Unfortunately, not," she admitted.

"Do you really like him for this?" Tracy asked. "Kyle Roberts is a very successful, well-connected man, with top-level connections in the city, and he's never been in any trouble."

"That's true. But the fact that Hayley didn't struggle, and Grace identified the ring on the kidnapper's hand as looking like the one her father wears, I thought it was worth having a conversation with him."

"Well, you won't be speaking to Mr. Roberts again," Tracy said, unable to hide the note of satisfaction in her voice. "We've had a complaint from his attorney. He says you have a conflict of interest, and if you attempt to contact his client again, he'll bring charges of harassment."

"Excuse me?" she asked in surprise.

"Mr. Roberts said that you know his wife and brother-in-law. That you're going after him to avenge some problem you had with his wife years ago."

"That's ridiculous. I followed up on what his own daughter told me."

"But it would have been helpful if you'd taken one of us with you, or even called us as soon as you got the information, in light of the fact that you apparently have a relationship with our only witness's family. You conveniently left that out of your briefing."

"It wasn't relevant, and I haven't had a relationship with the witness's family in over a decade. I knew Mr. Roberts's wife and brother-in-law when I was in my teens. But I didn't even realize Josie Roberts was the Josie Bishop I knew until I went to interview her daughter Grace."

"What problem did you have with Mrs. Roberts?"

"She stole some money and jewelry from me. She was a teenager and a drug addict at the time."

"Did you press charges?"

"No. Look, it was not that big of a deal. She gave some of it back to me, and I'm certainly not carrying out some personal vendetta."

"I would hope not, but Agent Hobbs asked me to let you know that while we appreciate the insight you bring to this case, you won't be doing any further interviews with potential suspects or witnesses unless one of us is with you."

"He's benching me?"

Tracy shrugged. "Call it whatever you like. You can still be helpful, of course. But we'll take the lead; we'll do the field work. You find clues, bring them to me. We want to work with you, but we're also much more versed in the minefield of Chicago politics than you are. If you make a wrong move, this agency risks alienating people, who might be instrumental in finding this child."

"I grew up here, Tracy. I understand Chicago politics. And I am the one who got Grace to remember something," she couldn't help adding.

"Good job on that," Tracy said with a complete lack of sincerity.

"Do we need to talk about Quantico?" she asked.

"Why would we need to talk about the academy?"

"Because if anyone seems to be holding a grudge, it's you."

"You think I've given you even one thought over the last five years?" she asked incredulously. "I've been busy building my career, and I've done that on my own, unlike you, who still seems to be getting into trouble with your gang of friends."

"You're talking about New York, about Damon and

Wyatt."

"And Alan Parker, our fearless mentor at Quantico, who turned out to be a double agent. That was quite remarkable. And amazing that you and Damon and Wyatt were all taken in by him. You thought he was so fantastic."

"Alan changed over the years," she said, trying not to rise to Tracy's bait. "And the only reason you hated our gang, as you liked to call it, is because you weren't one of us."

"I didn't want to be one of you. You relied too much on each other. A good agent should be able to think and act completely independently."

"Teamwork can also be effective."

Tracy shrugged. "We can agree to disagree." She got to her feet. "I heard about Jamie Rowland's memorial celebration. Is Diego going to that?"

"He was invited, but I don't know if he's going. Last I heard he was in Ecuador." She gave Tracy a thoughtful look, remembering how interested in Diego she'd always been. "Have you stayed in contact with Diego?"

"No. I haven't stayed in contact with anyone." She paused. "I'd appreciate it if you would keep me updated on any leads you stumble upon."

"Of course," she said, very aware that Tracy thought her break in the case was pure accidental luck. But she didn't care. She wasn't looking for credit, only answers. She was, however, relieved when Tracy walked away.

Glancing at her watch, she saw it was past five. She'd never been one to leave the office early, but it had been a very long day. She decided to head back to her hotel and work from there.

She'd just gotten into her hotel room when the phone rang. She was relieved to see it was Dan. She could use a friendly voice. "Checking up on me?"

"I hear you're causing problems in Chicago. I had no idea you ever lived there. Why didn't you mention it?" he asked.

"It wasn't a happy time in my life. Who did you speak to?"

"Hobbs. He asked me if you were a loose wire that needed to be cut."

"What did you say?"

"That you're one of the smartest and most intuitive agents I've ever worked with, and he'd be a fool not to listen to you."

"Thanks, I appreciate that. But at the moment, I seem to be benched. Apparently, he is a fool," she said dryly.

"He's trying to keep a lot of people happy."

"Keeping people happy is not my concern. Finding one ten-year-old girl is. We both know Hayley doesn't have a lot of time. And it's frustrating not to be able to just run my investigation the way it needs to be run."

"Are they making mistakes, missing things?"

"I wouldn't say that. They're following all the protocols we follow, but it's just not enough, at least not for me."

"I get it. You work better from the front."

"I do," she admitted, knowing that was one reason why she liked working with Dan; he respected her need to cross boundaries when necessary.

"You want my advice, Bree?"

"Always."

"Do what you do. That kid needs you at your best. Sort out the politics later."

She appreciated his words, because Hayley was the only one who mattered right now. "That's exactly what I'm going to do."

"Good. Now tell me something else."

"What?" she asked warily.

"What's the deal with this family you're at odds with? They're related to your eyewitness?"

"Yes. Josie is the mother. Josie's husband Kyle is a person of interest. And Nathan Bishop is the child's uncle. Josie and Nathan and I knew each other as kids."

"Got it. Hobbs said you have a grudge against one of them."

"Which is a complete fabrication created by Kyle's lawyers. A long time ago, Josie stole some stuff from me. But it wasn't that big of a deal. We were street kids, Dan. We met at a time when we were all in survival mode."

"You were a street kid?"

"Yes."

"Tell me about it."

"You really want to hear all this now?"

"Considering how concerned the Chicago team is about you, I think I need to hear it."

"It's really not relevant, but here are the highlights. My mother had me when she was sixteen. She didn't know who my father was or if she did, she didn't tell me. Her father, my grandfather, was a widowed military man, and he threw her out of the house when she came home pregnant. My mom had a lot of trouble taking care of me. She had problems with drugs, problems with relationships. We were broke. We were homeless. Sometimes, we lived in shelters. Eventually, my mom died of an overdose when I was ten. I went to live with my aunt then, who was not in much better shape than my mom. When I was fourteen, I ended up in foster care, and that's where I stayed until I aged out."

"That is a much rougher story than I was expecting."

"I survived, and it made me tougher. Anyway, there's no deal with Nathan and Josie. In fact, it was actually good to see them. I wasn't sure they'd make it. But they did. They're doing well."

"So are you."

"Most days, except today, when I managed to piss off the entire Chicago office."

"Only because you were better than them."

"Thanks, Dan. You always know what to say."

"Tell my wife that. She says I have a great talent for sticking my foot in my mouth."

"But she adores you. How is her pregnancy coming along?"

"She's doing all right now. But she's making a lot of noise about me being around more when the baby is born."

"Would you quit the team?" she asked, hoping that

wouldn't be the case but completely understanding if it was. Getting called out at a moment's notice was easier when you weren't leaving behind a family.

"I'm thinking about it," he admitted. "But nothing is decided. If I do change things up, you'd be a good leader for this team."

"I don't even want to think about taking your job."

"Well, you don't have to. Just find that little girl and that monster before he strikes again."

Thursday morning, Nathan hit the pavement just before seven, putting in a good six miles along the river, hoping each pounding step would drive thoughts of Bree out of his head. But it didn't work. He couldn't stop thinking about her.

She'd changed her last name from Larson to Adams. She'd changed her demeanor, too, not nearly as soft and kind and insecure as she'd once been. Now, she was a strong, determined, federal agent doing one of the hardest jobs in the world. And he found himself liking her more, which was exactly the opposite of the way he wanted to feel.

He'd spent far too much time in his life liking Bree, lusting after her, thinking she might finally wake up one day and see him, instead of every other idiot guy chasing after her.

She'd told him last night that he'd changed when they reconnected in high school after a few years apart. That was true. A lot had happened in those years that she hadn't known anything about—still didn't know anything about—and he hadn't been able to tell her.

But it wasn't just his secrets that had pushed them apart; it was realizing how much he wanted her when she clearly did not want him.

Instead, she'd chosen Johnny Hawke, the oldest of three boys born into a criminal family that ran a boxing gym as a front for their gambling and drug business.

Johnny was funny, charming, a talker who liked to flash his cash and his car in a part of town where that kind of money came with a lot of power. Bree had gotten caught up in Johnny's world. And for a short time, he had as well, mostly because he'd wanted to stay close to Bree, not because he'd wanted to hang with Johnny.

Frowning, he picked up his pace, trying to outrun the past, but that was going to be impossible with Bree in town. He'd already checked the news upon waking up, and Hayley was still missing, which meant Bree wasn't going anywhere.

He didn't know if she was truly done with Kyle; he hoped so—for Josie's sake. But there was nothing more he could do about it. He needed to keep his distance from Bree and from the past. When he ran out of path, he turned around and headed home. He'd just entered his apartment, when his phone rang. It was Adrienne.

Good. He needed a reminder that he had a different life now.

"Adrienne."

"You didn't call me back last night," Adrienne complained, a little whine in her voice that was starting to grate on him.

"Sorry. I was hanging with Josie." That wasn't really true. He had spoken to Josie again after the incident at Kyle's office, but he'd spent the rest of the night at home watching the Cubs and trying not to think about Bree.

"Is Grace okay?" Adrienne asked.

"She's hanging in there, but it's a bad situation."

"I'm sorry. I know you have a lot on your mind, but my college friend, Kari, is in town tonight. I really want you to meet her. Can you come to dinner or drinks after?"

None of that sounded appealing. "Maybe drinks," he hedged. "Can I call you later?"

"Sure. I just miss you, Nathan. It doesn't seem like we're seeing each other too often these days. I want to get back on track."

"We will," he muttered, feeling like the biggest asshole

when he hung up the phone. He hadn't given Adrienne one single thought since he'd run into Bree.

It was ridiculous. He should be over Bree by now. Hell, he should have been over her twelve years ago—fifteen years ago. He didn't know what it was about her that stuck with him...

Actually, he did know.

It was the girl he'd met when he was thirteen, who'd captured his heart. Her smile had felt like the sun coming out after a relentless series of storms. Her friendship had been sweet and generous. They'd whiled away the hours watching silly cartoons and then being ruthlessly competitive at card games.

They'd roamed the city streets, made up stories of how great their lives were going to be one day, pretending that the reality they were actually living would one day completely vanish.

She'd been his escape. And he'd been hers. But then life had gotten in the way.

Years had passed.

When they came back together, everything was different.

And then there was Johnny.

He'd thought she'd come out of her crush eventually. He'd thought she'd wake up much sooner than she had.

But then there was her secret, which had become his secret, too.

Shaking his head, he jumped into the shower. Running hadn't worked; maybe some ice-cold water would at least dull the memories.

Five

She was not cut out for desk work, Bree thought, as she sat through another briefing Thursday morning and then watched various agents head out the door to chase down leads in Hayley's case. After spending three hours reviewing surveillance videos near Hayley's school, answering the lead line, and running through the Cubs' list of ring owners, she was feeling frustrated and restless.

She was at her best when she was in the field. She was good at engaging people in conversation, at reading witnesses, at assessing situations. Dan had told her to do what she did and worry about the politics later. She needed to follow his advice.

Plus, sitting around the office was giving her way too much time to think about Nathan.

It had been so strange seeing him the day before. And their conversation outside of Kyle's office had been surprising on a lot of levels.

She felt guilty that Nathan had taken a beating for her. She'd forced him into helping her, so the fact that he'd also been hurt made her feel terrible. Now, she had a better understanding of why he'd been so angry when he'd first seen her, why he hadn't been able to answer a simple question as to whether they were friends or enemies or just people who used to know each other.

Obviously, he had very mixed feelings when it came to her. *How could she blame him?* She'd brought him into her crisis, gotten him hurt, and then never talked to him again. No wonder he'd thought she was selfish and made bad choices.

But she was different now. And seeing him again reminded her of the good times before all the bad stuff, the times when they had been the best of friends. They had had fun together. They had laughed and talked and dreamed together.

That connection had been broken when she'd gone into foster care and had had to live farther away. Three years had passed before she made it into the same high school as Nathan and by then everything had changed.

Well, it didn't matter now. She was happy he'd gotten his life together, that he was building houses and that his sister had a family who loved her.

She was also glad she'd come back a better person. At least, Nathan could see that she'd changed, improved, and turned her life around. His help had not been for nothing. She wished that she'd told him that the day before.

She also kind of wished that she'd have a chance to see him again, but that was probably unwise. He'd told her he didn't want to get dragged back into the mud with her, and while she had no intention of getting caught in the mud, maybe it was best if they just let things stand where they were.

Tapping her fingers restlessly on her keyboard, she shut down her computer. She needed to get out of the office and at least get some air. But what could she do that would be helpful?

The one place she hadn't been yet was Hayley's school and perhaps seeing the actual site of the abduction would help her figure something out. According to the investigators who had gone over the stage area with a fine-tooth comb, there was nothing to find, but they hadn't seen the school sites where the three other children had been abducted. Maybe she would view the scene differently.

Gathering her things together, she headed downstairs. She unsuccessfully tried to flag down a taxi, then checked her app for any available rideshare cars nearby, but prices were surging, and cars were scarce. It was one o'clock—lunchtime—and everyone seemed to be on the move.

The rumbling of the train a few blocks away told her she did have another option. She just really hated riding the L, which was short for Chicago's elevated train system. It was always crowded, usually hot, often dirty and smelly, and the rickety, rocking curves often made her feel sick.

In the past, the body-to-body cramming on the train had also brought forth some unwelcome touching, and she still shivered when she thought about those moments.

But she did need to get across town...

She'd give it another five minutes.

While she was waiting for the next light to change and hopefully send a taxi in her direction, her phone rang. The unidentified number sent a jolt through her system, and she mentally prepared herself to hear the creepy altered voice once more. But this time she was ready. She used a new app the tech had recently put on her phone to record and trace the call.

"Agent Adams," she said crisply, confidently.

"I missed seeing you at the news conference," he said.

"I was busy. Are you ready to tell me what you want?"

"That wouldn't be much fun, although at the moment, I feel quite bored. You seem to have no idea who I am, where I might be. How can I run if you don't get closer?"

"Why don't you give me a clue?"

"There's not much challenge in that," he said, the noise from a loudspeaker cutting off his last word.

Her brain sharpened. It sounded like he was at a train station.

Another rumble echoed through the phone. She strained to hear what the voice on the speaker was saying. It sounded like Park Station. She knew where Park Station was. It was, in fact, quite close to her old neighborhood. *That couldn't be a coincidence.*

"She's waiting for you," the voice said, sending a shiver down her spine.

It was the first time he'd mentioned Hayley.

"Don't hurt her."

"That's entirely up to you."

The phone clicked off. She drew in a deep breath as blood rocketed through her veins. She glanced back at the building behind her. She could go back inside and turn over the recording...but then what? Someone else would eventually get to checking out the train station? She could easily do that herself. She was going to take the train after all.

Turning, she walked down the block to the nearest station. She was probably playing into the kidnapper's game. He'd no doubt made the call knowing she would hear the speaker behind him.

But it was a crowded, public place. She wasn't worried he was going to go after her. She just needed to figure out if there was some area around that station where he might be keeping Hayley.

On the way to the train, she called Tracy. Thankfully, she did not pick up. She wanted to be up front with the Chicago team, but she also didn't want to get stopped in her tracks.

Leaving a voicemail, she said, "I heard from the kidnapper again. I'm going to check out a hunch. Call me when you get this, and I'll fill you in. The good news is that I think Hayley is still alive." She called the tech who had set up her phone next. When the woman answered, she said, "Eva," she said. "I got another call. I'll send you the recording." She punched a button to do that, and then slipped her phone into her bag. She bought a ticket from the machine and hopped onto the next train.

As she'd expected, despite the brisk weather outside, the train was hot and steamy, with tons of people on board. She grabbed a nearby rail as the train lurched down the track. Within minutes, she was regretting her decision.

Knots formed in her throat, and she felt a wave of motion

sickness as the train screeched around a corner. She could have just waited for a taxi and taken a cab to Park Station. But that could have taken too long.

Maybe coming back to Chicago was a good thing. Perhaps facing her past and fears like these were just what she needed to really break free of who she'd once been. She wasn't Bree Larson anymore. She was Bree Adams. She'd turned herself into her own person.

Mental pep talk over, she managed to stay on the train as the doors opened at the next stop. One more stop, and she'd be at Park Station. She could make another minute or two.

The train swayed again as it started to move. Thirty seconds later, she felt someone's hand on her back.

Turning her head, she looked down and saw a young girl tugging on the hem of her coat. The girl appeared to be about ten or eleven with straight, brown hair, a pale, dirty face and big, wide, green eyes.

"Mommy?" the little girl said.

"What?" she gasped, sure she hadn't heard her correctly. "What did you say?"

"How come you never came back and got me?"

Shocked at the question, she could barely draw a breath. "I—What?"

"I was waiting," the little girl said. "For a long time."

"I'm not—I'm not your mother," she finally bit out.

The train came to a halt, and the little girl slipped away from her as the doors opened, and a mass of people exited.

She hesitated one second, then got off the train, and ran after the girl, wondering who she was, why she'd said what she'd said. There were so many people, she quickly lost sight of the child, and when she went down the stairs to the sidewalk, the girl had vanished.

The train rumbled overhead as it continued on its way. She looked back up, seeing a sign on the stairs—*Park Station*.

She'd gotten to where she needed to go, and it had been a trap.

She'd just never expected the trap to include a young

girl—a girl who wasn't Hayley.

Who was she? How had she known to get on the train? Why had she said what she'd said? And where the hell was she now?

She looked up and down the street, feeling unseen eyes upon her.

He was close by. She could feel it.

He'd lured her to this spot, and the stakes had just been raised in a manner she never could have anticipated.

Her phone buzzed, and she reached for it. *Was he calling her again?*

No. It was Tracy returning her call. She sent the call to voicemail. She couldn't talk to Tracy right now, not while she was feeling so raw and so very confused.

The kidnapper had done his research on her. He obviously knew more about her than just about everyone else in the world—except one.

She'd had a feeling her good-bye to Nathan was not going to stick.

Nathan stood on the third floor of the duplex he was building in Lakeview. As a general contractor, he ran a crew of two and subbed out the rest of the work. One of his employees was on vacation, and his foreman, Joe Kelly, was about to run out and pick up some supplies, leaving him with not much to do until Joe got back.

With the framing done, and no drywall up yet, he had a good view of the surrounding neighborhood. Being up high and outside reminded him of the times he and Bree had sat on roofs overlooking the city, dreaming about a different life.

As he heard Joe speaking to someone, he walked closer to the edge and peered down at the street. It was Bree. *She was back.* Just like that, every resolution he'd made about not seeing her again, not letting her get into his head, not allowing himself to be dragged into the past, went out the window.

She was dressed in black slacks and a white shirt and a black blazer. Her hair was down today, falling in pretty waves around her shoulders.

His chest tightened, along with just about every other part of his body.

Why did Bree have to be so damned beautiful? Hell, she even looked sexy in her serious federal agent clothes—clothes he wouldn't mind stripping right off her body to find the curves he'd dreamed about as a teenager.

What the hell was wrong with him?

He needed to get a grip. If Bree was here, it was because something bad had happened. He needed to remember that. She certainly hadn't come here just to see him. She'd made it clear the day before she wanted to put the past behind her as much as he did.

He saw Bree show Joe her badge. Then his foreman gave him a quick glance.

He nodded, and Joe handed Bree a hard hat, and sent her up the stairs. He walked over to meet her.

"Hi," she said tentatively as she reached the top step. "All right to come in?"

"Looks like you're already in. What are you doing here, Bree? When you said good-bye to me yesterday, it didn't sound like you were planning on saying hello again any time soon."

"Things changed."

"What things?"

"I need to talk to you."

"About Kyle?"

"No. Something else."

"Hayley?"

"Not exactly." She cleared her throat, looking away from his questioning gaze. "This is a big house."

"It's a duplex, so it's two homes."

"And you're building the whole thing?"

"It's my job, but others work on it."

She turned her gaze to the view. "Is this the master bedroom?"

"It is."

"I wouldn't mind waking up to a view like this."

"Even if the view is in Chicago?" he said dryly.

"Good point. I would prefer it be somewhere else."

"Like maybe a beach in Southern California with colorful sailboats catching the wind and the waves," he murmured, the words coming from a lifetime ago.

Her gaze shot back to his, and he thought he saw pain in her eyes.

"I can't believe you remember that," she said.

"Really? You cut out magazine pictures of beaches in California and put them up all over your walls: Newport, Laguna, Santa Monica, Malibu. Did you ever get out there?"

"Not yet."

"I'm surprised. Why not?"

"I'm not ready for the beach yet. What about you? Have you ever thought about leaving Chicago?"

"I've thought about it a million times, but Josie got pregnant at nineteen, and even though she had Kyle, I wanted to stay close to make sure she could handle things. Plus, I adore her kid. Grace is a gutsy little firecracker. She's like Josie in some ways, but in other ways, she's completely different. She definitely has more confidence than her mother ever had, but then, thankfully, Grace hasn't had to live through what Josie did."

"Thankfully," Bree echoed. "How did Josie meet Kyle? It doesn't seem like they would have been running in the same circles. He's a lot older than her, and from what I learned about him, he's well educated and comes from a fairly wealthy family."

"Josie was working as a hostess at the Waltham Club and Kyle did a lot of networking there. She got pregnant by accident and was shocked when Kyle told her he was going to marry her. She couldn't believe that such a successful and smart man not only fell for her but wanted to take care of her.

To be honest, I was surprised that he stepped up. But Kyle said he took one look at Josie and fell hard. He didn't care that she came from nothing or she hadn't been to college."

"She is a beautiful woman. She always has been."

"Yes. That beauty got her into a lot of trouble, but in this case, it got her out of it. I have to give Kyle credit for helping Josie stay on a better path. I think he likes having someone who really looks up to him, which Josie does. But I worry that things aren't as good as they once were."

"Because Kyle works late a lot?"

"That's part of it." He paused. "Why are you here, Bree?"

She gave him a pained look. "I probably shouldn't have come. You're just the only one I can talk to."

"I'm the only one you can talk to?" he asked in surprise. "Isn't there an entire building of FBI agents you can talk to?"

"Not about this."

"About what?"

Before she could answer, Joe came up the stairs. "I'm going to take off, Nathan. You need anything before I go?"

"No, I'm good." He ignored Joe's very curious look.

"All right."

As Joe left, Nathan folded his arms across his chest and gave Bree a thoughtful look. "You're stalling. This must be bad."

"It is bad," she admitted. "I didn't mention this before, but I've had a couple of calls from a man who I think is the kidnapper. He alters his voice, so it's difficult to decipher any kind of tone or accent."

Her words shocked him. *The kidnapper was talking to her?* "What does he say?"

"Each call has been short and cryptic. He is basically taunting me, making it sound like he's watching me, playing some sort of game with me." She licked her lips. "Anyway, the third call came in about an hour ago. He was chatty this time. He said he was a little bored, that he wondered why I didn't seem to know where he was. He sounded impatient, like I wasn't smart enough to keep up with him."

"That's crazy," he muttered, not sure what to think about the calls.

"I wasn't sure it was the kidnapper in the beginning. The first time, the voice just said I'd be sorry. The second call came when I was walking over to Josie's house. He implied that he could see me. He mentioned my hair being up. He said he wanted a worthy competitor. And then he hung up. But he never mentioned Hayley in those two conversations."

"But he did this third time?"

"Not by name. But he said she was waiting for me."

He frowned. "Okay. Then what happened? I assume there's more and it has something to do with why you're here. You don't think it's Kyle, do you?"

"No, I don't. While I was on the phone, I heard the announcement for a train coming into Park Station. I decided to go down there, to see if I could locate a place where he might have stashed Hayley."

"It sounds like he wanted you to hear that."

"I'm sure he did. But I figured I'd be safe enough at a crowded train station in the middle of the day. So, I got on the train."

"You got on the train?" he echoed. "You hate the train. You always preferred to walk whenever you could avoid taking it."

"Well, it was the fastest way to get there. Anyway, it was really crowded as always, and I was almost to the stop, when this little girl tugged on my coat and asked me if I..." Indecision flashed through her eyes.

"Well, don't stop there. What did she ask you?"

"I can't believe I'm going to say this out loud."

His pulse started beating faster at the look in her eyes. "Just say it."

"She called me *Mommy*, and she asked me why I had taken so long to come back for her."

Shock waves ran through his body. "What?"

"You heard me, Nathan," Bree said, panic in her voice. "She thought I was her mother. I told her I wasn't, and she just said she'd been waiting for me for a long time. She had brown hair and green eyes—just like me. And then the train stopped, and she jumped off. I followed her, but she disappeared into the crowd."

"Are you sure about what she said to you? Sometimes the train is loud."

"I'm absolutely positive, Nathan. She looked right at me. And she wasn't confused. There was a purpose in her eyes."

He had no idea what to say. He was completely stunned.

Bree stared back at him, her heart in her eyes. "The kidnapper set me up. He knew I would go down to the train station. He wanted me to meet her. He wanted me to think—"

"You can't think that. It's ridiculous."

"How can I not? She was about the right age. I saw myself in her, Nathan, I swear I did." Her gaze filled with anguish. "What if that girl really was my daughter?"

Six

—➤➤◄◄←—

His heart pounded against his chest, and he struggled to take a breath, Bree's words spinning him back into the past.

Bree had barely been showing when she'd gotten on the bus eleven years ago, despite the fact that she was almost six months pregnant. He'd been worried about her that day. She'd been so scared, so pale, and she could barely keep food down, throwing up twice in the bathroom before getting on the bus. He hadn't wanted her to go, but he knew she had to leave.

He'd wished he could go with her, at least help her get settled somewhere, but Josie was having a hard time. He couldn't leave his sister for Bree. And it wasn't as if Bree had asked him to go. All she'd wanted from him was a bus ticket, a ride and a promise not to tell anyone.

"Nathan?" Bree asked, her voice bringing him back to the present.

He looked into her anguished green eyes and said the first thing that came into his head. "I didn't know you had a girl."

"Oh." Her mouth trembled, as she fought against what had to be an overwhelming rush of emotion. "I guess you wouldn't have known that."

"You said you didn't know when you got on the bus."

"I had an ultrasound a week later."

It was so strange to think that Bree had had a daughter,

that there was a little girl somewhere in the world, with her hair and her eyes. But he didn't think it was the girl on the train. "You said the girl on the train spoke with purpose. Did it sound like she was coached?"

"Maybe." Bree nodded. "Probably."

"How did he know you'd actually take the train and not just cab it over there?"

"All I can think is that he was watching me."

"Or someone else was. If the call came from the location of the train station, and you were in front of the FBI building at the time you were speaking to him, then there are two people involved in this."

"As well as a little girl. Maybe they were just going to have the girl come up to me at the train station, but when I got on the train, they decided to make it happen there." She blew out a breath. "I don't know. But it's bad. It's all bad. This person knows way too much about me. And if he's trying to freak me out, it is definitely working."

"Why don't you just change your phone number? Stop talking to him?"

"Because I can't cut him off. The more he talks, the more likely it is he will make a mistake and reveal something that will help us find him."

He wasn't so sure about that. It sounded like the kidnapper knew exactly what he was doing.

Bree tucked a strand of loose hair behind her ears, as she adjusted the hard hat on her head. "What shocks me is how deep he's dug into my past. He's found a secret that no one else knows. How did he figure it out?"

"I never told anyone, Bree. Did you?"

"I told two people when I was at Quantico."

"Really?" He was surprised by that.

"I didn't have a choice. We did an assignment where we had to discover each other's secrets. That's when it came out. But one of those people is dead, and the other person, Parisa, is not in Chicago, and she would never set anything like this up. She's my friend."

He hoped that was true, but seeing the pain and uncertainty in her eyes, he had a feeling that the thought that someone she trusted had betrayed her was worse than whatever mind game the kidnapper was playing on her.

Bree wrapped her arms around herself, and the familiar gesture tugged at his heart. There had always been a lonely quality about Bree. She hadn't had many people in her life who'd hugged her, protected her. He'd wanted to put his arms around her a million times, but he'd always stopped himself, always thought it was a line he couldn't cross...*shouldn't* cross.

But now she looked so lost and alone, he found himself breaching the distance between them. He wrapped his arms around her shoulders and pulled her close.

She stiffened in surprise, her gaze widening, but she didn't push him away.

"Just take a second," he whispered, pressing her head against his shoulder, his mouth so close to her ear, he could smell the sweet, sexy scent of her shampoo. "Breathe."

She didn't just breathe; she surprised him by sliding her arms around his back and taking the hug to another level.

He could hardly believe he was holding her and that she was holding him back.

Now *he* was the one having trouble catching his breath.

What the hell had he just started?

And how was he ever going to let her go?

Before he could come up with an answer, Bree pulled out of his embrace, giving him a shaky, uncertain smile.

"Thanks," she said.

He didn't want her thanks; he wanted her back in his arms. But the moment had passed.

"Nathan, I need something else," she began.

"What? What do you need?" Right now, he wanted to do anything that would take the anguish out of her eyes.

"I need you to tell me it wasn't her. I need you to make me believe it."

"It wasn't her, Bree. It wasn't your daughter on the train."

He didn't know who the girl was, but he just didn't believe that it was her child.

"It couldn't be, right?"

"No. And just because someone found out you had a child doesn't mean they know where that child is. You took steps to make sure your child didn't end up in Chicago."

"I know. I was so careful. I didn't even go to Cleveland like I told you; I went to Detroit. The woman from the agency you set me up with suggested I do that, so that no one, not even you, would know where I was."

"I had no idea."

"The woman—her name was Diane—said my child would not be adopted by a family in Illinois. That she would be kept far from Johnny's sphere. But now I don't know if that's true. I need to find the girl on the train, Nathan."

"I don't think she's your daughter, Bree. A kid wouldn't act like that unless someone told them to. And if she really thought you were her mother, she wouldn't have run away from you."

"Then someone used her to get to me, which means she could be in trouble. I need to find her."

"How?"

As she pondered his question, he could see the fear receding from her gaze, replaced by strength, determination, fight—another side of Bree he remembered very clearly. She knew how to put her emotions away, to compartmentalize, to focus on the reality of the moment and nothing else. It had been a necessary trait to survive the unpredictability and sadness of her childhood.

"I'll check the security cameras at the train station," she said. "Maybe they caught the girl leaving or meeting up with someone else."

"Good idea. But is it possible that the kidnapper wants you to chase this girl instead of Hayley?"

She met his eyes. "Oh, I'm sure that's part of his goal. But at least I know what this girl looks like. If she can lead me to the kidnapper…"

"Then you're right—she might be in very big trouble," he said somberly. "Can I ask you a question? How did this kidnapper get so fixated on you?"

"I found his last victim in Philadelphia. I saved her before he could kill her. The press was on the scene. I was on the news. I became the face of his adversary."

He did not like the idea that some deranged kidnapper was stalking Bree. "What is the FBI doing to protect you?"

"I can protect myself. At the moment, he is not trying to hurt me; he just wants me in his game."

"For now. This could end with him trying to kill you."

"My concern at this moment is for Hayley and the unknown girl on the train. I should go."

"Bree, wait. I haven't heard you say anything about another person who could be involved in this."

Her face paled. "Johnny doesn't know about the baby. You said so."

"I said I didn't tell him, but beyond that..." He shrugged. "Have you looked him up? Do you know what he's doing now?"

"No. I have never wanted to know anything about him."

"Because you were afraid you'd go back to him?"

Anger flashed in her gaze. "Definitely not. I would never have gone back to him. I may have been young and stupid and lonely when I first got together with him, but I was sixteen, Nathan. Two years later, I knew a lot more about him, and I had seen his dark side."

"You were way too good for Johnny."

"I didn't think I was back then," she whispered. "I didn't think I was good enough for anyone."

His heart turned over at the candid admission. But then how could he blame her? Bree had been thrown away by a lot of people who were supposed to care about her. "You were always good enough. You just didn't pick the right people."

"I didn't."

"You might need to look into him now."

"I really don't think he's part of this. This kidnapper has

been operating out of the Northeast. Johnny is in Chicago."

"He could have expanded his operations. You don't know."

"My gut says he's not involved."

"Well, forgive me if I don't completely trust your gut where Johnny is concerned."

"I guess I can't blame you for that. But for now, I'm going to assume he's not involved. And whether or not that girl on the train is my daughter, I am going to find her. Now, I better get back to the office."

"Will you call me if you get a lead on the girl?"

"I thought you wanted me to stay out of your life."

"Well, that doesn't seem to be working, does it?"

"I didn't know who else to go to."

"I'm glad you came here. And now I'm intensely curious as to what's going on." He pulled his phone out of his pocket and handed it to her. "Put in your number."

She punched it in and then sent herself a text, so she'd have his number as well. "I'll let you know if I find out anything," she said.

She'd barely finished speaking when his phone rang. He saw Adrienne's name flash across his screen as Bree handed him back the phone.

"You can take that if you want," she said. "I'm going to go."

"It's fine." He silenced the call and put the phone back in his pocket. "I'll walk you down."

When they reached the bottom of the stairs, he took her hard hat and then walked her out to the sidewalk.

"I'm going to call for a car," she said. "I think I'll stay off trains for a while." She glanced down at her phone. "There's one only five minutes away."

"I'll wait with you."

A minute of silence followed his comment, and then she said, "Is Adrienne your girlfriend?"

"We've gone out for a few weeks; I wouldn't call her a girlfriend."

"Still noncommittal when it comes to relationships?"

"I've never liked labels."

"That's true. Have you ever come close to getting married?"

"Nope. I've been busy building my company. What about you?"

"There was someone in my life a few years back, but he died."

He thought about her words. "Was that guy at Quantico with you? The other person who knew your secret?"

"Yes. His name was Jamie Rowland. He was a military man turned FBI agent, and we clicked for a while. I don't know if it was a forever kind of thing; I certainly wasn't looking for that, and he wasn't, either. But he was funny and generous and just a really good person. His death was a tragedy. It happened during a training exercise. I almost quit after that. But I knew Jamie would have wanted me to keep going, so I did."

He found himself feeling a little jealous of this unknown man. At least when she'd been with Johnny, he'd had someone to hate for a lot of reasons, but this military hero and justice fighter seemed to have had a lot of things going for him.

"Sorry," he muttered.

"I only knew him a few weeks, but he made an impact on my life. He encouraged me to turn my painful secret into something positive. That's why I decided to get involved in finding missing kids. I know my child isn't missing, and I gave her up by choice, but I do know what it's like to lose a piece of yourself. And if I can help some other family get whole again, I will."

"I'm sure you do a lot of good. I'm sorry I was an asshole when you first showed up at Josie's house. You threw me," he said candidly.

"I was shaken, too. I was not expecting to see your face. I honestly had no idea that Grace's mother was Josie. I just had Grace's name. I don't even think I saw the names of her parents. But then everything was happening really fast. I got a call at six a.m. yesterday to get on a plane and come to Chicago. It's been a lightning blur since then."

"When did you first hear from the kidnapper?"

"Actually, I got that call right before my boss got in touch with me about Hayley's disappearance."

"That's interesting. The kidnapper knew they were going to call you in."

"Sometimes, I think this whole case is about me and my past. And that's why he picked Chicago and moved out of the Northeast. He wanted me in his game, and this is where he could make me the most vulnerable. But I'm not going to let him win. I'm going to find Hayley and this girl on the train, and I will make sure this kidnapper ends up in jail for the rest of his life."

"I believe you."

She checked her phone and groaned. "Now it says five more minutes."

"There's a lot of traffic this time of day. That's why the trains are usually faster." As he spoke, he glanced around the neighborhood, wondering if someone was watching her even now.

She followed his gaze. "I didn't see a tail," she said. "I watched on the way over here."

And he didn't see anyone sitting in a car or hanging out in the doorway of a building, but he had to admit he felt decidedly tense.

"So, what does Adrienne do?" Bree asked.

"She's an event planner."

"That sounds fun."

"She seems to like it." Standing next to Bree, he could barely remember what Adrienne looked like. *How was that possible?* Two days ago, he'd been thinking she might be someone he could think of as a girlfriend. Now, she seemed like a very pale comparison to Bree and all her fiery passion. Of course, that passion also came with a lot of problems. Bree was drama and pain. Adrienne was light and fun.

Hadn't he had enough darkness in his life?

"Have you told Adrienne about your childhood, your stepfather?" she asked.

"Why would I? It's not important to our relationship. And we're definitely not to the point where we're sharing secrets. Hell, I haven't even told her I don't like Brussels sprouts."

Bree raised an eyebrow. "You don't like Brussels sprouts?"

"No. I don't care if they're roasted or steamed or covered in garlic and cheese. I just don't like 'em."

"That sounds very definitive," she said with a light smile. "Why haven't you told her that?"

"Because she loves Brussels sprouts—all vegetables, in fact. She is passionate about her health. And it seems too soon to confess such a dark secret."

"How are you going to have an honest relationship, if you can't come clean about a vegetable?"

"Honesty is overrated."

"I don't agree with that."

"Really? You think telling people what they don't want to hear makes them like you more?"

"I wouldn't say that, but maybe Adrienne needs to date a guy who shares her love of Brussels sprouts."

"So, I'm depriving her of the opportunity to find her perfect vegetable match? I guess I need to break up with her."

"Or come clean. How long have you been dating?"

"Two months."

"That's a fair amount of time."

"Is it?"

"What is she like?"

"Why are you so interested?"

"Because I just am. You used to date a lot of blondes. You had a new girl every week in high school."

"Well, I always heard blondes had more fun, and I was a teenage boy."

"Do you ever think about getting married?"

"Whoa, you are getting way ahead of yourself."

"You're not getting any younger, Nathan. You're thirty years old."

"That's not that old. I'm busy with my career. What's your excuse?"

"I'm busy, too. I'm always on the go. I get called out of town on a moment's notice. Not many guys appreciate that." She paused as a silver Prius came down the street. "There's my car."

He felt both relieved and unhappy that it was time for her to go.

She gave him a grateful smile. "Thanks again for talking me off the ledge, Nathan. I feel better now."

She might feel better, but he felt very conflicted.

He didn't know what to make of the mysterious girl on the train, but one thing was clear. Bree was in trouble.

Was he going to go back to his old ways and try to protect her, rescue her? Or was he going to walk away and let her take care of herself?

She was more than capable of doing that. He just had to let her.

Yeah…it wasn't really a question…

After Bree left, Nathan tried to work. But as the afternoon shadows deepened, and five o'clock approached, he put his tools away and got into his truck. He started toward home, but halfway there, he turned around and made his way toward Craig's, a small sports bar in River North.

He'd met Alan Craig in middle school, and they'd been friends during most of their teen years, but after Johnny's beat-down, he'd left his old neighborhood and gone dark on all of his friendships.

Ten years had passed before he'd run into Alan at a market last year. Since then, he'd hung out a few times at the bar, happy to see Alan had taken his grandfather's bar in the old neighborhood and moved it to River North, where he'd found a good clientele of locals and tourists.

When he entered Craig's, he was immediately enveloped by a warm, friendly feeling. The wood-paneled walls featured sports memorabilia from all of Chicago's teams, the Cubs, the Bears, the Bulls, the White Sox, and the Blackhawks. In addition to a long bar with three TVs behind it, there were a dozen or so tables in the middle of the room facing additional flat-screens, most of which were currently playing a White Sox game that was just about to start.

There were about fifteen people in the bar: a group of young male executives who looked like they'd just left an accounting or law firm, a trio of twenty-something women who were working their way through a platter of Craig's famous chicken wings, as well as a few other couples and singles sitting at the bar.

He slid into an empty stool as Alan gave him a nod. Alan had dark-red hair, pale skin, and a multitude of freckles across his face. He'd added a few pounds to his square, stocky build, probably the result of testing out too many of those wings. Or maybe it was because he'd moved in with his girlfriend, Beth, a few months ago.

"Long time no see," Alan said with a grin. "Thought you'd ditched me again. And it was going to be another ten years before I saw you."

"Not a chance. I've been working a lot."

"Glad to hear business is good. I've got a Tank 7 Farmhouse Ale on tap."

"Sold."

"How are things going?" Alan asked, as he filled a glass and set it in front of him.

"Not great."

Alan's eyebrow shot up. "Problems with Josie?"

"Not this time. Well, not exactly. Did you hear about that girl who got kidnapped from the school concert?"

"Yeah, I saw it on the news. That's terrible. You know her?"

"I do. She's friends with Josie's daughter, and I know her

dad."

"I'm sorry. Are they close to finding her?"

"I hope so." He took a sip of his beer. "The FBI is involved."

"That's good, right?"

"It is good, but one of the FBI agents working the case is Bree."

"What?" Surprise flashed through Alan's eyes. "You're kidding me. Not Bree Larson?"

"She changed her last name to Adams, but it's her. She came to interview Grace, Josie's daughter, because Grace was a witness to the abduction. I could not believe it when I saw Bree standing on the porch."

Alan shook his head. "I can't believe she's in the FBI. That's something else. How did she look?"

"Really good," he said, taking another long draught of beer.

Alan laughed. "Man, you still have a thing for her."

"Don't be ridiculous."

"Come on, Nathan. I knew you back then. You and her always had some weird dance going on. I never knew exactly what was between you, but there was something."

Alan's words echoed Bree's from the night before when she'd said she didn't know what they were—friends, enemies, or people who used to know each other. It seemed that they had been all three at some point or another. But she definitely felt more like a friend after their last conversation, after she'd shown her vulnerability, after she'd admitted that dating Johnny was a huge mistake.

"Is she single?" Alan asked.

"That's what she said, but that's not important."

"What is important?"

"Johnny Hawke."

"I should have figured his name was coming after you mentioned Bree." Alan glanced around, making sure that the other bartender was taking care of the customers and then leaned forward. "Does Johnny have something to do with the kidnapping? Is Bree going to take him down?"

"I don't know if he's involved, but someone is messing with Bree, someone from our past, and Johnny is a good suspect. Unless you can tell me he's in jail now, or better yet—dead."

Alan frowned. "Sorry, but from what I hear, Johnny's business is better than ever. He's taken over his dad's boxing gym on Hayward. He and his brothers also run an automotive shop. I heard he operates his side gigs out of there—drugs, guns, gambling...the usual. He's made the family more powerful than it used to be. I don't think he lives in the old neighborhood anymore, though. He has other, more expensive, properties."

He sighed. "Not what I wanted to hear, but thanks."

"He's living with Sierra Littman now. Remember her?"

"Sure." Sierra had been friends with both Josie and Bree. She had always been looking for love in all the wrong places, and apparently, she'd found it in Johnny. "I'd like to say I feel sorry for her, but she was not a nice person. She was always lying and stirring up drama."

"That's true."

"Do they have kids together?"

"Not sure. His family has been expanding, but I don't know if they're his kids or his brothers' kids."

That was interesting. While Bree didn't think Johnny was involved, if he was, he probably had access to all kinds of kids who could pull off a con job like the girl on the train.

"Don't mention to anyone I was asking," he said.

Alan gave him a disgusted look. "You think I'd do that? I know what Johnny did to you. My advice is to do what you've been doing: stay out of the neighborhood, stay out of the past, and stay away from Bree. She almost got you killed once."

"It wasn't her fault."

"You were protecting her."

He tilted his head, giving Alan a speculative look. "I never told you why Johnny beat me up."

"It didn't take a rocket scientist to figure it had something to do with Bree, especially since she disappeared around the same time. Hey, if Bree is an FBI agent, maybe she can arrest Johnny's ass and put him away for good. Unless you think she still has feelings for him?"

"I don't think that, but I also don't think she wants to go anywhere near Johnny."

"Probably wise if she doesn't. Speaking of women, how are things going with the tall blonde you brought in a few weeks ago?"

"Damn. Adrienne," he muttered, looking down at his watch. He'd told her he wasn't going to do dinner, but she was still waiting to hear from him about drinks, and the last thing he wanted to do was hang out with her and her college friend when he was completely and utterly distracted.

"She went right out of your mind when you saw Bree, didn't she?"

"I didn't say that."

"You didn't have to. Do yourself a favor, Nathan. Figure out what you want from Bree once and for all. And then go get it."

"It's not that easy."

"It might just be. You won't know until you put it all on the line, but that's not something you've ever been willing to do with her."

"I didn't think I'd ever see her again." His phone buzzed, and as he took it out of his pocket, he saw Bree's name on the screen. "It's Bree."

Alan smiled. "Maybe this is your second chance to get it right."

"Or screw it up again."

"Looks like you're going to have an opportunity to find out." Alan moved away as he took the call.

"Hello?"

"The security camera caught the back of the little girl as she left the train station. She went into a café down the street, but I never saw her come out," Bree said, excitement in her voice. "I'm heading there now. Someone might have seen her or know who she is."

"I'd like to go with you. Why don't I pick you up?"

"I'm sure it's out of your way."

He was sure, too, but he wasn't letting her do this alone. "I can be at your office in about fifteen minutes."

"I'll meet you in front of the building."

"Stay inside until I get there. I'll text you." Getting up, he took a ten out of his wallet and put it on the bar. "I'll see you soon, Alan."

"That's way too much."

"It's cheap for the therapy session you just gave me."

Alan laughed. "Good luck."

"Thanks. I think I'm going to need it."

Seven

—➤➤◄◄◄—

Despite Nathan's suggestion that she stay in the office until he arrived, Bree packed up her things and walked quickly to the elevator.

The Chicago team was even less happy with her now than they had been earlier. When she'd returned to the office, she'd had a rather heated discussion with both Tracy and the ASAIC. They didn't like that the kidnapper had called her or that she'd gone down to Park Station on her own. They were happy that she'd recorded the call, but that analysis was still going ongoing and the trace had led to a café that was miles away from Park Station. No phone had been found dumped in the trash or anywhere else in the café. So, once again the kidnapper had played his hand very well.

One thing she had omitted from her story was what had happened on the train with the little girl. When she'd requested access to security cameras around the train station, everyone had assumed she was looking for Hayley. And, of course, she had looked for Hayley, but she had also looked for the brown-haired, green-eyed girl in the ragged gray sweatshirt and ripped jeans.

Maybe it was wrong not to have come completely clean with them, but she hadn't been able to summon the will to confess her personal secret to people she barely knew. Plus, she had as much experience, if not more, than anyone on the

Chicago team, and the second she thought her secret would save Hayley's life, she would tell it, but right now she needed to play things out on her own and try to find the girl on the train. If she could get to her, she would be one step closer to the kidnapper.

When she got downstairs, she waited in the lobby for Nathan, her thoughts turning to the man who had played such a pivotal role in her life at various times. She probably shouldn't have gone to him this afternoon, but he had seemed the perfect person to turn to.

It wasn't just that he knew about the baby; it was because he knew her—the real her, the person that no one else knew.

And it had felt so damn good to lean on him. Even now, she could feel his arms around her, and the memory made her nerves tingle. She and Nathan had had odd moments of attraction over the years, but they'd never acted on them. *They certainly couldn't act on them now.*

She really shouldn't have called him. She was pulling him into a dangerous situation.

Was that fair? Hadn't she already put him through hell once before when Johnny had almost killed him because of her?

But it was too late now. She could see his truck pulling up in the loading zone, and her phone buzzed with his text. She typed in a quick *ok* and headed out the door.

When she hopped into the truck, she gave him a nervous smile, and felt another jolt of attraction as his brown-eyed gaze met hers. *This was not good.*

She looked away and fumbled with her seat belt, reminding herself that she needed to focus on finding the girl and nothing else.

"Are you okay?" Nathan asked her.

She forced a neutral expression onto her face. "I'm fine."

"Did you tell the other FBI agents about your experience?"

"I shared the call with them, but not the rest. I will tell my secret if it will help Hayley."

"I know you will," he said evenly.

"You do?" she asked with a bit of surprise. "You haven't always liked my decisions."

"That's true, but I'm okay with this one. I know you won't jeopardize Hayley's life for any reason, not even to protect your secret."

"Thank you. The one good thing about this sick game is that I'm pretty certain Hayley is alive, and that gives us a chance to find her."

"I hope you're right. What's the name of the café we're going to?"

"It's called the Hummingbird Café. I looked it up, and it's open til nine; they serve breakfast, lunch, and dinner. It's owned by Viola and Jonas Montclair, a middle-aged, African-American couple, who opened the restaurant five years ago."

"You did your research. Is that important to know?"

"I have no idea. But I'm trying to find a way to get ahead. Since the girl went into the café and never left, she's either still there or there's a back door."

"If that's the case, she could have gone through the place in two minutes, and it's possible no one saw her."

"That would be depressing, but I'm hoping that's not the case. The girl was no more than ten or eleven, and she was alone, so I'm thinking she lives nearby, knows the area. She walked with confidence."

"Interesting that you said earlier that she spoke with purpose and now you say she walked with confidence. It doesn't really sound like she's scared or in trouble."

"No, it doesn't, but maybe she's too young to know she's being used."

"True." He paused. "By the way, I saw Alan Craig earlier. Do you remember him?"

"I do, but I thought you said you didn't see anyone from our past."

"Actually, I do see Alan now; I ran into him last year after not having seen him since we were teenagers. He runs a bar in River North. He named it Craig's after the one his grandfather used to run in the old neighborhood. He has a girlfriend he lives with. Beth is a sweetheart."

"You were good friends with Alan. How come you let that end?"

"Because once Johnny beat the crap out of me, I didn't want to hang out with anyone who might get hurt in my wake. Alan knew what had happened to me. I actually stayed at his house for a night before I was able to get Josie and move out of that neighborhood."

As Nathan was telling the story, she sensed there was a reason behind it that she wasn't going to like. "Where are you going with this?" she asked, pretty sure she knew.

Nathan gave her a quick look. "I wanted to find out if Alan knew anything about Johnny's current activities. I know he has a few friends who still live in the neighborhood."

"Did you tell him why you were asking about Johnny?"

"Not really."

She didn't like his answer. "You told him I was in town, didn't you?"

"I told him you were looking for the missing girl."

"And then you asked about Johnny. Dammit, Nathan, he's going to start putting things together. You said he knew you got beat up. Did he know why?"

"No. I told you I didn't tell anyone. He did say earlier tonight that he figured it had something to do with you, because you disappeared, and Johnny was going crazy trying to find you."

She shook her head. "I wish you hadn't brought him into this."

"He's not into anything, and aren't you a little curious as to what he said?"

She really didn't want to be, but if it could help the case... "Fine. What did he say?"

"Johnny has taken over for his dad. He's grown the family business of criminal activities. He's very powerful now."

"Awesome."

"He's with Sierra Littman."

"Well, things really haven't changed all that much, have they? She was always trying to get Johnny's attention. Are they married? Do they have kids?"

"I think they're just living together. But Alan said there are a lot of kids around. Could be Johnny's or they could belong to his brothers."

"Johnny always talked about having sons, carrying on the family legacy. I tried to tell him that he could be better than his family. I thought there was more good in him than there was in his brothers. He used to say I was crazy; there was nothing better than power, and that's what his family had."

"And what he wanted more than anything."

"I suppose so. But isn't that what we all wanted back then? We were in our late teens, looking at adulthood. We wanted to control our destinies, but we still needed money and school and opportunities." She turned her head, looking out at the city streets passing by. "Do you remember all those nights we used to just walk around? Especially in the summer when it was so hot? It seemed like we'd walk for miles, but we never got anywhere. It was like we'd run into those invisible fences that keep pets from leaving their yard. We couldn't step beyond a particular curb, go past a corner. The future was always just beyond where we could get to."

"That's a good way to describe it." He paused. "I know you don't think Johnny is part of this, but he would know how to get a kid to play a con like this. He used to do this kind of shit when he was a kid."

She frowned as she turned back to him. "I still don't think it's him. But I take your point."

"Just something to consider."

A moment passed, and then she said, "I feel like I should apologize again for what happened to you after I left, Nathan. I was caught up in my own problems, but I should have seen how much danger you put yourself in for me. I shouldn't have called in my debt."

"You kept Josie out of jail; I owed you. I paid up."

"Yes, you did. But you paid more than you owed. And I shouldn't have forced your hand like that."

"Well, maybe someday I'll need a favor, and you can pay me back."

"I would try, Nathan. You probably don't believe that, but I would."

He looked away from the road to meet her gaze once more. "Actually, I do believe you."

His words warmed her heart. "I'm glad."

Their gazes clung together for a long moment, and she felt as if whatever had been holding them apart suddenly fractured.

Then Nathan squared his jaw and turned his attention back to traffic.

Maybe there was still a wall between them after all.

As they neared Park Station, she realized how close they were getting to the old neighborhood. They weren't there yet, but it was only a mile or two away. She was quite sure the station had been picked for a particular reason, and perhaps that was it.

It took Nathan a few minutes to find a parking spot. Then they walked down the street and under the train tracks. As the train rumbled overhead, her mind went back to earlier that day. She could hear the girl's voice so clearly, see the question in her eyes, but then she was gone.

"I assume the café is the building with the bird on it," Nathan said, waving his hand toward the end of the block.

"Yes."

As they headed toward the restaurant, she wondered if someone was watching them, if someone was waiting, and she found herself moving closer to Nathan.

Or perhaps he was moving closer to her...

His hand suddenly covered hers, and she jumped, startled by the unexpected touch, by the surprising heat.

"I just want to keep us together," he said, in answer to her unspoken question.

She should let go, but her fingers seemed to have a mind

of their own, curling around Nathan's. And it felt right…better than right, if she were being honest.

She was so used to being on her own but at this moment it felt really good to have Nathan with her.

When they reached the café, Nathan opened the door for her, and she stepped inside. Despite the fact that the restaurant was bright and charming, with a dozen or so tables and a glass display case by the register filled with cakes and cookies, she felt as if she were walking into a trap. She scanned the restaurant quickly. There were about fifteen people seated at various tables, but no girls of the right age.

She moved over to the counter, where a young woman in her early twenties greeted her.

"Can I help you?" the woman asked.

"Yes. I'm looking for this girl." She took out her phone where she'd captured a screenshot of the little girl. It was of her back, but she was hoping the woman might recognize her from her clothes. "She was in this café a few hours ago, between one and two o'clock. Were you working then?"

"Right. Yeah, I saw her. You're her mom? The FBI agent?"

Her pulse leapt at the question. "Who told you that?"

"The kid. She said you'd be in, and I should give you this." The woman reached underneath the counter and pulled out a piece of paper.

She took what appeared to be a flyer out of the woman's hand. "What's this?" she asked in confusion.

"Beats me. The kid gave me $20 and said to give it to her mom, the brown-haired FBI agent with the green eyes. The kid looked just like you." She paused. "If you don't mind, I have some other customers..."

Bree stared down at the flyer in confusion but stepped to the side as the clerk helped a young father and his son.

"Open Heart Refuge," she murmured, her stomach twisting into another painful knot. She felt hot, sweaty, dizzy, weak… "I have to sit down." She stumbled a few feet away to an empty table.

Nathan sat down across from her and took the paper out of her hand, a deep frown crossing his lips. Then he lifted his gaze and met hers. "He is pushing all your buttons. Someone is seriously screwing with you. Someone from your past—*our* past," he added, a hard light entering his light-brown eyes. "Open Heart Refuge is where we met."

"I know. I was twelve. I was there with my aunt. You were thirteen, and you were there with Josie and your mom."

"One of several times she tried to leave my stepfather," he said, a harsh note in his voice. "It just never lasted longer than a few weeks. She always went back, and she always took us with her. But for that short time…"

"Everything felt almost normal," she murmured, meeting his gaze. "We played cards after school—hearts and spades."

"And poker," he reminded her. "I taught you how to play seven card stud."

"And you made up stories to entertain Josie, so she wouldn't be scared. There were a lot of tales about soldiers and white knights and magical spells that would protect us."

"But they weren't real." He set the flyer down on the table, giving her a speculative look. "You know what you're supposed to do with this."

"I'm supposed to go to the shelter."

"Do you really want to walk through those doors again, Bree?"

She thought about his question for a long moment. "I really don't."

"But you're going to."

"It's the next move. I have to find that girl. Maybe she's there."

"She's not. That would be too easy. I think you should stop playing his game."

"I've had the same thought."

"I sense a *but* coming."

"But the Chicago office has a lot of manpower on Hayley's case, and if I follow these clues, maybe he'll make a mistake. Perhaps he'll reveal something that will lead us to

Hayley."

"He doesn't seem like someone who is going to make an easy mistake."

"No, but if I don't go, I'm just going to spend all night wondering what I would have found there." She paused, glancing down the hall. "There's a back door. The little girl must have left through that door. Although, it appears to be locked now." She got up and went over to the counter, waiting for another opportunity to speak to the cashier. "Do you have a security camera off the back door?"

"We did, but it broke last year, and the owner hasn't gotten it fixed."

"You didn't see anyone with the little girl? She didn't meet up with someone here in the café?"

"Nope. As far as I know, she was alone. Sorry."

"Thanks."

Nathan got up as she returned to the table. "I'll drive you to the shelter."

"You don't have to do that. I can take a cab." She licked her lips, knowing she should send him away, but she wasn't quite feeling it. She liked having him around.

"You're not taking a cab, and you're not going there alone."

"You're not the one in charge," she said, feeling it necessary to remind him.

"You're not, either, Bree. The person in charge is the one sending you on this sick scavenger hunt."

She frowned. "You're right. It is sick, and I need to find that girl, because she's a pawn in this game, and even if she isn't my daughter, I need to make sure that she's safe."

"Then we'll go to the shelter, and we'll take it from there." He grabbed her hand. "And, yes, I am going to hold onto you until we get to the truck, so get over it."

She didn't have to get over it, but she wasn't going to tell him that. "If it makes you feel better, fine."

Eight

—➤➤◄◄◄—

Nathan only felt better until he had to let go of Bree's hand and usher her into his truck. As he walked around the vehicle, he felt a cold chill and a deep sense of foreboding that only got worse as he got behind the wheel and started the engine.

Bree was being targeted in a destructive, terrifying manner, forcing her to walk back through the darkest moments of her past. He didn't know if he agreed with her decision to keep the Chicago FBI team out of this, but she knew her business more than he did, so he had to go along with it. What he wasn't going to do was let her go to the shelter on her own.

He rationalized that helping her was also helping Hayley, but deep down, he knew he was still with Bree because he couldn't walk away from her. He'd never been able to do that completely. Sure, he'd kept his distance at times, especially when she was with Johnny, but he'd always been close enough if she'd ever needed him.

And she had. She'd needed him to help her leave town. Even though he'd let her believe that she'd blackmailed him into helping, it wasn't really true. And helping her exit his life had been one of the hardest things he'd ever done. Even when she'd been with someone else, she'd still been in his life; he could still see her smile, hear her laugh...

Knowing that he would probably never see her again had

gutted him.

But knowing that she'd be out of Johnny's power and that she and her child would be safe, would have better lives, had helped him get through it.

He really didn't want her to get sucked back into the quicksand that had once been her life.

But she wasn't going to quit—at least, not yet.

Neither was he.

Glancing over at her, he wondered what she was thinking. She hadn't spoken a word since they'd gotten in the car, and her gaze was on the dark city streets, blocks that were becoming more and more familiar. Mack's Deli, where they'd saved up change to buy a Mack special, which was really just a lot of processed meats and cheese: bologna, pepperoni, Swiss cheese, a mound of lettuce, a couple of tomatoes, and a lot of red onions. They'd loved those sandwiches, usually sharing a half-footer, washing it down with a soda, chasing it with some gummy worms.

It was any wonder they'd survived on the food they'd eaten.

But some days there hadn't been much food at all…

He could still vividly remember the feeling of hunger in the pit of his soul, gnawing away at him, making him feel hollow. But the hunger hadn't been nearly as bad as some of the other emotions he'd had to get through. He'd take an empty stomach any day over the alternative—having to deal with his stepfather, a mean-assed son-of-a-bitch.

Clearing his throat, he was tempted to turn the truck around and speed away as fast as he could.

Bree turned her head, gazing back at him, as if she sensed his sudden discomfort.

"I know," she murmured. "All this sucks. We both have our lives together and now we're going to relive a painful time in our past."

"Are you sure you want to do this now? Maybe you should think about it, sleep on it, come back in the daylight."

"I can't afford to waste any time, Nathan. There's a clue

at the shelter, and I have to get it."

"How can you be sure?"

"Because he wouldn't be sending me there unless he has something else to show me."

"Or he wants to hurt you."

"I don't think he's ready to do that yet. He's still in the slow build...savoring the game that he has so carefully put together. He wants to watch me twist in the wind, wonder if this girl is my daughter, worry if I'll find her in time."

"Okay, I have to bring something up," he said abruptly.

"What is it?"

"You've become fixated on the idea that the girl on the train is your daughter."

"That's not true. I know she's probably not."

"There's a part of you that is unsure."

"Well, you did hear the cashier at the café say she looked like me, didn't you?"

"Yeah, I get it. She has brown hair and green eyes. Lots of girls do."

"What's your point?" she snapped.

He made a quick decision and took a turn at the next intersection, then pulled over.

"Why are we stopping?"

"Because we need to have this conversation, and I don't want to be driving while we're having it."

"Okay. What do you want to say?"

He threw the truck into park and turned to look at her. "What about Hayley?"

"What do you mean?"

"If this kidnapper has Hayley, why didn't he just use her to get to you?"

"Well...because she probably wouldn't have done it. This girl might have been paid. She could have been a street kid, who was ready to make some cash. She wasn't afraid. Hayley wouldn't have been able to pull this off."

"All right. That makes sense. But what about Hayley?" he repeated. "Come on, Bree. It has to have crossed your mind that Hayley is also the right age to be your daughter. And she was adopted. If this kidnapper knows you had a kid, and wants to torture you in the worst way possible, how can you not consider the fact that Hayley might be your child?"

Her eyes glittered in the shadowy light. "I did think about it. But her birthdate isn't the same. Hayley was born in Joliet, Illinois, five days before I had my daughter."

"Five days isn't very long."

"But my child was born in Detroit. And the mother listed on Hayley's birth certificate checked out. We verified that she did give birth in that hospital on that day. Nothing points to Hayley being my kid. She doesn't even look like me."

"Then why did the kidnapper pick her? Why did this person, who you said has been working in the northeast, come to Chicago and pick Hayley as his next victim?"

"I think he came to Chicago because of me. After I botched his last abduction, he wanted revenge, and obviously he did a lot of research on me. He probably thought I'd be weaker here in Chicago, not just because of my past, but because I wouldn't be with my normal team, the team that has been chasing him for months."

He supposed that made sense.

"As for why he picked Hayley?" Bree continued. "All I can say is that she matches the other victims for the most part. Her hair is brown, not blonde, but she has brown eyes, just like the other three girls, who were also around the same age. She lives in an upper-class neighborhood, goes to a good school, and comes from a happy family—also just like the other three girls. Her abduction follows the same patterns as before. She was taken from a school, a place where she should have been safe."

"Were any of those other girls adopted?"

"No, but I'm not sure how he would know that in advance."

"So that's different."

"Yes, and the other difference is that he's pulling me into his game, as well as this other little girl from the train." She blew out a breath. "When I say it all out loud, it sounds crazy. I know that. But there's a good chance this kidnapper is not sane."

"All right. I get it. Hayley fits the pattern. But if he knows you gave up a kid, why didn't he try to find her, take her?"

"Because he can't find her. He might have found out I got pregnant and left town and had a baby, but he doesn't know where my child is. My daughter is safe and far away from here," she said, a desperate note in her voice.

He knew she needed to believe that, and he didn't want to take her hope away, but he wasn't as convinced as she was.

"Can we go now?" she asked.

"One second. Tell me about Detroit."

"There's not much to tell. I lived in a studio apartment about as big as a closet. I had a part-time job in a taco shop, and I was there for three months until I gave birth." She sucked in a deep breath, slowly letting it trickle out. "Giving up my daughter was the most difficult and painful thing I've ever done. I was in labor for hours, and I was all alone. I should have been used to it by then, but it was still so lonely and terrifying. And when she was born, I heard her cry, and then she was taken away."

A tear slid out of Bree's eye, and his heart ached for her.

She ruthlessly wiped it away with her fingers. "All I saw was a tiny bundle in a hospital blanket. I didn't even see the color of her hair or her eyes."

"Why not? Why didn't they let you hold her—say good-bye?"

"Before I went into labor, I had told them I didn't want to see her, but after she was gone, I really wished I hadn't said that. I thought it would be easier if she just disappeared, but it wasn't. I cried the whole night and most of the next few months."

"You shouldn't have been alone. I wish you had called me."

"I couldn't call anyone. I had to make a clean break from

my old life."

"What happened after that? Did you stay in Detroit?"

"No. I left three weeks later. It was too painful to stay in the apartment where I'd been pregnant. For months, it had just been me and her. I didn't make any friends there. It was too risky. At night, I'd read to my baby, play her music, tell her she was going to have a great life. Once she was gone, I couldn't stand being there."

"You left Detroit and went where?"

"Colorado. I was given a bonus of five thousand dollars for delivering a healthy baby. I enrolled at a community college and got a part-time job and eventually made it to the University of Colorado Boulder, where I majored in criminal justice and psychology. I made a new life for myself, and several years after graduation, I got into the FBI. That's when I really came into my own. Now I'm trained in multiple weapons, I understand criminal behavior, and I can win at hand-to-hand combat. I don't need anyone to rescue me anymore. And I've been doing good work the last five years. I like who I am now."

"I like who you are, too," he admitted.

She flashed him a smile. "Really? I know I disappointed you a lot back in the day. You were pretty critical of my choices."

"Johnny was bad for you."

"I didn't find out how bad for a long time. I hate that we're going down this road into the past, Nathan."

"I think you're supposed to hate it."

"I still don't understand how the kidnapper knows my secrets. But it doesn't really matter. I just have to find him before he hurts Hayley or this other little girl. We only have a couple of days at most. The other girls didn't make it past the seventh day."

"Then we better get to it."

—➤➤◄◄—

She couldn't believe she'd told Nathan about the night she'd given birth to her child. She'd never told anyone, and now she was feeling overwhelmed with emotion, remembering those first few minutes after the birth, when she'd yearned to see her baby's face, her eyes, her first look at the world.

For that entire first year, she'd thought about her child every single day, hoping she'd made the right choice. As time went on, she'd never forgotten, but she had found a way to move on, secure in the knowledge that she'd done the right thing. She'd imagined her child with loving parents, a beautiful home in a nice neighborhood, pretty clothes and good food and nothing but joy.

Had that been a fool's dream?

Had choosing total secrecy to protect the child from Johnny actually put her daughter in more danger because she'd used someone working outside of the law?

She needed to know. She needed to find her daughter. She'd told Nathan that her child was not the girl on the train and not Hayley, because none of the facts supported either scenario. He hadn't tried to argue with her, but she'd seen the doubt in his eyes.

She wanted to believe that her child was still living the dream life she'd given her away to get, but she needed to find out for sure. And the only way to do that was to keep playing the game, until she had a chance to make her own move.

A few moments later, Nathan parked under a streetlight, a block away from the shelter. She hoped the tires, the rims, and everything else would still be there when they were done, but in this neighborhood, you never knew.

Nathan took her hand again as they hit the sidewalk, and she didn't quite know what to think about that. She just knew that she liked it, probably a little too much. But she had enough to worry about right now, and her relationship with Nathan—whatever it was—would have to be dissected later.

When she saw the bright-blue door with the sign Open Heart Refuge, her heart sped up again. This particular shelter, housed in an old three-story hotel, was for single mothers with children, and instead of one or two big rooms filled with cots like most shelters, each of the eighteen hotel rooms could house one to four family members.

Having a room that she only had to share with her aunt had made her feel more normal. There had also been a large multi-media room downstairs with card tables, a big television, and plenty of games, as well as a smaller quieter room for reading and homework. Adults had their own computer center and private room for when they needed a break from the kids. There was also a kitchen and a dining room that actually provided decent meals.

They'd spent four months at the shelter before moving into an apartment. She'd been sad to leave, but the shelter was very good at helping their residents move into longer-term situations. Unfortunately, longer term for her and her aunt had been about seven months. Then her aunt had ended up in rehab, and she'd been put in foster care, the first of several homes, all of them disappointing.

As they drew nearer to the door, Nathan's steps began to slow, and his fingers tightened around hers.

She paused, giving him a curious look. "Everything okay?"

His lips tightened. "I never thought I'd be back here."

"Nothing bad happened at this place," she reminded him. "Right?"

"Right."

"The director—what was her name?"

"Lucy Harper."

"Yes. Miss Lucy, we called her. I wonder if she's still here. Although, she seemed like a hundred years old when I was twelve."

"She was probably fifty," he said with a tight smile.

"She was fierce. I remember her chasing off bad boyfriends and bad husbands and just anyone who seemed like a threat. It was the first time I'd really seen anyone do that."

"She had a baseball bat behind the desk. She threatened to use it on my stepfather when he showed up one night. I only wished she'd done it. It would have saved us all a lot more pain."

She didn't know all the ins and outs of Nathan's life, but she knew he'd had a lot of trouble with his stepfather, and that hadn't ended until his stepfather had died when they were in high school.

"How is your mother doing now?" she asked tentatively.

"She's in a good place, but we don't need to talk about her. Let's get this over with."

She nodded, and they headed toward the door.

As they stepped inside the building, she felt as if she were stepping back in time. She had to remind herself she wasn't a scared kid looking for shelter or a safe place anymore. She was an FBI agent trying to save a child's life. That was what mattered.

She walked up to the desk, which was manned by a woman with a nametag that read Christie. She had blonde hair, blue eyes and appeared to be in her late thirties.

"How can I help you?" Christie asked.

"My name is Bree Adams. I'm a special agent with the FBI." She showed her badge to Christie, whose expression immediately turned wary. "I'm working on a case involving a missing child."

"The one on the news?" Christie asked.

"Yes, but there's another little girl that we're concerned about at the moment, and I have a lead that she might be staying here at the shelter. This is a photo of her. It's obviously taken from the back, but maybe you recognize her?" She handed her phone to Christie.

Christie looked at the picture. "I'm sure you know that I can't give out any personal information on our residents. It's for their safety." She gave Bree back her phone. "I'm sorry."

Judging by the uncomfortable gleam in Christie's eyes, she had recognized the girl.

"I completely understand," Bree said. "But this is a

matter of life or death. And I know you would want to help us."

"This little girl is in danger?"

"Yes."

"I can ask the director..." Christie began, stopping as the door to the office behind her opened.

Bree was shocked to see the older woman with white hair and piercing blue eyes that she and Nathan had just been talking about. "Miss Lucy," she muttered. "You're still here."

Lucy Harper's gaze swept across her face and then moved on to Nathan. "Well, well. You two look familiar. Let me think." She gave Bree a long look. "Bree Larson."

"I can't believe you remember me."

"Brown hair, beautiful green eyes that were always hopeful," Lucy said, then turned to Nathan. "And you are Nathan...oh, what was your last name?"

"Bishop."

"Of course. Nathan Bishop, the very protective big brother and devoted son."

"You have an excellent memory," Nathan said. "I was thirteen years old when I was here. That was a long time ago."

"I like to think of the people who stay here as family. And I have to admit your mother's face still haunts me, Nathan. When she left, I was very worried about her. She never came back. I didn't know if that was good or bad," Lucy said with concern in her gaze. "Dare I ask?"

"She's okay now," Nathan said tightly.

As Bree heard the words, she wanted to feel relieved. But she felt like there was something Nathan wasn't saying. Now, however, was not the time to get into it.

"Oh, I am so happy to hear that," Lucy said. "Now what brings you two back to our shelter? You don't look like you need help anymore."

"They're with the FBI," Christie put in.

"Actually, I'm with the FBI," Bree corrected. "I'm looking for a little girl. She's in danger, and I need to find her.

I know you can't give out confidential information, but this is really important. I have a picture of her. I just showed it to Christie."

Lucy gave Christie a nod of encouragement. "Go ahead."

"The girl's name is Emma Lowell," Christie said. "She came in two nights ago with her sister Tasha. Tasha showed me her ID. She's eighteen years old. Emma said she was ten. They told me that their mother was sick and couldn't pay the rent and they needed a place to stay until she got out of the hospital."

"You didn't call DCFS?" Bree asked.

"Since Emma was with her adult sibling, we did not," Christie said, a defensive note in her voice. "We try to help families stay together, not get ripped apart."

"She knows that," Lucy said, giving her a pointed look. "Don't you?"

"I do. And I'm not here to make trouble. I just want to find Emma. Is she here now?"

Christie shook her head. "She and her sister checked out a few hours ago. They said they'd found a better place to stay. They seemed quite happy, as if things had turned around in an unexpected way."

"Did they say anything else? Like where they were going?"

Christie thought for a moment. "Emma said something about getting a part in a play. That's all I know."

A part in a play or a part in a con?

"Have the cleaners gone through their suite?" she asked, wondering if Emma had left anything behind. It seemed unbelievable that the flyer would bring them to the shelter and then there would be nothing. "Did they leave anything behind?"

"The cleaners won't be in there until morning. We don't have a full house right now, so there wasn't a rush."

"Can I see where they were staying?"

"Well, I suppose there's no harm in that," Lucy said. "But you'll have to wait here, Nathan. As you might recall, no adult men are allowed upstairs."

"I understand," he said.

She gave Nathan an apologetic look. "I won't be long."

"Take your time. I'll be here."

As Bree walked up the stairs with Lucy, she noticed that the shelter had definitely been updated. There was fresh paint on the walls and tiled floors instead of the old, stained carpet that had always smelled bad.

"How does it feel to be back?" Lucy asked, giving her a sharp look.

"Weird. But this place was good for me and my aunt for the time we were here."

"What happened to your aunt?"

"I'm not sure."

"You don't keep in touch?"

"No. I haven't seen her in years. She fell apart after we left here. Like my mother, she was toxic. She just couldn't get herself together, and she certainly couldn't take care of me. I ended up in the system. I kept thinking she would get better and come looking for me, but that never happened."

"Well, I'm glad you're doing well now. How do you like working for the FBI?"

"I love my job. I spend most of my time looking for missing kids, and while it's difficult at times, it's also rewarding."

Lucy smiled. "I'm sure they are all very lucky to have someone like you on their side. You were always a stubborn girl. I bet that works well for you now."

"I'd like to think so."

"And Nathan. You two are together? I remember you were very close when you were here."

"How do you remember us? So many people come through here. It seems unbelievable."

"I look at people. I listen to them. I almost always remember their names and at least some part of their story. It's actually much harder to forget some of the things I see and hear than to remember."

She saw a sadness in Lucy's eyes and could only imagine some of the horror stories she'd had to hear, to live through. "The people who come here are lucky to have you."

"I was on the streets when I was a little girl. I understand the needs, the despair, the dreams of the people who come here. I do what I can to make life a little better for a short while."

"You do a great job. This is the best place I ever stayed." She paused. "Do you know any more of Emma's story than what Christie told us?"

"Unfortunately, I don't. I didn't meet Emma or her sister. I've been in and out the last couple of days." Lucy paused in front of Suite 2102. "This is it."

Bree sucked in a quick breath. "This is it? But this—this was my suite."

"Is it? I didn't realize. That's odd."

She didn't think it was odd or a coincidence. "Did they ask to be in this suite?"

"I don't know. I can check with Christie. I don't know why they would have. They'd never been here before. It's not like they wanted to go back to a favorite room." Lucy opened the door and waved her inside.

As she stepped into the room with two double beds, it felt much smaller than she remembered. Both beds were unmade, covers tossed about. There was a pizza box on the dresser and a couple of empty soda cans.

There was also something on one of the pillows—a large white envelope.

She walked across the room with a growing sense of trepidation that worsened when she saw her name scrawled across the front of the envelope. She'd just found her clue. Inside, she found two newspaper clippings. It took her a moment to realize the clippings were actually of one photograph that had been ripped down the middle. And that photograph was of her. After high school, she'd done some modeling to make some cash, and she'd made it into the newspaper while walking the runway at a charity fashion show.

She couldn't believe someone had dug up this old clipping, ripped it in two and left it for her.

"Can I ask what's going on?" Lucy enquired.

She saw the concern in the older woman's eyes. "Someone is trying to drive me mad."

Lucy frowned as she showed her the ripped photo.

"I don't understand. What does this mean?" Lucy asked.

"That someone knows my past and is digging it up piece by piece. I got a lead to come here, and now I find this. Only problem is I don't know where to go next."

"How are Emma and Tasha involved?"

"I don't know. Emma told Christie she had a part in a play. Maybe they were paid to come here, ask for this room, leave me this note, and then they left. I just hope that means that they're safe." She took another look around the room and the adjoining bathroom. There were no other items of interest. "Thanks for letting me up here," she told Lucy as they made their way downstairs.

"If I can be of any more help, I'll certainly try."

"Will you let me know if Emma or Tasha come back?"

"Of course."

She left her phone number with Lucy and then joined Nathan, who got up from the bench by the door, a questioning gleam in his eyes.

She handed him the ripped photo.

His gaze narrowed. "I remember this event."

"Yes. I thought I was going to be famous when I made the paper."

"Johnny called you his supermodel," Nathan said, a terse note in his voice. "What the hell is this supposed to mean? Was there a note?"

"Nope. I think it means that they can rip me apart whenever they want, or am I being too literal?"

"Let's get out of here," he said, giving her back the clippings.

She put the envelope in her bag and they headed outside.

She shivered as the wind gusted down the street, the temperature having dropped at least ten degrees. It was after seven now, and she was happy that the truck was close by, also happy that no one had tampered with it.

"What do you want to do?" Nathan asked, as they fastened their seat belts.

"I have no idea," she said with a sigh. "I need to think, but I'm tired, I'm hungry, and I'm pissed off that I am playing puppet to some master I don't even know."

"I can't do anything about the puppet master, but I can do something about food. You want to get some dinner?"

"I would like to eat something, but you don't have to babysit me, Nathan."

"I'm hungry, too. Where are you staying?"

"In a hotel by Michigan Avenue and the river."

"I know a place in that neighborhood, which is not tied to our past in any way."

"Thank goodness for that." Maybe after some food, she'd be better able to put some of the clues together in a pattern that made sense and would hopefully lead them to whoever was sending her on a sad trip down memory lane.

Nine

—➤➤◄◄◄—

In a cozy restaurant, over one of Chicago's infamous deep-dish pizzas laden with vegetables and spicy pepperoni, Bree felt her tension begin to ease. Part of that was because of the pizza and the glass of wine she'd consumed, but most of it had to do with Nathan.

She'd forgotten how much she'd liked him when they were kids, how easy he was to talk to, how he seemed to know what she was thinking or where her brain was going even before she got there. Since they'd tabled all subjects involving the past for the duration of their pizza, it had been fun to hear him talk about his construction business and the triathlon he planned to do in the spring. He also clearly adored Grace, talking with great affection about his niece's love of reading and drama, how she was always roping him into playing imaginary games when he babysat for her.

Nathan had always loved his family beyond compare. She didn't think she'd met anyone who would go to the kind of lengths that Nathan had to protect the people who shared his blood. Certainly, her family had never done that for her.

But she shoved that thought aside, preferring now to concentrate on Nathan's very attractive face, his light-brown eyes that darkened with his moods, his strong jaw that could be incredibly stubborn, his sexily tousled brown hair, his full mouth that could utter both incredibly sharp but also incredibly kind words.

The years had put a few lines around that mouth, but his lips looked full and inviting, and she wondered what it would be like to kiss him. She had a feeling a lot of women wondered that. Their waitress had certainly made more than the normal number of stops by their table to ask if they needed anything, her gaze always on Nathan when she asked the question.

She'd always thought Nathan was attractive, but he'd put up a lot of walls between them as they'd gotten older. Actually, he'd put up a lot of walls around himself in every area of his life. He'd been much more open and outgoing in his early teens. By the end of high school, he'd been closed off, guarded, always on the edge of anger, and her behavior had certainly annoyed him.

"Where are you?" Nathan's voice cut through her reverie.

She started, realizing she was still staring at his mouth. "Sorry. Just thinking."

"About what?"

She raised her gaze to his. "I was actually thinking about you—how different you seem now in some ways, and yet very much like your old self in others."

"Do I want to ask you to explain?" he asked dryly, taking a swig of his beer.

"I'm not sure I could. It's weird how we seem to meet up at critical junctures in our lives. The first time we met was at the shelter. My mom had died a few years earlier, and I was living with my aunt, who had her own struggles. You and your mom and sister were escaping from an abusive situation. But being friends with each other made everything seem better. You were like Grace back then. You loved to tell stories, too, act out imaginary scenes, and I liked being part of that. You made me believe things were going to get better."

He tipped his head. "You made me believe that, too."

"No way."

"Yes, you did. You had the ability to compartmentalize in a way that I didn't even understand back then. But you could turn all your focus onto whatever we were doing, and that's all you cared about, whether you were beating me at board games or conning some street vendor out of a pretzel with some pretty real tears. You were a brilliant and competitive genius."

"I'm glad you said genius. For a minute there, I thought you might go with freak," she said with a smile.

He grinned back at her. "That might have been a better word, but it's what you're doing right now that always made my day better."

"What's that?"

"It's your smile. It didn't come that often in the beginning, and it became a challenge to me to see if I could make it appear."

"Really?" She couldn't imagine he'd cared that much.

"Yeah. Because somehow when you laughed, when you were happy, I felt happy, too."

She was touched by his words. "I think it worked both ways." She paused, tilting her head, as she thought about their past. "But that changed when we met up again in high school. We hadn't seen each other in several years, and I was so excited when I first saw you. I'd been in three foster homes by then and two other high schools, but when I saw you in the gym, it was like my world tilted upright again. I thought, this is going to be okay—Nathan is here."

His gaze darkened. "You never told me that."

"Well, I didn't want it to go to your head. But that first great feeling faded over the next year. Once I got involved with Johnny, you didn't want much to do with me."

"I couldn't believe you couldn't see what he was really like."

"But was it that obvious then?" she challenged. "I mean, Johnny was funny, right? He was popular. We knew his parents were probably criminals, but a lot of kids had parents who did bad shit—yours and mine included."

Nathan frowned. "He was funny, but there was a core of ruthlessness and cruelty that you didn't see or that he didn't show you. I thought your relationship would be over as fast as it started, because just about nothing lasted back then for more than a few weeks, but you and Johnny just kept getting closer. I tried to warn you a lot of times, but you stopped talking to me."

"You stopped talking to me," she countered. "You were super critical. And when I wouldn't do what you wanted, you were done."

"You were throwing yourself away; I couldn't watch it," he said harshly. "I'd seen that show before. I hated that helpless feeling of watching someone I cared about heading straight for pain and suffering."

Seeing the dark depths in his eyes now, she sensed they were talking about more than just her. "You haven't told me anything about your mom. Is she well? Does she live in Chicago?"

He cleared his throat and sat up straighter in his chair. "We weren't going to talk about the past, remember?"

"That was during pizza." She tipped her head toward the empty platter. "We're done."

"Yeah, and we should probably get going," he said, picking up the check.

"We can split that."

"I've got it." He pulled out his wallet and put some cash down on the table. "Ready to go?"

She wasn't ready to go. She'd been having a lovely conversation with him, and he'd just pulled the plug. But he was already on his feet, so she had no choice but to put on her coat and follow him out the door.

"I can walk to my hotel," she said, as they stepped onto the sidewalk in front of the restaurant, which was situated along the river and only a few blocks from where she was staying.

"I'll walk with you."

"I don't need a bodyguard. In fact, I could probably take someone out faster than you."

"Oh, yeah?"

"I'm very well trained."

"I didn't notice a weapon tucked under your jacket."

"Well, I don't usually need one when I've been relegated to desk work."

"Maybe you should think about actually staying at that desk, considering everything that is going on."

"I probably should," she agreed, as they headed along the path that wound itself along the river.

A party boat came down the dark canal with its lights on and music wafting across the water. "I really like this area. I don't know why we never came down here."

"That invisible fence," he reminded her.

"I guess so. And if we did come, it was to pick some cash from some distracted tourist."

His eyebrow shot up. "You never told me you did that."

"It was once or twice, and I wasn't very good at it. I felt bad that I was taking someone's money. You never did it?"

"Nope."

"Well, you always walked a higher moral ground than I did."

"That's not true," he said sharply, anger suddenly filling his voice.

"What did I say?"

"Nothing. Never mind."

"Really? It seems like you had a rather intense reaction just now."

"I have a lot of intense reactions when you're around," he said dryly.

"I do seem to set you off." She paused along the rail, seeing her hotel just up ahead and not wanting to get there quite yet. "This is pretty. In my head, I only remember the ugliness of Chicago, but this is nice."

"They've made a lot of improvements along the river: new restaurants, bars, lots of space for walking and jogging and just hanging out." He leaned against the rail, and then gave her a curious look. "I've been wondering about something. When did you change your name to Adams?"

"In Detroit. The woman who helped me with the adoption also helped me with the name change. She got all my paperwork updated and said I was going to have a new start. I definitely needed that to complete my escape from my life, so I went with it."

"I'm sure the FBI did a background check on you. Surely, your old name came up."

"Of course. But it didn't matter. I hadn't changed it because I had done something illegal. I just wanted a new name."

"How did you pick Adams?" he asked, then a smile spread across his face. "Wait, I know the answer. It was because of that movie—*The Addams Family*. We must have watched that tape a dozen times at the shelter. You liked that girl—what was her name?"

"Wednesday. She was so weird and magical at the same time. And she always spoke her mind. But I do not spell my last name with two *d's*. That would have been odd, and I wanted to be even for the first time in my life," she said with a laugh. "I'd been odd far too long."

"You were not odd. You were beautiful; you still are, Bree."

His gaze swept across her face, bringing with it a rush of heat.

"You shouldn't say things like that, Nathan."

"Why not?"

"Because..." She had no idea how to finish her statement. "We—we're friends, well, maybe not friends, but we..." She stumbled to find appropriate words.

"You can't define us. We defy definition."

"Well, that's true." Her mouth went dry as his gaze settled on her lips. "But I don't know what you want."

"Yes, you do."

He straightened suddenly, his hands sliding around her waist, setting off a wave of anticipation. He gave her a long look that made her heart race. And then he lowered his head—so slowly her nerves were screaming.

Finally, his mouth was on hers.

She felt like she'd been waiting for his kiss forever.

Nathan took possession of her mouth as if he owned it, and she couldn't quite believe how much she liked that. His need for her was compelling, drawing forth a deeper need for him than she had expected.

And as he slanted his head to get a better angle, she went with him, putting her arms around his neck, opening her mouth to his, letting go of all the reasons why they shouldn't be doing this and grabbing on to all the reasons that they should.

Nathan, the imaginative boy, and Nathan the somewhat angry teenager, merged into this Nathan, this incredibly sexy, powerful, strong man who kissed her like he was never going to let her go.

But, of course, he did eventually let her go, raising his head, his eyes gleaming in the moonlight.

She stared back at him in amazed confusion. "So, that happened."

His hands dropped from her waist, and he took a step back. "I'm not going to apologize."

"I didn't ask you to."

"You kissed me back," he said, a hint of surprise in his voice.

"Didn't you want me to?"

"I did. I just…" His voice drifted away. Then he said, "I didn't know if you would." He ran a hand through his hair. "I've been wanting to kiss you for a long time."

His words sent her heart racing again. "I—I didn't know that."

"I think you did," he said quietly. "But you wanted someone else."

Their gazes clung together. *They had been so close at times but also so distant at others. Was he right? Hadn't she known he liked her as more than a friend? Hadn't she thought at times that his teenage anger was jealousy? But sometimes it had also just felt like dislike.*

"You were hard to read in high school, Nathan."

"Maybe." He turned and looked out at the water. "It doesn't matter."

She could feel him pulling away, and she didn't like it. She put her hand on his arm and his gaze swung around to hers. "Putting our past aside, what happened just now...it was good."

His eyes brightened. "It was."

"So maybe we just agree on that, and let it be..."

"I don't know if I can just let it be—that's the problem." His phone buzzed. Taking it out of his pocket, he frowned and then silenced the call.

"Who was that?" she asked.

"It doesn't matter."

"It was Adrienne, wasn't it?" She let out a breath, seeing the answer in his face. She'd completely forgotten he was seeing someone. "You should call her."

"We're not done here."

"We should be. You have a woman in your life, and I'm leaving as soon as this case is over. We can't start anything now."

"We started all this a very long time ago, Bree. One of these days we're going to finish it."

"Maybe we finished it now. We had our kiss. It was good. That's it." She started walking, and he reluctantly fell into step alongside her.

They didn't speak until they got to the front door of her hotel. Then he said, "What if I told you I don't want this to be it? What would you say?"

She let out a breath, wrestling with reckless temptation. "I want to say—then come up to my room."

He drew in a sudden breath.

"But," she added quickly. "You have someone in your life who cares about you. Your home is here, and I'll never ever want to live in this city. This can't go anywhere, Nathan. And when I saw you at Josie's house yesterday, you said, 'let's try not to mess up each other's lives.' So, I'm going to try not to mess up your life, and I'm going to say good night."

His mouth tightened. "I liked your first answer better."

She smiled, then stole a quick kiss. "One for the road," she said, and then she turned and walked into her hotel.

Ten

~>≫◄◄◄<~

Bree took the elevator to her room and then bolted the door behind her. She tossed her bag on the dresser and flopped onto the bed, staring up at the ceiling, her senses spinning, her emotions in utter turmoil.

She'd kissed Nathan. She could hardly believe it. Talk about the past and the present colliding...

She wished she could say she felt good about her decision to end things with a kiss, but she didn't.

Her senses were clamoring for more Nathan, and even though her brain knew she'd done the right thing by shutting it down, her body was tingling with the idea of Nathan's mouth on hers and his hands all over her body.

Groaning, she sat up, knowing she was going around in circles.

And she had many more important things to think about.

She took her computer out of her bag and turned it on. She had no emails that needed to be answered immediately, so she went on the internet and entered the baseball forum, wondering if anyone had answered her earlier message.

Smiling, she saw a message from Parisa.

Sorry I missed you at the Rowlands' house today. Still at the same number if you want to talk. Spending a boring night watching Wyatt pick up women. Could use a break. Call me.

Seeing that the message had come in a half hour earlier,

she scrambled off the bed and dug out her own burner phone to call Parisa.

Parisa had been her roommate at Quantico. A beautiful, dark-haired, dark-eyed woman, Parisa had the ability to blend into many different cultures. She also had the language skills to back up her appearance—fluent in French, Portuguese, Spanish, and Farsi as well as various Russian dialects. Parisa was the daughter of a former diplomat and having traveled the world, she brought an international experience that served her well. Parisa spent a lot of her time overseas, and it had been over a year since she'd last seen her.

Parisa picked up the call a moment later. "Hello?"

"It's me, Bree."

"Hang on a sec."

Bree heard some music in the background and then it got quieter, although there was now street noise in the background.

"That's better," Parisa said.

"Where are you?"

"Some bar by NYU. We came here after Jamie's celebration of life."

"How was it?"

"Sad but also oddly happy. It was bittersweet to see so many old friends, but not to see our dearest friend Jamie."

"Were there a lot of people there?"

"More than I expected—not just our tight group, but a lot of the people we went through Quantico with. It was fun to catch up. Now, however, Damon and Sophie are snuggled up together and Wyatt has two grad students hanging onto his every word. I miss my wing-woman, Bree."

"Those days feel like a long time ago."

"It has been forever," Parisa agreed.

"What about Diego?"

"He didn't make it."

"That's too bad. How are the Rowlands doing?"

"They tried to make it a joyful dinner, but I could tell that Vincent is still destroyed by the loss of his son. Cassie seems to be doing better."

"Vincent blamed himself because he'd always wanted Jamie to follow in his footsteps at the FBI. If Jamie hadn't made that decision, he might still be alive."

"Yes. He seems to carry a lot of guilt," Parisa said heavily.

"How is Wyatt doing? He wouldn't tell me where he was going after the big dust-up in New York last summer."

"Same old Wyatt—mysterious, brooding, can't really figure out what he's thinking or what he's doing. He said he's been doing some special assignments—whatever that means. Beyond that, I have no idea. Since we came to this bar, he's been all about finding some babe to hook up with." Parisa paused. "It has been nice getting to know Sophie. She's a good match for Damon."

"She is. I've gotten to know her better since she and Damon came back from their summer archaeological digs."

"Yes, they described some of their findings in great, boring detail," Parisa said with a laugh. "I never thought Damon would be into digging up old bones."

"He's in love."

"And love makes you crazy," Parisa said.

"What about you? What are you up to?"

"I'm heading to London on Sunday."

"To do what?"

"I'm not sure yet," Parisa said. "But let's get back to you, Bree. Your post had a slight note of desperation in it. Everything okay?"

"No," she said with a sigh. "I came to Chicago to consult on a kidnapping case."

"Damon told me you've been tracking someone called the White Rose Kidnapper."

"Who had been working his evil in the northeast until he made a sudden jump to Chicago. Now it seems that the kidnapper has decided to put me in the middle of his twisted game. He dug up my secret, Parisa, the one I told you about during training. He's forcing me to go back into my past, and

I can't seem to stop him."

"Seriously? I thought all that was buried as deep as it could go."

"I did, too. There's a girl's life on the line, maybe the lives of two girls, and I don't know if it ends there. The kidnapper is trying to make me think that one of these girls is my daughter, the one I gave away."

"My God, Bree. That sounds bad."

She could hear the worry in Parisa's voice. "I don't know how he got all this information on me. Worse, I don't know where he's going with it."

"Maybe someone from your past is helping him. Have you run into anyone?"

"I have. But Nathan isn't helping this guy; he's trying to help me."

"Nathan, huh? Where do you know him from?"

"We grew up in the same neighborhood. He's actually the one person who knew about the baby. He helped me get out of Chicago. He helped me find a private adoption agency."

"Are you sure he's really helping you, Bree? It sounds like he could be the leak."

"It's not Nathan. I trust him completely," she said, realizing how true that was.

"Your voice just changed," Parisa said. "It got a little softer, sultrier. Is this Nathan more than a friend?"

"He wasn't…until about twenty minutes ago."

"Now we're getting to the good stuff," Parisa said with a laugh.

"Not really. I put a stop to everything."

"Why on earth did you do that?"

"There's no point in starting something that can't be finished, right?"

"Oh, I don't know. Living in the moment isn't always bad, especially in our line of work. But don't ask me about love; I never seem to make the right call." She paused. "Hang on, Wyatt is talking to me."

A moment later, Wyatt's voice came over the phone.

"Where the hell are you, Bree? You should be here tonight."

"I wish I could be. How are you, Wyatt? What have you been doing?"

"Laying low."

"Is someone paying you to do that?" Of the five of them, Wyatt did the most undercover work, although his last stint had almost killed him.

"You don't think I work for free, do you?"

"Good point."

"Everything okay in Chicago?"

"I'm not sure yet. Still figuring things out. You know who is here, though? Tracy Cox."

"Cool, calculating Tracy?" Wyatt said. "Has she warmed up to you?"

"Not even a little bit. She's definitely enjoying having me report to her."

"That's a change for her. You were always out in front of her at the academy. But I have to say that even though she was a pain in the ass, she was smart."

"I'm trying to remember that. She asked me about Diego. I always wondered if something went on with those two."

"Not that I ever heard. I have to run. Keep us posted if you need anything."

"I will," she promised.

Parisa came back on the line a moment later. "As Wyatt said, if you need any help, Bree, I'm here for a few more days. Call me or post a message in the forum."

"Thanks for the offer. You guys sound like you're having fun," she said wistfully.

"We'd be having more fun if you were here. We'll have to reunite at another time."

"Definitely."

"Stay safe. And this guy—Nathan? Be careful of men from your past. It's always better to look forward than to look back."

"I'll keep that in mind." As she set down her phone, she felt both better and worse.

It had been nice to talk to Parisa, but now she felt more alone than ever. She wished she could be with her friends, celebrating Jamie's life. She wished Hayley was home safe with her family and that a little girl named Emma had never been brought into this twisted game. Most of all, she wished she knew where her daughter was, and if she was still safe.

And she really wished she knew what to do about Nathan...

———————

Bree, Bree, Bree...

Her face went around in Nathan's head all night. He tried to shake her with every toss, every turn, but he couldn't get her or the kisses they'd shared out of his mind.

He'd wanted to kiss her forever, and it had been far better than his best dream. What had really surprised him was the way Bree had kissed him back. There had been no hint of shyness or restraint—just passion and fire and need.

And when she'd told him she was tempted to invite him upstairs to her room, he'd been tempted to push the idea, to follow her through those hotel doors and make her see that it didn't matter what happened tomorrow when they had tonight.

But he hadn't done that.

Some age-old self-defense mechanism had kicked in, reminding him that this woman had stomped on his heart more than a few times.

At dawn, he gave up trying to sleep, threw on track pants, a sweatshirt and his running shoes and headed out the door. He ran down to the lake and then along the shoreline, hoping he could outrun his thoughts, but every mile brought new ideas.

What if he kissed her again? What if he took her to bed? What if he showed her what she'd been missing out on all these years?

But where the hell would that get him?

She'd eventually say good-bye again, and he probably wouldn't see her for another decade, if then.

It was just a fluke that she'd come back now. It certainly wasn't because she'd been dying to see him.

And he certainly hadn't been dying to see her. He'd gone on with his life. He'd put her out of his head. He had Adrienne.

Adrienne! He'd never called her the night before, nor had he answered any of her texts. She was going to be pissed that he hadn't met up with her and her college friend, but he hadn't been able to bring himself to go see them. Not after what had happened with Bree.

He'd never been one to fool around with more than one woman at a time.

And the fact that he could barely remember Adrienne now that Bree had returned was probably a sign that he needed to end things with her.

But was that the smartest idea?

Adrienne was easy, fun, light, bright. She came from a normal family. She didn't have dark secrets. She didn't carry emotional scars and still-healing wounds. She wasn't a magnet for trouble.

That's who he should want.

But, no, he had to be hung up on a woman who had always been a thorn in his side, who had almost gotten him killed. And it wasn't like the present was any different than the past. She was surrounded by danger and shadows, and he was getting tangled up again in her problems.

So, what was he going to do?

Walk away from Bree? Let her figure things out on her own?

Call Adrienne back and apologize? Meet her after work? Tell her he'd make last night up to her?

He picked up his pace and sprinted the last mile, hoping the right answer would come to him.

When he got home, he took a quick shower and got dressed, debating his next move—a move that didn't need to include either Bree or Adrienne.

He wanted to do his part to help Hayley, so maybe he'd go by the Jansens' house.

While Bree had dismissed the possibility that Hayley was her child, he still wasn't completely convinced. And since the Chicago FBI investigation team had decided to keep Bree out of the field, maybe he could discover something on his own. It was probably a long shot, but he was going to take it.

He stopped to pick up coffee and pastries from a bakery that he and Mark occasionally went to after a run and then headed to their house.

He was surprised to find the street empty and quiet. For the past two days, there had been tons of news vans and reporters. He hoped that didn't mean the media was losing interest in Hayley's story. But it was only nine a.m., so maybe they'd be arriving later.

When Mark answered the door, Nathan's first thought was that his friend had aged ten years in the past two days, with dark shadows under his eyes, pale, pasty skin, and desperate eyes.

He felt terrible that all he had to offer were sweets and coffee. "I wanted to drop these by, Mark. I thought Connor and Morgan might like the sweets, and I got you your usual coffee."

"Thanks." Mark took the coffee container out of his hand. "That was thoughtful. Do you want to come in?"

"If I'm not intruding."

Mark waved him inside and shut the door. "I'd welcome the conversation. Lindsay's parents took the kids to their house last night. I was glad to get them out of here. I thought I'd be happy with fewer people around, but now the silence is…terrifying."

"Is Lindsay here?" he asked, following Mark down the hall to the kitchen.

"I'm hoping she's getting some sleep now. She was up all night sitting in Hayley's bedroom, holding her stuffed animals and rocking back and forth. She's not doing well."

"I'm so sorry, Mark."

"Thanks."

Nathan sat down on a stool at the kitchen island. Seeing the boxes of donuts, pastries, cookies, and pies on the counters, he realized he'd had a very unoriginal idea. "Looks like you were already well stocked."

"People don't know what to do so they bring food. You should see all the casseroles in the refrigerator. And the irony is that I've never felt less like eating in my life. I will take the coffee, though. I was about to make another pot." Mark pulled one of the coffee cups out of the cardboard container and sat down across from him.

"Is there any news?" he asked.

Mark shook his head. "No. I don't know if you saw, but we made a public plea on the news last night. It generated some leads, but none of them have panned out. I spoke to both the police and the FBI this morning, and they assure me that they're still devoting every minute of every hour to Hayley's case. There's going to be another full-scale volunteer search starting in about an hour, expanding the grid that was searched yesterday. The last kid who was taken was found in an abandoned building so they're concentrating on properties like that." He ran a weary hand through his hair. "I can't bear the thought of Hayley sitting in the dark and the cold in some condemned building. But then, I can't bear the thought of anything that could be happening to her."

Mark's pain rolled off him in thick waves, and Nathan had never felt more helpless to comfort someone in his life. There was nothing he could say to make Mark feel better and trying almost seemed insulting.

But seeing Mark's grief also made him more committed to doing whatever he could to help find Hayley. "It sounds like there are a lot of people looking for your daughter," he said quietly, wanting to give Mark some reassurance, no matter how hollow it might be.

"The police have been good. Better than I expected."

"Why do you say it like that?" he asked curiously.

"I haven't found the cops to be too helpful in the past. We've had a lot of car break-ins on this street the last month, and they can't seem to catch anyone."

"Your car was broken into?" An uneasy tingle ran down his spine.

"Actually, it was Lindsay's SUV. Luckily, she didn't have anything of value in there, just some kids' toys and soccer shoes and a pair of expensive sunglasses. But they hit five other cars that night, and one of our neighbors had left a computer tablet in the car, so they lost that." Mark paused as Lindsay came into the room.

She wore black leggings and an over-sized long-sleeve sweater that enveloped her thin frame. Like Mark, she looked completely exhausted and emotionally spent, her eyes and nose bright red from crying.

"Oh," she said, stopping when she saw him. "Nathan. I didn't know anyone was here."

"He brought us coffee and pastries," Mark put in.

"Thanks," she said, without much meaning in her voice.

Mark grabbed the second coffee from the cardboard holder and handed it to her. "Why don't you start with this?"

She took a grateful sip. "Caffeine has become my best friend."

"Is there anything else I can do for you guys?" he asked.

"The FBI said that Grace remembered that the man had a World Series Cubs ring on his finger," Mark said. "Has she remembered anything else?"

"No. I'm sorry."

"It's not her fault," Lindsay said, leaning against the counter.

"You want to sit down?" he asked, ready to give up his seat.

She put up a hand. "It's fine. I need to move around, find some energy. I have to be strong for Hayley."

"You are strong."

A phone rang on the counter, and both Lindsay and Mark jumped, but Mark reached it first.

"Is it the police?" Lindsay asked impatiently.

"No. It's work," Mark said. "I'm just going to take it, all right?"

"Sure," she said in a dull monotone.

Despite Lindsay's earlier statement about wanting to find some energy, when Mark left the kitchen, she took her husband's seat.

"Is Grace all right?" she asked. "We were practically yelling at her the other night. She must have been scared. I feel badly about that."

"Don't feel bad. Grace is okay. She just wants Hayley to come home."

"Even though they're a year apart, they've really become close since they started ballet together. They both love to dance, and that bonded them."

"Grace can't seem to stop twirling, even when she's supposed to be doing her homework."

"Hayley is the same way."

"Did you dance as a kid?"

"No, not at all. I have two left feet, and it never interested me, but Hayley was drawn to ballet from the time she could walk. She just loves it." Lindsay bit down on her bottom lip. "But I keep thinking that if I hadn't pushed her to be on stage, none of this would have happened. Hayley didn't want to perform. She was nervous about being in front of people. She really just likes to dance for herself. But I didn't want her to miss out, and all the kids were doing it. If I hadn't pressed—" She stopped abruptly. "Everything would have been different if I had just made other decisions."

"What you're going through, Lindsay—I can't imagine. It must be hell on earth."

"It really is. I feel her calling out to me, Nathan. Every time I close my eyes, I hear her voice asking me to come and find her, and it just breaks my heart. She was such a miracle baby. It was just by chance that I became her mother, and now I feel like I failed. I didn't protect her the way I was supposed to. I was going to give her the better life that her own mother couldn't. But I didn't do that."

He was shocked that Lindsay was talking about Hayley's adoption. According to Bree, no one except the family knew about the adoption, and Hayley was completely unaware that she had different birth parents. But clearly Lindsay was distraught. She was rambling on, and he wasn't sure she was even aware of what she was revealing. However, now that she'd given him the opening he needed, he had to squeeze through.

"I didn't realize that Hayley was adopted," he said, thinking that was the most normal response he could make.

"Oh." She suddenly realized what she'd said. "Yes. I shouldn't have said anything. Not a lot of people know. I haven't really thought about it in years, but since she was taken, and the police asked a lot of questions about her birth parents, I can't stop thinking about it."

"Do they think the birth parents have something to do with this?"

"I don't believe so. The mom died very soon after Hayley was born. No one knows who the father is. And no one has ever reached out to us."

"What do you know about the biological mother?"

"She was young, seventeen, I think. She didn't have parents around. She said she wanted to give up her child, so she would have a better life."

"Did you meet her?"

"No, it was a closed adoption done through an agency. Mark handled most of the details. After so many disappointments, it was hard for me to keep getting my hopes up."

"I can't imagine how tough that was."

"But after we got Hayley, I did write the birth mother a letter. I was sitting in the nursery that I never thought I would fill, and Hayley was sleeping so peacefully in her crib, and I picked up a pen and paper, and I told this young teenager how grateful I was. I said I would guard Hayley's life with my own. I would give her everything I could. But I didn't do enough." Lindsay blinked back tears. "You'd think I'd be out of tears, wouldn't you?"

"I don't think there's a limit when it comes to heartbreak. Did you ever send the letter?"

"I didn't know where to send it. I was going to give it to the agency, but Mark didn't think it was a good idea. He said we should let things be the way they were set up—no contact whatsoever. We didn't want to risk the birth mother changing her mind, so I put it away. One day I'll give it to Hayley. I hope she won't hate me for not telling her she was adopted all these years."

"When are you planning to tell her?"

"I don't know. We didn't want to do it when she was really young, so we kept putting it off. She's only ten, but it feels almost too late and yet too soon at the same time. I can't think about it right now." Lindsay gave him another pained look. "Do you think it's wrong that we haven't told her?"

"I wouldn't presume to say what's right or wrong, but I do know that you're a great mother, Lindsay. And this isn't your fault."

"How can it not be? It happened on my watch." She drew in a breath. "I keep thinking that she must be terrified, and she doesn't even have her bunny."

"Is that her favorite stuffed animal?"

"Yes. It's a tiny little thing, but she always has it with her—in the car, in her backpack—it goes with her everywhere. She loves it so much. My mother gave it to her when she was a baby. Unfortunately, it was lost a few weeks ago, so it didn't go with her to the school concert."

"How did she lose it?"

"It was in our car when it got broken into. I don't know why anyone would take it, but then they took everything that belonged to the kids that had been left in the car. I guess they sell the stuff somewhere. Hayley was so sad. It was the first time I'd seen her cry in forever. She's usually a pretty happy kid." Lindsay paused as Mark returned to the kitchen.

Nathan was surprised by the change in Mark's

appearance. He'd changed out of his sweats into slacks and a shirt. His eyes were bright. He looked like he'd found some energy and a new purpose.

"Are you going out?" Lindsay asked in surprise.

"I have to go to the office for about a half hour."

"Why? What could possibly be important now?" she demanded.

"It's my biggest client, Lindsay. All I have to do is pull something off my work computer, and hand it off to Brian. Then I'm home again."

"Brian can't do that himself?"

"He can't. I'm sorry. I swear I'll be back soon. And to be honest, I need the break, Lindsay. I need a few minutes out of the house. I'll have my phone. If anything happens, you'll call me."

"I just don't understand how you can think about work right now."

The doorbell rang, interrupting their tense conversation. "Why don't I get that?" he suggested, sensing that the two of them had more to say to each other. He jogged out of the kitchen and down the hall. When he opened the door, he was surprised to see Josie on the porch. "Josie—what are you doing here?"

"I wanted to check on Lindsay and Mark. What about you?"

"The same."

"Is Bree here, too?"

"No."

She gave him an assessing look. "But you've been talking to her, haven't you? Is she still going after Kyle? He told me what happened in his office. He said his attorneys are on it, and I shouldn't worry. Should I believe him?"

"You should."

"Good, because I can't believe anyone could think that Kyle would take Hayley. I really hope no one suggested that to Mark or Lindsay."

"They did not mention that to me, so I don't think they

did."

Relief filled her eyes. "Thank goodness. Are they here? Are they busy?"

"They're here. Actually, Mark has to run into work for a brief time, and Lindsay isn't happy about it. Maybe you can stay with her."

"Of course. Are you going to work?"

He hesitated. "Eventually."

His sister gave him a knowing look. "It's Bree, isn't it? You're getting tangled up with her again. You took one look at her and you were right back where you were before."

"Bree is focused on finding Hayley. And so am I."

"I don't want to see you get hurt again, Nathan. You have Adrienne now."

"You don't have to worry about me. I know what I'm doing."

"You always say that, and most of the time I believe you. But when it came to Bree, you never knew what you were doing. You were blinded by love or lust or something very, very strong."

He let Josie have the last word, because there was a big part of him that knew she was right. He'd made a lot of mistakes when it came to Bree. And there was a good chance he'd already made one more by kissing her the night before. "I'll see you later."

As he walked across the street to his truck, he was surprised to see Bree get out of a car a few doors down. He walked down to meet her. "I thought you were benched."

"I need to talk to the Jansens."

"Has something happened?" he asked quickly.

"Yes. I received two texts this morning." She turned her phone, so he could see a photo.

The picture was of a baby about a year old. The child was sitting in front of a Christmas tree. She was dressed in a pink dress with a pink bow on her head, and a happy smile on her face. Across the photo, someone had scrawled the letter *I* in black marker.

"Who is this?" he asked.

"I don't know. There's one more." She swiped the screen.

He found himself staring at a toddler, probably about three. Her back was to the camera, but she was blowing soap bubbles in the middle of a playground. Her hair was brown, but he couldn't see her face. Across this photo was the word *am*.

"What does this mean?"

"I think he's going to tell me who my daughter is, starting with the words *I* and *am*," she replied. "I'm pretty sure the next word is going to be *your*. The texts came in thirty minutes apart. I was waiting for the next one, but it's been sixty minutes. What I need to know is if this is Hayley. All the photos in her FBI file are of her at age ten. I know Lindsay had a baby photo she showed me the first time we spoke, but I didn't look at it closely enough to know if that child is the same as this one. I need to see it again, and I need Lindsay or Mark to tell me if these photos are of Hayley."

"Who else could it be?"

"Emma," she said, giving him a helpless shrug. "I know you don't agree, but I can't ignore what happened on the train."

"It's possible. But I still lean toward the idea that Emma is more of a little con artist, and that she and her big sister are just pawns in the game. Her sister could even be involved with the kidnapper."

"I have considered that. Frankly, it's not a huge leap to think my daughter could be a con artist. When I was ten, I would have taken money and told some woman she was my mother without thinking twice about it. I just hate the idea that my child might be living my horrible childhood."

He felt a wave of compassion at the pain that filled her eyes. "This is what the kidnapper wants—to get in your head, to make you second-guess your decision, to drive you crazy with guilt."

"Unfortunately, it's working. But I am trying not to focus on myself and my feelings. This is about Hayley."

"Have you showed your fellow FBI agents these texts?"

"I forwarded them to Agent Cox. Tracy is my main contact within the Chicago team. I told her I was going to stop by the Jansens and verify that the photos are of Hayley."

"What did she say?"

"She hasn't answered yet. I didn't want to wait."

So, Bree had decided to take things into her own hands. He couldn't blame her. These photos were the biggest clues they'd had so far.

"Are the Jansens home?" she asked. "Is there a big crowd at the house?"

"Actually, no. My sister Josie just arrived, and she's with Lindsay now. Mark got a phone call when I was inside the house, and he told Lindsay he needs to go down to his office for some quick hand-off of files or something. Lindsay is not happy about it. But then they're both exhausted and stressed out. I think Mark is probably looking for an excuse to get a little air. He said Lindsay sat up all night crying."

"This situation is awful."

"It is. But I did find out a little information. I was actually going to call you when I saw you."

"What did they tell you?"

Before he could reply, the front door opened, and Mark walked quickly out of the house. Instead of heading straight to his car, which was parked in the short driveway, he walked around to the other side of the house and grabbed a backpack from the ground.

"What's he doing?" Nathan muttered.

"Nothing good," Bree said, a frown on her lips.

Mark jogged toward his car, threw the backpack onto the passenger seat and peeled off down the street.

"What the hell was that about?" he wondered aloud.

"We have to follow him," Bree said, running toward his truck. "Give me your keys, Nathan. I want to drive."

"I can drive," he protested.

"You don't know how to follow someone; I do." She held out her hand.

He tossed her his keys and got into the passenger seat as she slid behind the wheel.

He winced as she crunched the gears, then braced his hand on the door as she sped down the street and around the corner.

Eleven

―→ ≫ ≪ ←―

"There he is," Nathan said a moment later, spotting Mark's car up ahead. "He's turning on Crawford."

"I see him."

"Why are we chasing him?"

"Because he's acting suspiciously."

She maneuvered her way through traffic with confident speed, but his truck wasn't built for a car chase.

"He could just be going to work," he suggested.

"With a backpack he hid in the side yard?" she challenged. "I don't think so."

He didn't think so, either. "Then what?"

"I think he lied to me the other day when he said he hadn't heard from the kidnapper. Or he was contacted after our conversation. I'm betting there's a lot of cash in that backpack."

"He's delivering ransom?" That idea seemed incredible to him.

"That's my guess. He told you and Lindsay he was going to work?"

"Yes. He got a call when we were together in the kitchen, but he took it in the other room. He was gone about fifteen minutes. When he came back, he had changed, and he looked like he was energized."

Had Mark gotten a call from the kidnapper? But why

wouldn't he have said anything? Why wouldn't he have told the police or the FBI or his wife?

He pressed his hand against the door as Bree took another turn on two wheels. "You might want to slow down."

"I've got this. Trust me."

"Hard to do that when I'm the one who taught you how to drive."

"I'm a lot better now."

He could see that. There was no hesitation in her decisive movements, no doubt. She was a woman on a mission, and she wasn't going to lose her target. For the first time, he really saw her as she was now: a well-trained, fearless and determined FBI agent.

"Where is he going?" he questioned, as Mark made another unexpected turn.

"Probably someplace deserted, empty. The kidnapper likes abandoned buildings."

"Has there ever been a ransom demand before?"

"No, but this case has been different in several ways. I just wish I knew Chicago better. It's changed since I was last here."

"Somewhat and yet not that much," he said, one destination coming to mind as they headed toward the outskirts of the city. "He could be heading to the Damen Silos," he said referring to the abandoned and once majestic fifteen-story grain silos. The silos had been abandoned in the seventies, but they had been a target for graffiti artists, homeless encampments, and other criminal activities over the years. "You said he likes abandoned buildings, and those have certainly been a favorite criminal destination for decades. Although, I thought they had shut them down, locked them off awhile back."

"We had a team check the silos the first night, but the kidnapper could have moved Hayley, or he just chose that location for the ransom drop, and Hayley is nowhere nearby. I need to call this in to the team. Can you grab my phone out of my bag?"

As he opened her bag, he saw a 9 mm Glock, and his gut tightened—another reminder of how Bree had changed her life. His hand slid past the gun to grab her phone. He handed it to her and set her bag on the console between them.

She punched in a button and said, "Tracy? Yes, I want to talk about the photos, but not right now. Why? Because I'm in pursuit of Mark Jansen. I think he's meeting the kidnapper."

Bree paused, and he could hear a torrent of conversation coming from the other end of the line.

"I will call you as soon as I know for sure where he's going," she said. "I'm guessing he might be going to silos, but I'll have to let you know."

Nathan heard more loud comments on the line, then Bree disconnected the call and tossed the phone into her open bag.

"Tracy didn't sound happy," he said.

"Tracy is never happy with me, but I don't care. This could be the break we're looking for. I don't have time for office politics. I don't have time to make someone feel better. It doesn't matter who finds Hayley; we just need to save her life. And I can do this job as well, if not better, than any of the agents in Chicago."

He smiled, and Bree gave him a sharp look.

"What?" she demanded.

"I like your confidence, that's all. You are a different person now."

"I'm proud of that."

"Me, too."

She cleared her throat. "So, you said you found out something at the house. What was it?"

"Oh, right. Lindsay told me Hayley was adopted."

"She just volunteered that?"

"Not exactly. She was rambling on about letting down Hayley's birth mother. She said she was supposed to protect Hayley and give her a better life. She didn't realize what she'd said until I asked her about it. Then she admitted it."

"Well, okay, but that's not really new information."

"I'm getting to the new information," he said dryly. Bree

had never had a lot of patience when she was ready to act. "Lindsay mentioned that Hayley is probably missing her favorite toy, a small bunny, that she always had with her, except Tuesday night, because it was stolen from Lindsay's SUV a few weeks ago."

"Wait. There was a car break-in? That wasn't in the file."

"Mark said they reported it to the police several weeks ago. There were other cars on the block broken into that night that had more valuables taken. He said the police didn't seem to think they could do much about it."

"They usually can't," she murmured. "But the fact that Hayley lost her favorite bunny…"

"Do you think it's tied to the kidnapping? That means the abduction was planned weeks in advance."

"Every abduction by the White Rose Kidnapper has been meticulously planned out. I definitely think it could be connected. Hayley was lured out of her school by someone who didn't cause her to panic or scream or struggle. She either knew him, or he used something she loved to entice her, to make her trust him. I'm thinking it's this special bunny that he took out of her mom's car."

"That makes sense." He braced himself again as Bree pressed her foot down on the gas pedal and they took another turn at full speed. He didn't know if Mark had any idea he was being followed, but he was certainly driving fast, running red lights to get to where he was going.

As the silos came into view, his blood began racing as fast as the car. "What are we going to do when we get there?"

"I'm not sure."

"Really? You're not sure? You don't have a plan?"

"I'm making it up as I go along."

"I've seen how great that worked for you in the past."

"This isn't the past, and you're going to have to trust me, Nathan. I have better instincts now. They don't usually let me down."

It was the second time she'd said that to him since they'd gotten into the car, and he realized she needed to hear the words. "I trust you, Bree."

She gave him a hard look, then nodded and turned her focus back to the road.

—➤◀—

As Bree neared the silos, she eased back on the gas, not wanting Mark to catch sight of them. It was possible he might recognize Nathan's truck, although he seemed more intent on getting to his destination than looking over his shoulder.

But even if Mark wasn't looking for a tail, whoever he was meeting with would be. She didn't want them to get spooked.

She didn't know if Hayley would be at the drop; she didn't think so, but she couldn't discount the possibility that the kidnapper would swap Hayley for ransom. It didn't seem likely based on her work experience and also on the fact that the kidnapper was looking for more than money. Why else would he be threatening her, sending her through the painful places of her past and sending her baby photos?

The ransom call just didn't make sense, unless she was off base on where Mark was going, and what he was doing, but she couldn't get the sight of that large backpack out of her head.

"Looks like he's heading toward the south entrance," Nathan said, breaking into her thoughts.

She took out her phone and connected with Tracy once more. "He's about to enter through the south entrance of the silos," she said. "We're not far behind him. Come in quiet. We don't know if Hayley is there."

"Wait for us to get there," Tracy said.

She didn't reply. She might wait, or she might not. She was going to play this out in whatever way was necessary to ensure a good outcome.

She slowed down even more, staying a good distance behind as Mark drove through a broken-down fence a quarter of a mile away. She pulled off on to a side road and hid the truck behind a dumpster at the back end of a warehouse and turned off the engine.

Grabbing the gun out of her bag, she looked at Nathan. "I'm going to check things out. Stay here."

"I don't think so," he said, immediately following her out of the truck. "That agent told you to wait."

"Nathan, I don't want anything to happen to you."

"And I don't want anything to happen to you. So, we're sticking together. If you're going, I'm going."

She didn't have time to argue with him. And if she didn't let him come, he'd just wait ten seconds and follow her anyway. "All right, but stay close behind me, and don't make any moves."

"Got it."

They crept along a brick wall, and then scooted between two pillars just before the entrance that Mark had turned in to. A few feet later, Mark's car came into view. It was in an open area surrounded and hidden by the towering silos.

Mark got out of the car and looked around, then glanced down at the phone in his hand.

"He's waiting for a call," Nathan murmured.

Bree nodded as they stayed out of sight.

Her nerves were screaming at the silence. All she could hear was the wind blowing through the large, abandoned cement structures. It felt as if they were the only ones there, but that wasn't true. Mark was also present, and he was waiting for someone—someone who might already be here.

She needed to get closer. Moving with sure-footed confidence, she kept Mark in view as she got closer to the scene. She wanted the kidnapper to show his face before she showed hers. One wrong move, and the situation could go bad in any number of ways. She had to protect Mark, keep the kidnapper alive long enough to tell them where Hayley was, and then find Hayley. At any time, the FBI and the police could storm in at the wrong moment and create more chaos.

She wished she was in better communication with them, but at this point even the slightest whisper could carry.

A car turned in to the entrance and pulled up thirty feet away from Mark's vehicle, a cloud of dust hiding the identity of the driver. As the dust cleared, the man stepped out. He had on a dark ski mask, a gun in his hands, and he kept the door of his vehicle open in front of him.

She could feel Nathan's tension as his body slid forward next to hers.

"Just wait," she murmured, sensing his impatience. "We need to know where Hayley is." The little girl didn't appear to be in the sedan, but it was possible she was in the trunk.

"I've got the money," Mark yelled.

"Show me," the man said.

While the two men were engaged with each other, she crept forward another few feet, then settled into position, putting the gunman in her sight. She would take him down but not kill him. She needed to keep him alive, so he could be forced into telling them where Hayley was.

Before she could pull the trigger, Mark moved into her line of fire.

"Where's Hayley?" Mark yelled.

"Give me the money, and then you'll get your daughter back," the man said.

"I want to see my daughter. Where is she?"

"She's safe. Throw the bag to me."

Mark tossed the bag into the air, and it landed about five feet from the kidnapper. "I did what you wanted. Now give me my daughter."

Bree shifted position, trying to line up her shot, but Mark kept moving around, making it impossible for her to hit her target.

The gunman came from behind the car door and walked forward to get the bag. She waited for her opportunity.

"Tell me where she is," Mark demanded. "Please. She's just a little girl."

The man grabbed the pack off the ground and started backing away.

He was going to leave, and Mark was going to get

nothing.

She held her breath, ready to fire… One more step, and she'd have him.

But then Mark let out a blistering, frustrated yell of rage, as if he'd just realized his last hope was leaving and he charged toward the kidnapper, right into her line of fire.

The man fired his weapon, and Mark fell to the ground.

She immediately fired back, hitting the gunman in the right shoulder. He dropped the gun and stumbled backward in surprise, the bag of money hitting the ground.

She jumped up and ran forward.

Mark was alive, writhing on the ground in pain.

"I've got him," Nathan said, right behind her. He dropped to the ground next to Mark, as she moved toward the kidnapper.

The man's face was still hidden by the mask, but she could see panic in his eyes as he struggled to get up.

"Where's Hayley?" she demanded, aiming her gun at him. "You've got one second to tell me before I kill you."

"You'll never—"

His words were cut off as a bullet blast hit him right between the eyes. He fell backwards, dying instantly.

She whirled around.

Where had the shot come from?

Nathan was applying pressure to Mark's wounds and there was no FBI, no police, in sight.

There was a second shooter. But why had he shot this guy and not her? Not Mark? Not Nathan?

She needed to protect them. She scanned the surrounding structures, looking for some glint of metal in the sunlight, but the shot could have come from anywhere.

And another shot could be coming any second.

Twelve

Nathan stared down at Mark, fear racing through him when he saw his friend's glassy, shock-filled eyes. He was clutching his abdomen, and there was a massive amount of blood dripping through his fingers.

He heard Bree call for an ambulance, and prayed it would get there fast, because he didn't know how much time Mark had. Taking off his jacket, he pressed the material against Mark's wound. He didn't know what was going on with the shooter. He assumed he was dead or unconscious.

Bree had checked the trunk of the shooter's vehicle, which had apparently been empty.

Now, she seemed to have taken up a protective stance in front of them, and she was as tense as she'd been before.

She didn't think the danger was over.

He didn't want to think about what that might mean, because there was no way they were moving Mark to a safer location. He'd bleed out before they could do that.

"It's going to be okay," he told Mark, lying with as much sincerity as he could muster. He'd seen a few gunshot wounds in his life, and this one was bad. But he needed Mark to hang in there.

"Hayley," Mark choked out. "Love her so much. Tell her."

"You're going to tell her yourself. You have to be strong,

Mark. Stay with me."

"I—I was desperate."

"I know."

"Tell Lindsay...I'm sorry. Had to...take the chance. Said they'd kill Hayley if I didn't come alone...and bring the money. Should have known...trap."

"We'll find Hayley. Don't worry."

Relief flooded through him as police cars and unmarked vehicles came screaming through the entrance, followed by pounding feet, officers with guns drawn, and paramedics running toward him with a stretcher. *Thank God!*

He got up and stepped back as the EMTs took over, stabilizing Mark, so they could get him into the ambulance. He could see his friend going in and out of consciousness, and he hoped he'd done enough to stem the bleeding. He glanced down at his blood-soaked hands and felt a wave of nausea.

A female police officer came over to him and handed him a towel. "Are you injured?" she asked.

"No, I was just taking care of him," he replied, wiping the blood from his hands.

"Can you tell me what happened?"

He drew in a breath. "I don't know where to start." Glancing across the way, he saw Bree and a circle of FBI agents surrounding the gunman, who appeared to be dead. As happy as he was that the shooter would not be able to hurt anyone else, he couldn't help worrying about what was going to happen to Hayley if this guy didn't come back with the money.

"Start with how you came to be here," the police officer said, interrupting his thoughts.

"I was following my friend, Mark Jansen. His daughter was kidnapped. I saw him leave his house in a big hurry, acting suspiciously, and I—we—decided to follow him. Me and Agent Bree Adams," he said, tipping his head to the group of FBI agents. "She can fill you in on the rest."

"I still need your side of the story."

"Wait, what's happening?" he asked, seeing not only more police cars coming into the area, but officers and agents heading up and into the abandoned silos.

"We're searching the area."

"For Hayley? Do you think she's here?"

"We don't know. But she's not the only one we're looking for."

It suddenly clicked in: the second blast, Bree's frenzied movements after that, the way she'd positioned herself in front of him and Mark. "There was a second shooter, wasn't there?"

The officer met his gaze. "Did you see someone?"

"No. But I heard the shot. I thought it was Bree—Agent Adams. I was rushing to Mark's side. I didn't see who fired the weapon."

"We're going to need you to come down to the station and answer a lot more questions," the officer said.

"Sure, whatever you need."

"Stay here." She walked over to speak to another officer, one who appeared to be in command of the scene.

Despite her suggestion that he stay where he was, as soon as the circle of agents around Bree broke up, he headed in her direction.

She must have also been told to stay put, because she was suddenly alone, her gaze on the deceased gunman.

He quickly made his way to her side. "Are you okay, Bree?"

"Fine," she said with distraction. "I know this man, Nathan."

"What?" he asked, wondering how often he could keep feeling complete and utter surprise. But as he moved around her to look at the shooter, an icy chill washed over him, an old memory tugging at the back of his mind.

The ski mask had been removed—and while blood from a forehead wound covered the man's face and had made its way through dirty-blond hair and a scruffy beard, the hazel eyes shocked open in death were very familiar. He knew this man, too, but he hadn't seen him since he'd left the old neighborhood. "Calvin—"

"Baker," she finished, meeting his gaze. "He used to run with Johnny. He was two years younger, and Johnny was his idol. He was always asking him if he could do jobs for him."

"This guy is tied to Johnny," he muttered.

"Or was tied to him," she said quickly.

He frowned. "Your go-to move—always defend Johnny, always look for another explanation."

Her gaze turned angry. "I'm not doing that. I'm just stating a fact. Neither one of us knows what Calvin Baker has been doing the last ten or eleven years."

She had a point, so he would let it go—for now. "The police said there was another shooter."

"Yes. He took the kill shot. I just wanted to disable this guy, so we could talk to him. I should have moved faster. I should have stopped Mark before he ever got here."

He could see the guilt rolling through her eyes, and he shared some of those feelings. But the situation had been tense, and dynamic, and completely unpredictable. "If you'd stopped Mark before he got here, we wouldn't have found Baker. He might be dead, but he's still a good lead. There could be a trail to who he was working with. That could take us one step closer to finding Hayley."

"I just hope Mark survives."

"Me, too," he said heavily. "Why do you think the second shooter took out Baker? Why not aim for you? You were completely in the open. Or he could have hit Mark or myself."

"He wanted to stop Baker from talking, and he probably didn't have time to take us all out. If he was up in one of the silos, he could have seen the police cars coming down the road."

"What's going to happen next?"

"Every inch of the grounds will be searched for evidence."

"You don't seem to be a part of that."

"I was told to stay out of it. Tracy said I've helped enough," she said grimly.

"How much trouble are you in?"

"Probably a lot. But I don't really care about that. What I want to do is keep working the case." She paused, looking around. "Let's get out of here."

"Can we just leave?" he asked, surprised by her suggestion. "The police officer I spoke to told me to stay close."

"Well, you're with me, and at the moment, I'm still a federal agent. I want to go to the hospital and get an update on Mark's condition. I'm betting Lindsay is already headed down there, and I still want to show her the photos I was texted earlier."

"If she confirms those photos are of Hayley, and you now know that Calvin Baker, a former associate of Johnny's, was involved in a ransom demand, are you going to consider the fact that Johnny is the one who is tormenting you?"

"I'm already considering that, Nathan. I'm not an idiot," she snapped.

"I know you're not, but it just doesn't seem like the Johnny blinders have come off yet."

"They've been off for a long time. Let's get out of here while we have the chance."

Bree only had to flash her badge once at a police officer cordoning off the scene before they were out of the silos and crossing the road. The truck was still where they'd parked it, and he held out his hand for the keys.

Bree gave them to him without comment and he slid behind the wheel. It felt good to be back in control of something. "So far, so good," he said. "No one stopped us."

She gave him a weak smile. "Not yet."

"For what it's worth, I think you handled yourself really well back there. It was Mark who kept getting in the way. He kept moving around, blocking your shot. And if you'd waited for backup, Mark would definitely be dead. He would not have made it out of there alive."

"I just wonder if I shouldn't have pulled him out of there before Baker arrived."

"There wasn't time, Bree. And if there hadn't been a second shooter, the gunman would be alive, and we'd have a link to find Hayley."

"But there was another person there, an associate of Baker's. And ruthless enough to take out his partner to stop him from talking," she said grimly.

"Yes," he agreed, worrying again about how the unfolding of events might affect Hayley.

"I don't understand the ransom call, either," she muttered. "It doesn't fit the pattern."

"I think you're going to have to throw out the patterns and the rule book on this case."

"I agree," she said, glancing over at him. "I'm not so sure the rest of the agency will consider that a good option, though."

"Won't your fellow agents understand and appreciate the complexity of the situation you just faced?"

"They should, but I'm not part of this office. It would be different if I were in New York. I have friends there who would support me. But the Chicago team has been annoyed with my presence since day one. They don't like that the kidnapper is obsessed with me. They don't like that I'm the one getting clues. They're not happy about my interview with Kyle or my relationship with you. And they definitely are not excited about what went down here. The more days that pass without us finding Hayley, the more pressure everyone is under. And now the missing girl's father is in the hospital, fighting for his life." She paused. "Maybe I did botch this."

"You didn't choose to be the kidnapper's target. You had no idea that I was connected to the Jansens or the only witness." He paused, thinking about that. "You know, if Johnny is behind this, it's pretty ironic that I am tied to Grace. He wanted me out of your life from the first time he realized we were friends. And now we're connected again."

"That is ironic. He didn't like me having any other

friends but him. As a teenager, I thought his possessiveness was sweet." She let out a heavy sigh. "I don't know. Maybe it is Johnny. If I had to pick someone who could really hate me, the only person I can think of is him."

He was glad she'd finally admitted that.

"At any rate, I will deal with the fallout of my actions, when I don't have a choice. Until I'm suspended, I'm going to do my job the best way I can. What else do you remember about Calvin Baker?"

"He got in a lot of fights. He was dealing drugs. Nothing more specific. He wasn't anyone I hung out with." He glanced over at her. "What do you remember? You probably saw him more than I did."

"He was always looking to score points with Johnny, offering to work at the gym or do whatever he needed done. Johnny would get annoyed that Cal would continually text him. And I would get annoyed that Johnny was always on his phone. But that wasn't just because of Cal. In the beginning of our relationship, Johnny was just running the gym for his dad, or at least that's what I thought. Obviously, I discovered later that he was engaged in a lot of other criminal activities and that he wasn't ever planning to get out of the family business."

"I didn't realize he'd ever said he would do that."

"Usually, it was in response to me suggesting he do something more with his life. Johnny was smart. He just didn't use his brain in the right way. He was too ambitious and too greedy." She took a breath. "Back then, I thought Johnny had so much more than I did. He had money and a car, and he had a legitimate family home. Granted, it wasn't that great, but it was better than anything I'd lived in. In retrospect, I can see now that Johnny was a small-time thug in a small-time organization that didn't make enough money to get its owners out of the lower-class neighborhood they were living in. The Hawkes might have run our neighborhood, but they weren't running the city—not then anyway. I need to find out how much power he has now. And I want you to know, Nathan, that if Johnny is involved in this, he will pay, and I will go after him with everything I have. Please don't have any doubts about that."

"I believe you."

"Thank you." She straightened in her seat as her phone buzzed with an incoming text. "Oh, God."

"Is it from the kidnapper?"

"Yes. It's another photo."

He pulled over to the side of the road as she handed him the phone. It was a picture of a girl about six or seven. Her back was to the camera, but she was wearing a soccer uniform with the number eleven on it. Across the picture was written the word *your*.

He stared at the photo for a long moment and then handed it back to her. "I'm pretty sure this is Hayley."

"We can't see her face."

"No. But the park she's at—it looks like the place where Grace plays soccer, and that's about two blocks from Hayley's house."

"You know what the next word is going to be, don't you?"

"I think so, but I don't believe it's coming for a while. He wants you to wait, to wonder, to worry."

"I won't stop worrying or wondering, but I'm not going to wait."

He could see a new fire in her eyes. The picture might have been meant to discourage her, but it had actually had the opposite effect. Bree was charged up, ready to do battle, and failure wasn't an option.

Bree put her phone into her bag when they turned into the hospital parking lot. She didn't know how much time she would have before Tracy and the other agents caught up to her, but she hoped to speak to Lindsay before then.

They checked in at the information desk and then headed to the fifth-floor surgical center. There was a police officer stationed outside a small waiting room. Bree was happy to see that someone was watching out for Lindsay.

She showed her badge to the officer, who then allowed her and Nathan to enter the room.

Lindsay was sitting with her father, who looked angry and protective of the fragile woman he had his arm around.

When Lindsay saw them, she jumped to her feet. "Did you find Hayley?"

She hated to dash the hope out of her eyes. "Not yet," she said emphasizing the second word of her reply.

"I don't understand what has happened. The police said that Mark went to pay a ransom at the silos and that someone shot him. He told me he was going to work. He told you that, too," she said to Nathan.

"He did," Nathan agreed. "But he didn't do that. He apparently answered a ransom call."

"Who shot Mark? Where is Hayley? What's going on?" Lindsay asked, her eyes pleading for more information.

"Why don't we sit down, Lindsay?" she suggested. "I have a couple of questions."

"More questions?" her father interrupted. "Isn't it about time someone brought us some answers?"

"We're doing everything we can," Bree said, knowing her words would do nothing to console them. "I can tell you that the person who was meeting Mark is dead. But it looks like he was not acting alone. And Hayley was not with him."

Lindsay bit down on her lip. "Is she more in danger now, because they didn't get the money?"

"I wish I could answer you; I just don't know. I hope not."

"You hope not," Lindsay's father said scornfully. "Like that does us any good."

"It's okay, Dad," Lindsay said. "Let me talk to them. Maybe you could call Mom and check in on the kids. Make sure they're not watching the TV. I don't want them to see any news about their father."

"Are you sure you want to do this alone?"

"Yes, I'm fine."

"All right. I'll be back in a few minutes."

As her father left, Lindsay turned back to them, her gaze running down Nathan's shirt. Her face paled. "That's blood on your sleeve. Is that—" Lindsay put a hand to her mouth and then stumbled back into the chair she'd recently vacated. "It's Mark's blood, isn't it? I can't lose my husband, too. I just can't."

Bree took the empty chair next to her, while Nathan pulled over a chair and sat across from them.

"This is a really good hospital, Lindsay, and the doctors are going to do everything they can to save Mark's life," Nathan said.

"Were you there when Mark was shot?" Confusion filled her eyes again. "How were you there, Nathan? You were at my house. But you left before Mark did."

"Yes, but I ran into Bree across the street. While we were talking, we saw Mark come out of the house and grab a backpack out of the side yard. He was acting oddly, so we decided to follow him. I wish we could have prevented what happened. But I know Mark is a fighter."

"Did he say anything?"

"He said he was sorry that he hadn't told you where he was going, what he was doing, but he was desperate, and he hoped you would understand," Nathan replied.

Lindsay's mouth trembled. "That sounds like good-bye."

"He didn't mean it that way. He will do everything he can to survive," Nathan said forcefully. "I know he will."

"I pray that's true."

"I know you're scared," Bree said, drawing Lindsay's attention back to her. "And I hate to ask you more questions, but I need information, and you're the only one who can give it to me."

"Go ahead."

"I want to show you some pictures." She pulled out her phone.

"Pictures of Hayley?"

"I don't know. That's what I need you to tell me." She showed the first picture to Lindsay. "Is this Hayley?"

Lindsay nodded. "Yes. It was her first formal portrait. My parents took her to a photographer in town and had it done as a gift for me for Mother's Day." She licked her lips. "Why do you have it? Why is the word *I* written on it?"

"It was texted to my phone, Lindsay. There are two more." She flipped to the next one. "Is this Hayley, too?"

"Yes," she said tightly.

"And this one?" she asked, moving to the photo that arrived several minutes ago.

"Oh, God, what's going on?" Lindsay asked, putting a hand to her mouth. "Why is someone sending you pictures of Hayley through her life, and what do the words mean—*I—am—your...* What's next?"

Looking into Lindsay's eyes, Bree knew she had to tell her. It was not something she wanted to do. And she wasn't sure how to say it—especially in this moment, with Lindsay hanging on by a thread.

She gazed over at Nathan, silently imploring him to tell her what to do, but his eyes held the same uncertainty.

If they were wrong about her being Hayley's mother, then they'd be upsetting Lindsay for nothing. If they were right, then everything would change. Nothing would ever be the same.

Was she ready to take that leap?

"What's next?" Lindsay repeated, more strongly this time, her gaze moving back and forth between them. "What aren't you two telling me?"

"I don't know what the next word is," she said carefully.

Doubt filled Lindsay's eyes. "I don't believe you. You have some idea where this is going. Just say it. Tell me whatever it is."

She hesitated one last second and then decided that Lindsay had the right to all the information she had. "I think the next word is going to be *daughter*."

Lindsay stared at her in bemusement. "*I—am—your—*

daughter? But why would he send this to you? I don't understand. Was it meant for me?"

Bree licked her lips, knowing she was about to rip Lindsay's life apart one more time. "It was meant for me, Lindsay."

"You? What are you talking about?"

"Ten years ago, I gave up a baby for adoption, and the kidnapper seems to be saying that the child he has is my biological child—that I am Hayley's birth mother."

"What!" Lindsay's eyes widened, the blood draining out of her face, until she looked like a ghost. "That—that isn't possible."

She swallowed back a growing knot of emotion, knowing she had to find a way to get all the words out, to tell her secret to the one person who probably needed to hear it the most.

"I didn't believe it was possible, either. When I first met you, I had no inkling that Hayley could possibly be the child I gave up for adoption. I came to Chicago because Hayley's case was exactly like three others that I had recently worked. But I'm fairly certain now that the white rose was just meant to get me to Chicago."

"None of this is true." Lindsay gave a vehement shake of her head. "Hayley's biological mother is dead."

"It's probable that the records—the birth certificate— everything was doctored."

"Why?"

"Because you were going through back channels. You were working through the black market. Did you know that, Lindsay?"

"No. It was a legitimate agency. They did private adoptions. They had photos of happy kids and happy families on their walls."

"That agency went out of business a few months after you got Hayley."

"Businesses go under all the time. So what? You're mistaken. I'm sorry, but you're wrong. And maybe the message on the phone isn't going to end with *daughter*. It could be something else."

Lindsay was fighting hard to hang onto her reality, and Bree couldn't blame her, but in the end, the truth would come out.

"I'm not telling you any of this to hurt you. I am as shocked as you are that Hayley could be my daughter. I had specifically been told that my baby would not go to a family in Illinois."

"But we live in Illinois, and we picked up Hayley from a hospital in Joliet. Is that where you had your baby?"

"No. I had my child in Detroit. But you didn't pick up Hayley until she was several days old, right?"

"But she was born at that hospital." Lindsay paused. "I mean—I assumed she was born there." Suddenly, uncertainty was in her voice.

"We both made assumptions that weren't true," she said gently. "I was a teen mom. I willingly gave up my child, so she could have a better life. And I would have hoped beyond hope that she would have gone to a family like yours."

"Why did you give her up? Because you were young?"

She'd expected the question, but it was still difficult to hear. "I was eighteen, and I had lived a very difficult life. My mother had me when she was a teenager, and I grew up in chaos, poverty and crime. My mom died when I was ten, and I lived with my aunt for a few years, and then I went into foster care when she couldn't take care of me. When I realized I was pregnant, the only thing I knew for sure was that I didn't want my baby to live my childhood. I wanted her to have what you've given Hayley—two loving parents, grandparents, siblings, a pretty pink and purple bedroom with all the stuffed animals she could ever want." Her eyes filled with tears as she thought about Hayley's room.

A tear slid out of Lindsay's eye. "I tried my best. But now...you must hate me."

"I don't hate you. I hate the people who took Hayley. They're the only ones who are responsible."

"You're Hayley's birth mom," Lindsay muttered, as she

still tried to make sense of it. "But she doesn't have your green eyes. Hers are brown." She paused. "The father—we never knew anything about Hayley's father."

And the last thing she wanted to do was tell Lindsay about Johnny. "He's not important right now. I just want you to know that I'm going to find Hayley, and I'm going to bring her back to you."

"To me? Or to you?" Lindsay whispered, anguish in her eyes. "You're her mother. Maybe you want her back."

Did she want her back?

She shook her head, forcing the silent question out of her head. "No. You're her mother." She blinked back the tears that so desperately wanted to fall, and looking at Lindsay, she could see the same heartbreaking emotion. "And Mark is her father," she managed to add. "He's going to be all right, and Hayley will come home to you. We're going to put your family back together."

"Promise me."

It went against all of her training to make that promise, but she did it anyway. "I promise."

Tense silence hung between them, and then the door opened, and Lindsay's father returned to the room. She felt relieved at his interruption. Lindsay would have more questions, but for now she'd told her enough.

"Everything all right in here?" he asked, obviously noting the heavy atmosphere in the room and not sure if it had to do with Mark or Hayley or whatever else they'd been talking about.

Lindsay gave her a helpless look, as if she didn't know how to answer her father.

Bree didn't want to get into anything with Lindsay's dad, so she just said, "I'll be in touch, Lindsay."

"Just keep your promise. That's all I ask."

Nathan leaned over and gave Lindsay a hug. "I'm praying for Mark."

"Thank you," she said tightly.

As they left the room, Bree paused in the doorway.

Lindsay's father sat down next to his daughter and put his arm around her shoulders. Then Lindsay lost control and started to sob.

"I made things worse," she muttered.

Nathan took her hand and pulled her into the hallway. They moved a few feet down the corridor, away from the police officer. "You had to tell her, Bree."

"It was one of the hardest things I've ever done," she said, looking into his understanding eyes. "But I thought she needed to know."

"She did need to know. I just wished you hadn't made her a promise you might not be able to keep."

"I'm going to keep it," she said fiercely. "I'm going to save my daughter. Whatever it takes."

"I'm not arguing with you. I know you'll do everything you can, but I noticed you didn't tell her about Johnny."

"I didn't want to scare her more by telling her that Hayley's father is a criminal. But I'm going to have to tell everyone else. The pictures coming to my phone are putting together a phrase that will directly name me as Hayley's mother, and if I don't share my suspicions, I could be putting Hayley at more risk. I have to come clean. I have to get the police and the agency on the same page, so we can find her."

"I know it's not what you wanted, but it's the right thing to do. Do you want to get out of here before..." His voice trailed away. "I guess it's too late for that."

She nodded, seeing three members from the Chicago FBI office get off the elevator. They were followed by two men in suits. One was the lead detective on the case, Vance Cooper, but the other man was new to the investigation. He wasn't, however, new to her. "Is that Detective Benedict?" she asked Nathan, wary surprise running through her.

"I think so," Nathan said tightly. "What is he doing on this case?"

She didn't know, and she didn't like it. Benedict had been good friends with Johnny's father, and she'd always thought he was a dirty cop. The fact that he was suddenly showing up now when Calvin Baker, a former associate of Johnny's, had just been ID'd as the ransom negotiator made her very nervous.

Was he here to get information for Johnny?

"Be careful what you say to him," she told Nathan. "Don't let on that you remember Calvin."

"Don't worry. I know how *not* to talk to the cops."

"I don't know when I'll be in touch. The police will take over your questioning, while I'll be tied up with the agency. I wish I could protect you from the questions—"

"I'm not worried about it," he said, cutting her off. "I'll tell them exactly what happened, how we came to follow Mark to the silos, and how you took down the gunman before he could kill Mark."

"I shouldn't have taken you with me. I should have commandeered your truck and left you on the sidewalk."

"Like that was going to happen," he said dryly. "I will be sure to tell them I went willingly and actually forced you to take me. But don't waste your concern on me. I'm fine. And when you're done on your end, I'll be waiting."

She liked the sound of that.

"And, Bree," he added. "The promise I made to you at the bus station still stands. You tell your secret however and whenever you want. As far as anyone else is concerned, I know nothing."

"Last time you didn't talk, you got beat up. This time, you might go to jail. I don't want you to lie for me."

"The cops don't know as much as we do, and at the moment, neither does the FBI. My interview will probably be over before the police know you're Hayley's birth mother."

"You might be right."

"I'll handle myself," Nathan added. "You take care of you. And try to remember you didn't do anything wrong, Bree. You loved the wrong guy a long time ago, but everything else you did right. And you're still doing it right. You're Hayley's best chance at survival. Don't let anyone try to convince you otherwise."

Her heart swelled with gratitude. Nathan had always been the one person she could count on. "We'll meet up later," she said. But judging by the intent looks on her fellow agents' faces, she didn't think that would be any time soon.

Thirteen

—→→→←←←—

As Bree had predicted, the police detectives had zeroed in on Nathan, taking him down to the station, while the FBI had hustled her back to the office for a long chat.

She'd been in a conference room for the last five hours, having gone through every detail of her past: her relationship with Johnny, her teenaged pregnancy, the time she'd spent in Detroit, and the woman who'd set up the adoption. Then they'd moved forward in time to last year: the previous kidnapping cases, the news coverage in Philadelphia, and the text messages she'd received from the kidnapper. Finally, they'd zeroed in on her actions today: her arrival at the Jansens' house, her discussion with Nathan, which had led to them following Mark to the silos together, and the shots that were fired—one to disable and one to kill.

While most of the questioning was led by Tracy and/or ASAIC Hobbs, various other agents had come in and out of the conference room to ask questions and/or give updates on the investigation into the crime scene at the silos as well as Mark's condition. He was now out of surgery, still critical, but holding his own for the moment. She was tremendously grateful to know that he was going to make it.

The texts and the photos she had received from the kidnapper were being analyzed, but she doubted they would find anything. The kidnapper was too smart, always staying one step ahead. In fact, she wouldn't be surprised if he had some background in law enforcement. He seemed to know exactly how to mask his actions from the bureau, an agency with tremendous resources and technological expertise.

The fourth photo—the one she was sure would say *daughter*—had still not arrived. She had no doubt that another message would be arriving at some point. The game was not over. The kidnapper was not done.

As early evening shadows darkened the conference room, Tracy flipped on a light and sat down at the other end of the table as she took a call. It was just the two of them now, and Tracy seemed to be doing more listening than talking, which was unusual since Tracy always seemed like she had a lot to say.

Bree glanced at her watch. It was almost six. She was exhausted and starving. And she was getting tired of playing good little FBI soldier to Tracy and a bunch of colleagues who didn't like her much for mucking up their investigation and withholding what they considered to be important information. Never mind that it had been less than forty-eight hours since she'd arrived in Chicago, even though it felt like a lifetime had passed since she'd gotten on the plane.

Everything had been happening at lightning speed. Maybe they were pissed at being left out of the loop for a few hours, but she was getting angry about being cooped up in the office for so long and treated like a criminal instead of an agent.

"Are we done?" she asked when Tracy got off the phone and moved down the table to sit across from her.

"Almost. That was Detective Benedict. He said that Calvin Baker was living in an apartment on Hayward Street until a week ago."

"Hayward Street is where the gym is—the boxing gym that is owned by the Hawke family."

"We're aware," she said shortly. "The landlord said Baker moved out last week, leaving a half month's rent on the table. His whereabouts after that are unknown. Neighbors had nothing to say."

"No one on Hayward Street ever has much to say. Was there anything else?"

"Baker has been in and out of jail the past ten years. He's done just about everything from drug deals, to gun running, car theft, and assault."

"And his ties to Johnny Hawke?"

"Nothing recently."

Wasn't that convenient, especially since the information had come from Detective Benedict?

"What do you know about Detective Benedict?" she asked. "Because a long time ago, he appeared to be very close to Johnny's father. Suddenly today he shows up at the hospital. He hasn't been involved in this case at all, so why is he now a part of it?"

"Because he works organized crime, and he actually put Baker in jail four years ago after a drug bust. We contacted him looking for more information. We brought him into this, Bree."

She frowned. "It still seems odd to me. I'd swear he was a dirty cop when I lived here. I know I saw him talking to Johnny and his father. There was something between them."

Tracy shrugged. "If he's dirty, he's good, because he's had his job for over twenty years."

"Well, I need to talk to him. I want to speak to Johnny as well." She was dreading that, but it had to be done.

"No. You're not talking to anyone," Tracy said definitively. "My team will be conducting all the interviews."

"But I know Johnny."

"Obviously," she said sarcastically. "But you would be emotionally compromised in any interview with Mr. Hawke, so we will take it from here."

"He would tell me more than he would tell you."

"Would he? You did steal his child from him."

She sighed, knowing she couldn't argue that. "All right. Then let's end this now. There's nothing more to be said." She pushed back her chair and stood up.

Tracy gave her a hostile look as she also got to her feet. "That's not your call, Bree."

"I think it is. Despite the fact that you're treating me like a suspect, we are on the same side."

"It feels like you've been playing both sides," Tracy returned. "You should have told us that you thought this little girl was your daughter."

"I honestly didn't think that until about five minutes before I went to the silos. But we've been over all that a hundred times already. I didn't come to Chicago to make trouble; I came because this was a setup. I was lured here. Hayley's kidnapping wasn't done by the White Rose Kidnapper; it was just made to look that way, so I'd be called in. There's still a little girl out there we need to find, whether she's my daughter or not."

"I am very aware of that."

"Then why are you talking to me instead of looking for her?"

"Because you made a mess of things, and I have to clean it up."

"I didn't make a mess of anything," she snapped. "And if you weren't holding some grudge against me from the academy, you'd be acting a lot differently."

"No, I wouldn't. I go by the book, Bree. I follow protocol. I don't act out of passion and emotion. I always use my head. I'm logical. I plan my every move. I don't jump into trucks with a civilian friend and drive him to a ransom drop."

"I needed a vehicle, and Nathan was right there. At the time, I didn't know where we were going. But I'm done explaining my actions. This interview is over. I have told you everything I know. If I am out of the investigation, then I'm going to my hotel. But I will need my phone back. If the kidnapper calls again, I have to be able to answer."

They'd already argued about the phone several times, and while Tracy had disagreed, ASAIC Hobbs had decided Bree should hang on to the phone and keep her connection with the kidnapper alive.

Tracy reluctantly handed over the phone. "You will let us know if any calls come in?"

"As soon as it happens."

"I still think you should have protection."

Another topic they'd already discussed at length. "I don't need a visible presence between me and the kidnapper," she reminded Tracy. "He needs to think he can still get to me."

"Which means he *can* get to you," Tracy couldn't help pointing out.

"I can handle myself." She grabbed her bag and headed out of the room before Tracy could come up with any more reasons for her to stay.

When she got outside, she flagged down a taxi. As it pulled away from the curb, she stared at the phone, knowing there was another reason they'd let her keep it. They wanted to track her.

Not so fast. She quickly disabled the GPS. They could trace and triangulate any calls she made, but for now, she was free.

"I'm going to change my destination," she told the driver, giving him a new address. Then she sat back and looked out the window at the city that was continuing to beat her down.

Tracy's boastful words about being a better agent because she acted from a place of logic seemed laughable to her. She knew without a doubt that she wasn't going to get Hayley back by following protocols. She was going to have to get down in the mud and fight like the street kid she'd once been.

———⇒⇒⇐⇐⇐———

Nathan opened the door of his apartment just after seven on Friday night, thrilled to see Bree in the hallway. They hadn't been in touch since she'd left the hospital, and that had been hours ago. She looked exhausted. He pulled her into his apartment and into his arms, kicking the door shut behind her.

She rested her head on his shoulder and they hung onto each other.

He could feel the tension in her body, the stress of the last few days, the fear, the worry—everything. But then he'd always been in tune with Bree. He'd never really been able to divorce his emotions from hers. When she hurt—he hurt. It was just a fact. It had started when he was thirteen years old, and it didn't seem to be ending any time soon.

It didn't matter that they hadn't seen each other in years before this week.

This was Bree. This was the girl of his dreams.

She was here. And she was in his arms. And that was all that mattered.

She lifted her head and looked up at him with her beautiful green eyes. "Hi."

He gave her a smile. "I wasn't sure the FBI didn't have you locked up somewhere."

"They're not happy with me. There was talk of suspending me, but I'm the only link they have to the kidnapper, so for now I still have my gun and my badge. I'm not sure how long that will last." She let go of him and stepped away. "Let's see your place."

"It's not much."

She walked down the short hallway that led into his one-bedroom apartment and put her bag on the kitchen counter. Then she headed straight for the balcony.

"You have a view," she said with delight, moving through the small living room to the sliding glass doors.

He followed her outside, smiling at the change in her demeanor as she took in the city from the thirty-fifth floor.

"Oh, Nathan, this is amazing," she said, waving her arm toward the city skyline. "The lights are beautiful."

"Better than the rooftops we used to get up on?"

"So much better. We never had access to anything higher than twelve floors. This is crazy."

"I have to admit the view is what enticed me to pay more rent than I planned. Someday, I'd like to own a house and put down some deeper roots, but when I took this place, I was looking for a way to feel on top of things."

"You're on top of the world up here."

"It's not the beach. I don't see sailboats," he said, reminding her of her dream view. "But for now, this is good."

"It's better than good." She drew in a breath and let it out. "It's been a long day."

"That's an understatement."

Turning to look at him, she said, "I heard Mark came through surgery. How long did you stay at the hospital?"

"I was there until about an hour ago. Mark is not completely out of danger, but he seems to be holding his own."

"I'm so relieved."

"Me, too." He could see the unspoken question in her eyes. "Lindsay didn't say much about your revelation, except to ask that I not tell anyone else in her family. I assured her that information wouldn't come from me, but with the police and FBI being filled in on the connection between you and Hayley and the kidnapper, I didn't know how long anything was going to stay secret."

"Probably not long."

"I reminded her that the only thing that matters to anyone right now is finding Hayley. Everything else can be sorted out later." He paused. "She did ask me how I knew you. She wondered about our relationship and what I thought of you."

"What did you say?"

"I told her we met when we were kids and that you are a really good person. I said I was there when you decided to give your baby a better life, and I knew how much it cost you, but I also knew how sure you were that you were doing the right thing."

She met his gaze. "Thanks for the character reference."

"I told the truth. You are a good person. You're a good agent, too. I hope the bureau knows that."

She shrugged. "Time will tell." She paused. "Lindsay is probably worried I'm going to try to get Hayley back after all this."

"And/or blame her for what happened," he said. "She is

carrying a ton of guilt."

"I don't blame her or Mark for the kidnapping. That had nothing to do with them. The Jansens have given Hayley a great life. She has the family I always wanted for her. I just can't believe that she ended up in Chicago. I thought I was doing everything I could to keep my child out of Johnny's orbit. That's why I lived in Detroit, of all places. What was the point of me going there if they were going to give my child to someone in Chicago?"

"I don't know. Maybe the money was right. I'd like to know what Mark and Lindsay paid for that adoption."

"Ten thousand dollars," she said. "To a now defunct agency. I looked it up. But I'm guessing there was an additional cash payment that was not recorded."

"Probably."

She let out a sigh. "I've been keeping myself sane by telling myself that Johnny wouldn't hurt his own child. Family and blood are everything to him."

"I've been telling myself that, too. I also don't think he would feel a need to hurt Emma," he said, bringing up the little girl from the train. "I know you have been worried about her, but I think she's probably someone in the neighborhood, who was happy to make some extra cash. Her older sister might have put her up to it."

"It's possible."

"So, do you want to fill me in on what happened on your end?"

"A million questions. I answered many of them several times. The FBI and the police are working hard to track Calvin Baker's whereabouts over the past several months. He disappeared from his apartment last week. Detective Benedict, who works in organized crime, assured my colleague, Agent Cox, that Baker has no ties to Johnny Hawke's operation."

"But you don't believe him?"

"No. And I think Benedict is still on the Hawke's payroll."

"Good chance. I talked to Benedict, too. It was right after you left, so it was before he knew anything about Hayley being your daughter. His questions to me were about Mark leaving the house, our actions at the silos, whether Mark said anything to me before he was taken to the hospital. I think he wanted to know if Mark knew who the kidnappers were, and if he'd shared that information with me."

"I hope you said no."

"I did, because it was the truth. He didn't tell me anything. He just said he was sorry he'd done what he did."

"Did Benedict ask you anything about me?"

"Yes. He was aware that you'd grown up in Chicago, that you and I were friends in our youth, and that Kyle had filed a complaint against you."

She raised an eyebrow. "That's a lot of information for a detective from organized crime to have, especially since he had just come on the case."

"I thought so, too. I told him we reconnected when you came to interview my niece."

"Did he mention my relationship with Johnny?"

"He did not, and I didn't bring it up."

"Thanks for that."

"No problem. My impression of Benedict is that he's slick and smart. I don't like the timing of his entrance into the case, and I don't think we should underestimate him."

"I agree. I'm sure the bureau will share my relationship to Johnny with the police and with Benedict."

"And he'll tell Johnny."

"If he doesn't, the bureau probably will. They're going to interview him tonight."

"Without you?"

She nodded, anger in her eyes. "They think I would be emotionally compromised."

"I know you hate that idea, but it's probably true."

Her mouth tightened. "Maybe it is. I can't say that I'm not personally invested in the outcome of this case. Hayley is my daughter—my daughter," she emphasized, as if she were still trying to believe it.

"And you love her. That's why you're compromised. You'd do anything to get her back."

"I would," she admitted. "I'd even talk to Johnny."

"He's not going to be surprised when the FBI tell him about Hayley and their belief that she is his daughter with you. He already knows. He's not in the dark on this, Bree. He can't be. Baker had to be working for Johnny. I don't care what Benedict said. We know their past relationship. We were there."

She nodded. "I'm not arguing with you."

"That's a change. Usually, when Johnny is in the conversation, things get heated."

She made a face at him. "I'm not defending Johnny. And I'm not scared of him anymore. If I have to go through him to get to Hayley, I will."

He saw the steel determination in her eyes and had no doubt about that. "Any more photos come in?"

"Not since the third one. The agency let me keep the phone, because it's the only connection we have to the kidnapper." She paused. "I did, however, disable the GPS before I came here."

"So, they don't know where you are?"

"They could do some call triangulating if I get on the phone, but for the moment, I feel free. Not that they probably couldn't just guess I'm with you," she said with a wry smile. "But I need a little time to regroup, and it felt like I was taking back a bit of my power when I disabled the GPS. Silly, huh?"

"Completely understandable. While you're regrouping, do you feel like eating? I picked up some Chinese on my way home from the hospital."

"Chow mein and chicken fried rice?"

"You know it," he said, smiling as she named her long-time favorites. "Mongolian beef and potstickers, too."

"That sounds awesome, but right now I'm enjoying the fresh air. Maybe in a few minutes?"

"Sure. We'll have to heat it up anyway."

"You're being so great, Nathan. I didn't have a chance to say that earlier, but the way you handled yourself at the silos, taking care of Mark, dealing with the police, and then supporting me with Lindsay at the hospital. The past few days, you've listened to me ramble on and on about every new theory that comes into my head. You've gone above and beyond, and I feel a little guilty at how entangled you are in all this."

"Don't worry about me. I want to find Hayley—for her, for you, for the Jansens, for Josie, and for Grace, whose heart is still breaking for her friend." He took a breath. "I also want to help you, Bree. You don't deserve the gaslight treatment you've been getting. I want to help you find whoever is threatening you and make them stop."

"Thanks. It feels good to talk to you, Nathan. You always make things seem manageable. I was working myself into a lather on the way over here, furious with my agency for treating me like a criminal, irritated with myself for not handling the situation at the silos better, being unable to figure out the kidnapper is tied to Johnny, and being led astray by Emma instead of realizing that Hayley is my daughter until today. You saw it yesterday."

"Only because you couldn't bear the idea that your daughter had been kidnapped. Emma was a safer choice. You saw her as being okay, being part of a con, not being held captive."

"I guess. I know there is more coming Nathan. I told the agency that the game isn't over. He has more plays, and I need to be able to act. But they've taken me off the investigation. I can't even use agency resources anymore. They cut off my access, took away my security clearance. Because I'm the biological mother of the kidnap victim, I'm vulnerable to blackmail. I understand it, but I feel isolated, angry, frustrated and overwhelmed."

He could see that she was quickly working herself into another lather. "You can't do anything but live in this moment, Bree. You can't stop the thunder. You just have to let it roll over you. And then when it's done, you get up and keep going."

A smile suddenly spread across her lips. "Oh, my God. You just gave me a *Nathanism*."

"I'm afraid to ask what that is," he said warily.

"You used to have all these sayings that would make me and Josie feel better. We called them *Nathanisms*. You said that one about the thunder when we were at the shelter. I remember huddling with you and Josie in the downstairs room when the lights went off, and thunder was rocking the building. You sat between me and Josie, and you held our hands, and said, 'We'll get through this. We'll be okay. Just let the thunder roll over us and go on its way.'"

"I don't remember that," he lied, some self-protective instinct kicking in. In truth, that was the first night he'd ever held her hand, and he'd never been able to forget it.

"Well, I do. You were good for me. For a while, I was good for you, too."

"More than awhile. And we'll get through this round of thunder as well. You may not be officially on the case anymore, but I know that isn't going to stop you from working it, and I'll be there to help you. Tomorrow we'll get back on it. Or before tomorrow, if you get another clue."

"It seems to be taking a long time. I don't know if the kidnapper got put off their game because of what happened at the silos, but it's been hours since I received that third photo. Where's the next one?"

"Maybe they're afraid you're getting too close."

"Or they just want to drive me crazy for a while longer."

"You still don't want to call the kidnapper, Johnny, do you?"

"I know there were two people at the silos, and I'm guessing someone was left behind with Hayley, so right now I have to say *they*. Maybe Johnny is in charge, but I don't know if he's the actual kidnapper. I can't see him going into Hayley's school and grabbing her."

"No. That sounds like a job for one of his minions. He would have been somewhere else that night, with a perfect alibi ready to go."

She frowned but didn't say anything, turning her gaze back to the view.

He didn't know where she'd gone in her head, but from the set of her jaw, he could see it was nowhere pleasant. "You may be getting pulled back into the dark past, Bree, but you won't go under, you won't get trapped there. You won't let that happen and I won't let that happen. We're strong now. Stronger than we've ever been, and stronger because we're together. Johnny is no match for us. I don't care how big his army is now."

She turned her head, her tension easing. "You're right. And we don't just have each other. My agency may not be thrilled with me, but they will be there if we need them." She paused. "Do you mind if I hang out here? I don't want to go back to my hotel."

"I want you to stay. I was actually going to insist on it."

"Okay then. I'll stay."

As their gazes clung together, the air between them started to crackle and sizzle. He knew he should say something, but he had no idea what. And Bree, likewise, seemed to be suddenly speechless.

Thirty-five floors up, and he wasn't scared of falling over the rail; he was scared of falling into her.

He could feel the tug between them, the relentless pressure of desire and need that had gone unfulfilled for so many years. This wasn't the right time or the right place, but then what was?

In the past, he'd walked away from so many moments like this, and he'd always regretted it. He didn't want any more regrets, no more missed opportunities.

"Nathan?" she whispered, her voice like a soft song on the wind.

Was it a plea or a question?

"I want you, Bree." There it was—right on the table, out

in the light, words for her to stomp on or to embrace. He couldn't quite believe he'd said the words aloud after so many years of keeping them to himself.

Her green eyes darkened, and her lips parted, but it seemed to take forever for her to say something.

Would it be worth the wait?

"I want you, too," she said.

Definitely worth the wait.

He swallowed hard, not sure he'd heard her right, but her green gaze was gleaming in the moonlight. He bridged the distance between them, framing her head with his hands, his fingers sliding into the silky strands of her brown hair, his thumbs brushing the soft skin of her cheeks. Her lips parted, her breath a cloud of sexy heat in the cold night air.

He lowered his head, taking his time, wanting to savor every moment, because who knew if it would ever happen again?

When his lips covered hers, a wave of delicious warmth enveloped him. Everything else faded into the night—the lights, the traffic, the city. It was just the two of them, and that's really all he'd ever wanted.

She opened her mouth and invited him inside with an impatient sweetness that put him over the edge.

Bree had always been impatient to get what she wanted. She'd never been methodical or plodding; she'd always dived in—head first. And he'd always thought twice before he followed—*if* he followed.

But he wasn't following her now. And neither was he leading.

It was give and take, push and pull, one kiss blending into the next.

His hands moved through her hair, resting on her shoulders and then running down her arms to her hands. His fingers curled around hers as their mouths met again. It was the perfect kiss, the perfect touch, the perfection connection.

He didn't feel the chill of the night anymore.

He didn't feel the cold of his life anymore.

He just felt her.

Her mouth. Her hands. His Bree.

Maybe it wouldn't be forever. Maybe it wouldn't last until tomorrow. But he'd take what she was willing to give.

"Inside," he murmured against her mouth, pulling her back into his apartment, and closing the door behind them.

She took off her coat and tossed it over a nearby chair. Her gun and badge moved onto the coffee table, and then she went to work on the buttons of her blouse. He felt as if she wasn't just stripping herself of her clothes: she was stripping herself of the pressures and trappings of her life.

As she slipped her blouse off, he became entranced by the sheer white lacy silk of her bra. *She might look all business on the outside, but on the inside...*

"You're falling behind, Nathan," she said, a playful light in her eyes. "Just like that strip poker game we once played. I was down to my panties while you had only lost your shirt."

"That's because you were not very good at poker. Your excitement at getting a good hand always gave you away. You have very expressive eyes."

She made a face at him. "So, you were a better poker player. What's your excuse tonight?"

"I'm enjoying the show," he said, as she shimmied out of her black slacks, revealing a matching white lace thong and slender bare legs that he wouldn't mind having wrapped around his waist.

Despite his words, he was done watching. He moved forward, taking another kiss, as his hands cupped her sweet ass. And then she was doing just what he'd wanted, throwing her arms around his neck and wrapping her legs around his waist as he carried her into the bedroom.

He tossed her onto the mattress, then made quick work of his clothes while she took off her lacy lingerie.

Seeing her naked, in his bed, waiting for him, with her gorgeous brown hair spread across his pillow, her green eyes so intent and passionate almost stopped his heart.

"God, Bree," he murmured. "You're amazing."

"Get down here, and I'll show you how amazing I can be."

"We're really doing this," he muttered, still in a little disbelief.

"Oh, we're doing it, Nathan," she said, pulling him on top of her. "Kiss me already. I feel like I've been waiting forever."

He felt exactly the same way.

Fourteen

➤➤◄◄◄

Being with Nathan had been surprising and hot and really, really satisfying, Bree thought, as she snuggled against his side, her head on his shoulder, her arm across his waist, her leg over his.

She hadn't really known what to expect. Nathan had been many things to her. He'd been the kind, sweet, imaginative boy who had protected her and made her feel safe. He'd also been the fun, attractive teenager, who all the girls had wanted, but he'd still hung out with her. And then he'd been the brooding, mysterious, scowling man who seemed to disapprove of everything she did. And that had been the early years…

When she'd returned to Chicago a few days ago, he'd been angry and resistant, but then he'd gotten tangled up in her life and her problems, and he'd been a friend again, someone to lean on, someone to talk to, someone to trust…

Now, he was her lover.

She shivered at the memories of his hands on her body, his mouth on her lips and her breasts…his whispered words of passion as they moved together in perfect sync.

They hadn't always been on the same page, but tonight they'd both wanted the same thing—they'd wanted *everything.*

She hadn't felt so connected to anyone in a long time—if

ever.

It was almost shocking to think it was Nathan who had made her feel so complete.

And yet it also made sense.

He'd always been able to read her. He'd always known what she wanted.

She'd had a lot more trouble figuring him out, but not tonight—tonight hadn't been about the past, but the present, the *now*...and the now had been wonderful.

Her stomach suddenly rumbled, and she felt a wave of embarrassment when Nathan laughed.

Lifting her head, she looked into his smiling eyes, feeling a bit smug that he was so happy, and it was because of her. "I think I'm ready for that Chinese food."

"I'll get it just as soon as I can move again," he drawled. "That was something else, Bree."

"We were very good together. I want to do it again and again and again," she said, playfully poking his chest with each repeat of the word *again*.

"Sounds like an excellent plan."

"But first..."

He groaned. "Food?"

She nodded and got off the bed, smiling to herself as Nathan gave her bare ass a little whistle of appreciation.

After using the bathroom, she wrapped herself up in Nathan's soft dark-green robe and joined him in the kitchen.

He'd put on his boxer briefs and jeans but thankfully he'd left his shirt off. She moved up behind him as he opened the refrigerator and wrapped her arms around his waist, pressing a kiss on his back. "I'm glad you left your chest bare. I like a view while I'm eating."

He turned around in her arms. "I like a view, too. Maybe you should take off this robe."

"Not a chance. I know what will happen then, and I want my noodles."

He laughed and handed her a container. "I'll get us some plates, and we can heat everything up."

She opened the carton he'd given her. "I like it cold. And I'm too hungry to wait."

"You've reminded me several times tonight of how impatient you can be," he said with a wicked smile.

"I didn't hear you complaining a few minutes ago." She twirled some noodles around her fork and popped them into her mouth. "Yum. These are delicious."

Nathan poured food from several other cartons onto a plate, heated it up in the microwave, and then sat down next to her.

"Ooh, I want some of that, too," she said, eyeing the Mongolian beef on his plate.

He playfully pushed her fork away. "You like it cold, remember?"

"I like it hot, too," she said, making a quick move to spear a piece of beef. She put it into her mouth and savored the hot, spicy flavors. "Everything tastes so good when you're hungry."

"And you've just had really good sex," he said dryly.

"That, too," she agreed with a laugh. "Why didn't we ever do that before?"

A shutter came down over his eyes. "You know why. Do you want something to drink?" he asked, getting back up and moving toward the fridge.

She decided to follow his change of subject. "What do you have?"

"Beer, orange juice, water from the tap?"

"I'll take some orange juice."

He filled two glasses and brought them over.

"I'm sorry I brought the past up," she said, taking a sip of juice.

"We are our past. There's no escaping it. If anything has been proven the last few days, it's that."

"I know." They ate in silence for the next few minutes, and she didn't know how to get things back on track. By the time she had finished her noodles, she was starting to get annoyed. "You always did this," she said.

"Did what?" he asked warily.

"Get close to me, be all funny and sweet and then you'd shut it down. You'd back away, give me some scowling look, and disappear for a few weeks."

"I didn't do that."

"Oh, yes, you did—a lot. And you're doing it right now. You let me in and now you have to push me back out."

"It's not like you ever wanted to stay in," he said tersely.

"Why do you say that?"

"You were with Johnny."

"I'm not going to try to rewrite history. Yes, I was infatuated with Johnny for a time. We both know that. But he never had anything to do with you and me. It wasn't like he broke us up. You were shutting me out long before Johnny came along. I thought when I first saw you again in high school, when we reconnected, that I was so lucky because I had my friend back, this wonderful guy who I could count on, who I could be myself with. And you were back for a while. Then you disappeared again. It was actually while you were on one of your long breaks from me that I got involved with Johnny."

"So, now that's my fault?"

"I didn't mean it like that. I'm just telling you how it felt on my end."

He stared back at her, dark emotion in his eyes. He looked like he wanted to say something, but he couldn't get the words out. "Let's not talk about this now."

"Why not?"

"Because I want the *again* and *again* and *again* that you mentioned before to happen, and I don't think this conversation is leading in that direction."

"I actually think clearing up past misunderstandings would be a good thing. Let's be completely honest with each other."

He groaned. "Complete honesty, huh?"

"Yes. And we're not just going to discuss your hatred of Brussels sprouts, although I think I could convince you that they can be good if you eat them the way I cook them."

"I've tried every way."

"Fine. Getting back to more important issues. I know you disapproved of a lot of my choices back in the day. And I know that I deserved some of that disapproval. I acted impulsively. I jumped into relationships, so I wouldn't have to be alone. I was scared of the silence, the quiet. It gave me too much time to think, to stress, to be aware of how bad my life was."

"I know your childhood was hard, Bree."

"It was lonely," she said, feeling that deep, wrenching ache of memory. "I always felt as if I were on an island. There were people around me, but they weren't really with me. I wanted to be with them. I wanted to feel a part of someone else's life. But no one wanted me. Not my family, certainly, and the foster homes that took me in just wanted the cash."

His gaze narrowed. "I'm sorry it was so bad."

"You don't have to be sorry. It wasn't your fault. To be really truthful, it wasn't anyone's fault. I was just born to a mother who couldn't be a mom. And then I decided to make matters worse by following in her footsteps, picking the wrong men, making the same mistakes, getting pregnant when I had no ability to raise a child. I was stupid and reckless, and you could see I was heading for a cliff." She paused. "You were a mirror to my bad decisions. I'd take one look at your face and know I was on the wrong ride. But I couldn't seem to get myself off."

"Was I really that judgmental?" he asked quietly.

"You were—especially that last year before I left. That's why we stopped spending time together. I didn't want to look into your eyes and see everything I was doing wrong. And you probably didn't want to have to watch me screw up. You always walked a moral ground that was much higher than mine."

"That's not true," he said sharply. "You said that before, and it's just wrong."

She wondered why he was suddenly getting so heated. "How is it wrong? Isn't that the reason why you pulled away from me, why we stopped being friends? You didn't want to hang out with someone as messed up as me?"

"No. It's not the reason—not the whole reason anyway." He frowned and shook his head.

"Then why?" she asked, when he didn't seem inclined to continue. "What am I missing?"

He got up from his chair and walked over to the window, staring out at the night.

Suddenly she wondered just what she was digging up. An uneasy feeling was moving through her, but it was too late to backtrack. Whatever was in his head, whatever he was holding back, she needed to hear it.

She stood up and walked over to him. "Nathan, talk to me."

He turned to look at her, and there was a new torment in his eyes.

"What is wrong?" she asked in bewilderment. "What did I say?"

"You didn't say anything."

"Then why is there so much pain in your eyes?"

His jaw tightened. "I've never told anyone."

Her uneasiness deepened. "Told anyone what?"

"What happened."

"Then tell me," she urged. "Tell me now."

He hesitated for a long minute. "I didn't pull away from you because I didn't approve of your decisions. Not that I agreed with all of them, but I had a far more selfish reason. I didn't want to have to lie to you."

"Lie to me?" Now she was confused. "You're going to need to spell this out, Nathan. You're being too cryptic. Why would you have had to lie to me?"

He folded his arms across his chest, as if he were putting on some armor. "Because when we talked, we didn't hold back. We were honest with each other. Sometimes brutally so. No topic was ever off-limits."

"That was what was so great about us. What I missed the most. Why did you have to shut me down?"

"Because I had a secret."

"What kind of a secret?" she asked, surprised by his words.

"It had to do with my stepfather."

Her gut clenched. She knew his stepfather had been a horrible person, so whatever this secret was, it had to be bad. "Okay," she said tentatively. "Can you tell me now?"

"When my mother married my stepfather, I was ten and Josie was eight. My mom thought she was giving us a father after my real dad died. But she gave us a monster. She put us into a trap we could not get out of. My mother didn't have the strength or the will to get us away from him. She was convinced we couldn't survive without him. That's why she kept going back to him."

Her heart turned over in her chest, seeing in his eyes now the painful young boy she'd first met, the one who'd been so consumed with trying to protect his mom and sister from the evil that lived with them. "I know he hurt you all a lot."

"Yes. He almost killed my mom twice. I watched her go from a vibrant, happy woman to a sad, despairing shell of herself. And Josie was…" His jaw tightened. "She had to endure even more pain than I did."

She waited for him to go on, sensing that there was a lot more coming, because she had known most of what he'd just said already.

"So, you know he died in a car accident," Nathan continued.

She nodded. "We were having pizza when you got the call from your mom."

"It wasn't exactly an accident."

His dark words stirred her uneasiness. "I know you were not driving the car that hit him, Nathan. You were with me that night."

"Yes, but earlier that day, two men had come by the house looking for my stepfather. They worked for a bookie named Jose Ortiz. They told me if my stepfather didn't pay up, he was going to get hurt really bad. I guess they thought that I would encourage him to pay so that wouldn't happen."

She heard the hard note in his voice and had a feeling where all this was going, but she had to let him get there on his own.

"I almost didn't say anything. I almost let them leave. They were at their car when I ran out of the house and down to the sidewalk. I told them if they wanted to talk to him, they could find him at Smokey's Bar on Sycamore. And then I went back inside. My mom was in the kitchen. She was upset because she'd been so depressed she hadn't cleaned the house that day, and she was crying that my stepfather was going to be mad. I helped her with the dishes and told her not to worry, hoping that that night would end differently than the others." Nathan drew in a breath. "Nothing happened for hours. I waited for my stepfather to show up or for us to get a call, but neither occurred. I went to meet you for pizza, thinking that my big plan was a bust. I thought they'd let him off the hook. I thought things might be even worse once he realized I'd told them where he was."

"But they hadn't let him off the hook," she guessed. "They ran him down with a car."

"Yes. I heard they went into the bar, and my stepfather was stinking drunk and belligerent. Witnesses said there was an argument, but that my stepfather left on his own. He was hit two blocks away, and no one saw anything. He died in the middle of the street. And when my mom called me down to the hospital, she was crying, but I saw relief in her eyes. She wasn't going to have to worry anymore."

"You never told her you sent the men there."

"No. I never told anyone, not even Josie—until now."

She was humbled by his trust in her. "I'm glad you told me," she whispered.

He met her gaze. "I wasn't driving the car, Bree, but I knew they were going to hurt him, maybe kill him, and I helped it happen. When the police came around, I never mentioned the men coming to the house. I pretended I didn't know anything about his debts. My mom didn't have to pretend, because he had kept her in the dark. And Josie was so drugged out of her mind half the time, she was just glad she could finally sleep at home again." He drew in a ragged breath. "When I realized how much weight was lifted off of us after his death, I wished I'd found a way to get rid of him sooner. I'd had chances to kill him myself, but I never did. I hated myself for being weak."

"Oh, Nathan, you weren't weak."

"How else do you explain it?"

"You're not a killer. It's not easy to take someone's life. That's why most people can't do it."

"It should have been easy; he hurt us so badly."

Her heart went out to the guilty anguish in his eyes. "You were a boy. And your mother loved that man even when she hated him. I remember how conflicted you were when I first met you. You wanted her to be safe, but you wanted her to be happy. You didn't know how to make both happen at the same time, but that's because you were thirteen."

"I wasn't thirteen forever. Things got worse after we left the shelter."

"You were still young." She moved closer to him and put her hands on his shoulders. "I really wish you'd told me before."

"I couldn't get the words out. You thought I was your mirror of truth. You were mine, too, Bree. I didn't want you to be disappointed in me. I didn't want you to think I was capable of setting someone up to be killed. I was really no better than Johnny; I just didn't want to admit it."

"So many things make sense now—why you suddenly got so distant. I thought it was all about me. How selfish was that?"

"I wanted you to believe that."

"If I'd known, things would have been different."

"Maybe not."

She frowned at his words. "What does that mean?"

"Since we're being completely honest, I had another reason for staying away from you."

"Your hatred of Johnny?"

"No. My love for you."

Her heartbeat quickened. "You were not in love with me, Nathan."

"I was—helplessly and hopelessly in love with you," he confessed. "I didn't completely understand it at the time. You were my friend as a kid, but then in high school, I just really wanted to kiss you. But if I did that, I knew we wouldn't be friends…so I didn't know how to act around you."

"You never said anything. You never even hinted. You had other girls around, too."

"I knew you didn't feel that way about me. I had to hang onto a little of my pride. Then Johnny came into the picture, and there was no reason to say anything. You'd made your choice."

"Made my choice? You didn't give me a choice."

"You know what I mean." He raised a hand as she opened her mouth. "Before you say anything else, I want to make something perfectly clear."

"What's that?" she asked warily.

He wrapped his arms around her. "Tonight was not about the past. We have a history, yes, and it's complicated, but being with you tonight was about the present. I was living in the moment."

"So was I," she murmured, happy with his words. "And you're right; it wasn't about the past. We are not the same people we were when we were thirteen or sixteen or eighteen. We've grown up. We've built lives. We've become our own people. We weren't ready to be together when we were teenagers. I'm really glad we came together now. I don't have any regrets."

He leaned down and gave her a long, tender kiss. "I have never regretted a minute with you, Bree."

"That might be overstating things," she said with a smile.

"Not a minute—not when we were fighting, not when we

were making up games, not even when we were playing strip poker, which, by the way, just about killed me. I don't know how I got through that night."

"Our game got broken up."

"Right. That's how I survived." He tilted his head, giving her a thoughtful look. "I really can't believe you never knew how I felt about you."

"I knew things felt weird at times between us, but I wasn't the most perceptive person at that point in my life. I guess I was worried about hurting our friendship, too. I also didn't know how to connect with people. I didn't know what sex and love really meant. And I was never confident that anyone would really love me for longer than a minute. I think that's why Johnny swept me away. He was bold in his intentions. He didn't hide how he felt about me. I didn't have to guess. And it felt good to be wanted."

Nathan's gaze darkened. "I wish I'd been able to show you how I felt. I was juggling so many balls, trying to keep my family together, trying to hide my secret. I thought if I said anything about setting up my stepfather to be killed, I might end up in jail, and I knew my mom and Josie wouldn't survive without me."

"I totally get that. It all makes a lot of sense now. We were both broken, Nathan. But we're not broken anymore. We're whole and we're healed. We had our bad times. We got through them, and we'll get through whatever Johnny has in store for us."

"I like that," he said approvingly. "You're right. It's our time now."

"Tomorrow is a new day." She smiled. "Another *Nathanism*."

"I really did speak in clichés, didn't I?"

She shrugged. "They always made me feel better."

"Well, the sun won't be up for several more hours, so…"

"So…" she echoed, as he gave her a long, hot kiss that stirred her senses.

But it wasn't just the kiss, it was the honesty they'd

shared. She felt a deep connection to Nathan, a sense that being with him was where she was always meant to be.

"Let's take this back into the bedroom," he said. "I want to go slow this time."

"Seriously? You think you can manage that?"

"You're the impatient one," he said with a laugh. "I like to savor things."

"I can savor things, too."

The smile that came out at her words was like the sun appearing after a long, cold Chicago winter. And that's exactly where Nathan had spent most of his life, both literally and figuratively. She'd spent a lot of years there, too. But not anymore.

He kissed her again, and as he pulled her against him, she could feel his need building.

"No way you're going to last," she teased.

"That's because you're so damned beautiful. We'll go slow the next time."

"That's a lot of confidence for an old man of thirty."

He suddenly swept her up in his arms and carried her into the bedroom. "I'll show you what old is..."

"Show me," she said eagerly.

She didn't just want to make love with him—she wanted to drive all the bad away. She wanted to be the one to ease the pain of his life and make him happy.

But what then? They might have a past and a present, but did they have a future?

She shoved that thought out of her head. As Nathan had said, reality would be here soon enough.

Fifteen

$\longrightarrow\!\!\gg\!\!\ll\!\!\longleftarrow$

Waking up Saturday morning with Bree was a dream come true. But as Nathan watched her sleep in the early morning light, he couldn't help but wonder what condition his heart would be in when this all ended.

Which it would...

Bree was only in Chicago for her daughter, and as he thought about poor little Hayley, he felt guilty that he was worrying for one second about his happiness. Finding that little girl was all that mattered, and with the sun coming up, they needed to get back to it.

He just had to hope that Johnny's anger was toward Bree and not Hayley, that Hayley was safely tucked away somewhere.

Not that it made him feel better to know that Bree was a target, but having seen her in action, he knew she was very capable of defending herself. She didn't need him to protect her, and even though he wanted to do just that, it felt good to know that she wasn't looking for him to be her knight in shining armor.

He'd spent a lot of time in that role for his mother and his sister. Not that he wouldn't throw himself in front of a fist or a bullet to save Bree's life, but he also knew she would do the same for him.

Their relationship was the most honest one he'd ever had.

She knew him, really knew him, and after he'd shared his one last secret with her, he'd felt as if a huge weight had fallen off his shoulders, that the last brick in the wall between them had come down.

They'd made love for the second and third time with nothing in the shadows: no secrets, no lies, no misunderstandings.

And he wanted to be with her *again* and *again*.

He smiled, remembering her overuse of that very same word. Maybe they could get in one more round before they had to get up. But her phone buzzed on the bedside table, chasing that hopeful thought right out of his head.

Bree lifted her head, giving him a sleepy, happy smile, and he wished he could have captured that brief moment before she became aware of all the problems surrounding her.

He tipped his head toward her phone, which continued to buzz.

She jerked upright, pulling the sheet over her breasts as she reached for her phone. "Hello?" she asked, clearing her throat of the last bit of sleep. "Dan?"

She listened for a long moment.

"Oh, my God," she murmured. "But I guess I'm not really surprised."

He could hear a man's voice on the other end of the phone, and he assumed Dan had to be an FBI agent. Judging by the emotions playing across her face, there was news of some sort, and it wasn't good.

"Yes, I know I have a lot to tell you. Everything has been happening really fast. And this terrible news makes total sense now, because the case here is clearly a copycat. I wish I could help you, but I can't leave Chicago until I find Hayley." She listened once more. "I miss you guys, too. Keep me updated on your end, and I'll do the same." She set the phone back on the table.

"Who was that?" he asked, sitting up.

"Dan Fagan, my boss in New York, and one of my closest friends. There was a kidnapping this morning in

Brooklyn, a ten-year-old girl taken from a before-school program, a white rose left at the scene."

His body tightened. "That's terrible."

"It is, and it's another confirmation that Hayley's kidnapping was done by a copycat. I wish I could help my team find this girl in Brooklyn, but—"

"You need to find Hayley first."

"Yes. And I have a lot of respect for Dan and my fellow agents in New York; they'll do a great job even if I'm not there. I just really want to catch that guy, too."

He stared at her, a niggling feeling in his head that he couldn't quite shake. "It's so strange that Johnny went to such lengths to lure you back here. It seems like a very roundabout way to do it. Why impersonate this other kidnapper? How would he know for sure that you would come, that the Chicago agents wouldn't just handle the case?"

"Because I was on the national news during the last incident—I would assume. Maybe that's when he saw me, when he got the idea."

"But he'd have to have known about Hayley and then seen you and then concocted this plan."

She frowned. "You've been the one pushing for Johnny to be the kidnapper all along. Now you're having doubts?"

"Not doubts exactly. I still think, in light of Baker's appearance on the scene yesterday, that Johnny is involved. The setup just doesn't quite make sense to me."

"It has always felt off to me; that's why I was slow to jump on the Johnny bandwagon. The threatening phone calls were one thing, even the girl on the train. But why send me to the shelter, why give me that photo of me at the charity fashion show? What did that mean?"

"Well, the photo was ripped, which was threatening, too. He wanted you to know he knew a lot about you, where you came from, where you lived, what you did."

She nodded, but there was still serious doubt in her eyes. "I would have thought Johnny would be more direct."

"Maybe someone else brought the creepy creativity to

this plan."

"Someone else..." she murmured, grabbing on to part of his statement with a new light in her eyes.

"What are you thinking?"

"Sierra. You said she's with Johnny now. She definitely hated me at one point."

"She hated a lot of people. I was fairly high on the list of enemies as well."

"That's because you didn't want to sleep with her."

"I definitely did not," he agreed. "But I have to say that Sierra was not a particularly smart girl."

"She could be cunning and sneaky. I need to find her, Nathan. Sierra could be our way in."

"If she's with Johnny, she'd never turn on him."

"That might depend on what we have to offer."

"What do we have to offer?"

"I don't know yet. I have to think about it. But since I can't confront Johnny directly without going against agency orders, I have to try someone else, and she's a good choice."

"She'll go straight to Johnny."

"It's a risk. But at this point, I have to take it. I have to trust my instincts, and unfortunately, so do you."

"I do trust you. I let you drive my truck, didn't I?"

A slow smile spread across her face. "I think I took that decision out of your hands."

"Yeah, and my truck will never be the same."

"It needed a good, fast run," she said with a laugh. "Blow out the cobwebs."

"You are a very good driver now."

"I was one of the best at Quantico."

"What was training like?" he asked curiously, still having a little trouble seeing how she'd gotten from the girl she'd once been to the woman she was now.

"It was intense. I didn't expect them to get into our heads the way they did. There were a lot of mind games, a lot of ripping down of emotional barriers. And when you're living and working with people twenty-four seven, you get to know them really well. It's an incredible bonding experience. My best friends in life right now are from my training class."

He saw a hint of sadness in her eyes and remembered her friend who had died. "Do you see much of them?"

"Damon works out of the New York office, so I do see him. Wyatt used to be there, but his cover was blown, and he had to move on. Although, I guess he's back in New York this weekend. There was a memorial celebration for Jamie on Thursday night. I wish I could have been there. I talked to Parisa on the phone, but it wasn't the same."

"So, there's four of you now?"

"Five. Diego is the fifth. He's been working in South America the last year. We're spread out all over the world. But if any one of us is in trouble, the others try to show up. Last summer, that happened with Wyatt and Damon, and I was able to help them through their situation."

"Well, maybe we should call them and get them out here."

"I have thought about it, but I didn't want to take them away from Jamie's celebration. I know his family would have been very upset if a majority of the group didn't show up. Although, I'm sure they didn't mind that I wasn't there. Jamie's dad was never a fan of mine. He thought I distracted Jamie while we were in training, that Jamie wasn't completely focused on becoming an agent worthy of following in his father's footsteps."

"You can be a distraction."

She tucked her hair behind her ear. "You can be, too, Nathan."

"Want to distract each other awhile longer?"

"I do, but…"

"We need to get started on the day," he said.

"Rain check?"

"You got it." He pulled her toward him for a quick kiss. "I'll even let you take the first shower."

"Such a gentleman," she said with a laugh. She started to get up, then stopped. "I have a feeling today is going to get crazy, and I just want to say before it starts that last night was wonderful."

"It was."

"Whatever happens next…"

"Yeah," he said, knowing this wasn't the time to think too far into the future. "We'll figure it out. While you get dressed, I'm going to call Lindsay and see if I can get any information on Mark's condition."

"Good idea. I wonder if Lindsay told him I'm Hayley's mother yet."

"She might wait until he's stronger, but then again, he's her rock. She might not be able to keep it from him."

"I know she was shaken up by the news. I wish I'd spent another second reassuring her that I do think she's done a good job as Hayley's mom."

"I'm sure you'll have another chance to speak to her. Just like I'm sure she'd like another chance to thank you."

"Thank me?" Bree asked in surprise.

"She told me yesterday, when she first mentioned the adoption, that she'd written a letter to the biological mother a few days after they took Hayley home. She wanted to thank her for the beautiful gift she'd been given—the daughter she already adored. She wanted to express her gratitude. She knows how lucky she was that you gave up your daughter to her."

Shadows filled Bree's eyes. "I wish I could have read that."

"You might still be able to. She never sent it. She said Mark talked her out of it. He didn't want to open any communication in case it changed things."

"I can understand that."

"Bree, I have to ask you a tough question."

"A tough question?" she echoed warily. "Okay, give me what you got."

"Can you be objective? Can you make smart moves knowing your daughter's life is on the line? Would it be better to let your agency make those moves?"

"That's three questions," she said with annoyance. "And I don't think being objective is going to be helpful in this case, because it's not like the other kidnappings. It's different and it's personal and it's about me. I don't actually believe anyone else will be able to find Hayley but me."

"You think the kidnapper is going to tell you where Hayley is?"

She nodded. "Yes. When he's ready. He wants me to see Hayley. And if I can't find her on my own, he's going to keep dropping clues until I figure it out."

"And lure you straight into a trap."

"Not if I find him first."

"All right. Let's do it. Let's find him." He saw the sudden worry in her eyes. "Don't even think about trying to get rid of me. You may not have agency or police backup, but you have me, and where you go, I go. I helped save your child once from Johnny; I'm going to make sure she's safe now, too."

―――◆◆――

Nathan's protective and loyal words rang through her head as Bree showered and dressed. She'd never felt so loved as she'd felt the night before. And she was very grateful that Nathan was back in her life. She was also very, very aware of the bittersweet and probably short-term nature of her happiness. But she wouldn't regret the night she'd spent with Nathan, whether it was the first of many or just once in a lifetime.

When she walked out of the bedroom and into the kitchen, she smiled. "Bacon and coffee—my two favorite aromas."

"I made eggs, too," he said. "Have a seat. It's all ready."

"It looks great." She slid into a stool at the kitchen counter.

"Don't get too excited. I'm not in the running for any Michelin stars and breakfast is probably my best meal of the day," he said dryly, as he buttered toast. "What about you?

Do you cook?"

"I can make a few things, mostly salad and the occasional soup. I work long hours, and frankly, take-out in New York is fabulous. You cannot believe the different kinds of food you can get at any hour of the night."

"So, you like living there?"

"I do—for now."

"For now?" he echoed, as he set a platter of bacon and toast on the counter and took the stool at the end of the counter.

"Manhattan has a frenetic energy that I like, but sometimes it's a little too much. I still dream about my house by the sea. One of these days..."

"You'll get there," he said confidently.

"Maybe sooner than I want. Who knows where my career will be at when this is all over? I may have plenty of time to lay by the ocean and work on my tan."

"There are worse things in life."

"As we both know," she agreed, helping herself to some eggs. "Is Chicago going to be home for you forever?"

"I've thought about leaving a lot, but Josie is here, and I adore Grace. She's a great kid. She's funny, stubborn—like her mother, but much stronger than Josie. That kid is tough."

"I could see that during my first interview with her. She was a very composed nine-year-old. Josie has done a great job with her."

"Josie is a really good mother. I wasn't sure she would be, to be honest. But she's very attentive, and it's great that Kyle's career allows her to stay home."

"That is nice. I always wanted a mom who would be home when I got out of school, but mine was rarely there, and when she was, I never got the response I wanted. I know she cared about me, but she was absorbed in her own problems. And my aunt struggled from the same battles. I feel sorry for them now. I wish they'd both had better lives."

"Do you ever talk to your aunt?"

"No. I haven't seen or spoken to her since she bailed on

me and social services swept me up. I don't even know if she's alive. What about your mom, Nathan? I asked you about her before, but you didn't answer."

"She's in Texas. She moved down there a couple of years ago. She had a friend from high school who had a big house and her husband had just died, and she invited my mom down for a vacation. She never came back. She has visited a few times, but I think she likes being out of Chicago. If we want to see her, we go there. She's a different person now, too. She rides horses, for one thing. Who would have thought my city-raised mom would get on a horse? But she does."

"Well, I'm glad. She deserves to be happy. So, do you."

"I have been happy the last several years."

As he said the words, she realized that the one thing they hadn't talked about was the woman in Nathan's life, but she didn't really want to bring her up. Then she'd have to deal with the fact that she'd slept with another woman's man, and that Nathan had cheated on his girlfriend with her. Maybe they weren't as new and improved people as they thought.

"What are you thinking?" Nathan asked.

"Nothing," she said quickly. "Actually, I was wondering if you still run every morning."

"I don't believe that's what you were thinking, but yes, I still run. That's how Mark and I met."

"That's right. You were training for a triathlon. I guess that means you swim and bike, too."

"I'm a triple threat," he said with a smile. "What about you? Do you work out?"

"I run more now than I used to. I have to stay in shape for my job. You never know when you're going to have to chase someone down."

"Do you do that a lot?"

"I wouldn't say a lot, but I've definitely done it."

"I'm surprised you became an agent, knowing you'd have to run."

She made a face at his teasing comment. "It's not my favorite part, I'll admit, but I'm actually pretty fast."

"That's because you're trying to get it over with."

"You know me too well," she said with a laugh.

"I do know you well. I like that about us, Bree."

"I like it, too," she admitted. "I don't think I've ever been with anyone who knew everything about me. Not that we've been together in recent years. I'm sure there are still some things to find out about you, Nathan."

"Nothing that important," he said, finishing his eggs. Then he got up and took his plate to the kitchen. "Can I get you anything else?"

"No. I'm full. Thanks for breakfast."

"Any time."

"Were you able to get a hold of Lindsay?"

"No. Her phone went to voicemail."

"I hope Mark is hanging in there."

"Me, too." He set their plates in the sink. "I'm going to hop in the shower. What are you going to do?"

"I'm going to get on my computer and see what I can find out about Sierra."

"I thought you didn't have access to agency resources."

"I don't. But I can still get on social media, and if Sierra is anything like I remember, I'm betting she's online somewhere. She always loved attention."

Sixteen

Bree found Sierra's profile on three different social media sites in less than five minutes. As she'd predicted, the attention-getting Sierra, was still in the business of getting attention. She now ran a hair salon in Logan Square and when she wasn't styling hair, she was taking selfies of herself in lingerie and bikinis, with sometimes nothing more than her hands strategically placed over her very large breasts, which had to have been enhanced at some point.

Sierra had also transformed herself into a confident woman with black hair that hung down to her waist, dark eyes, and olive skin. She was also into jewelry: multiple rings on her hands, several piercings in her ears, and a nose ring. She looked nothing like the skinny, needy girl she'd once been—the girl who'd always been hanging around Johnny, wanting him to notice her, and sleeping with his friends when he didn't.

She was a little surprised that Johnny had finally hooked up with Sierra, but then Sierra fit Johnny's lifestyle more than she ever had.

Maybe she had been the anomaly in Johnny's life and Sierra was the kind of woman he'd always been meant to be with.

She typed in Johnny's name and while mentions of the gym on Hayward and the auto shop on Hudson came up, as well as some information on the Hawke family in general, there were no current photos of Johnny. Had he changed as well? She wished she had looked him up before she lost access to the FBI database. She'd been so determined to keep him out of her life, out of her thoughts, that she'd refused to go there. Now it was too late.

Thinking about Johnny made her wonder how his conversation with the FBI had gone the night before. Pulling out her phone, she called Tracy.

"Did you get another text or call?" Tracy asked, not bothering with a hello.

"No, nothing. I was wondering if you got any information from Johnny Hawke."

"I can't tell you anything, Bree. You're off the case."

"You can tell me something. Did he seem surprised that he has a daughter, that his daughter was kidnapped? That his former associate was killed at a ransom drop for that child?"

"Look, I understand that you're very invested in this case," Tracy said. "But I've also been instructed to keep you out of it."

"The kidnapper isn't going to keep me out of it."

"Well, when he contacts you, let me know, and we'll go from there."

"You're enjoying this, aren't you? Keeping me in the dark. Putting me a in box."

"Actually, not as much as I expected I would," Tracy replied, a note of candor in her voice. "I've learned a lot about you in the past twenty-four hours. I suspect some of our mutual associates at the academy already knew about some of what you lived through as a child."

"Some of them did," she admitted. "Friends confide in each other."

"It's usually those confidences that make people cross lines they shouldn't cross."

Which was another way of saying that Tracy wasn't going to cross any lines for her. She let out a small sigh. "Is there anything you can tell me?"

"I think you should watch your back and stay out of sight."

"Because Johnny will be gunning for me?"

"You said that; I didn't. If you want to reconsider protection, I'll talk it over with Warren."

"No. I can take care of myself."

"We're doing everything we can to find Hayley. Nothing that happened yesterday has changed that."

"Have you had a chance to speak to Mark Jansen? Was he able to provide any information on the person who contacted him for the ransom?"

"Bree. What part of I can't tell you anything don't you understand?"

She blew out a frustrated breath. "Fine."

"You're going to have to trust us to do our jobs. You need to stand down. Stay put wherever you are, although I suspect you're not too far from Nathan Bishop. Let us handle this. Don't go to Johnny. Don't get in the way. You have to think about your daughter, not yourself."

"Believe me, that's the only person I'm thinking about. I'll be in touch if I hear anything." She set down the phone, thinking that had gone about as badly as she'd expected. She was out of the loop. She was cut off from all communication. She definitely couldn't confront Johnny, which was what she really wanted to do. If he had done this, then this was between him and her. But if he had done this, then he wasn't ready to have that meet yet, or it would have already happened. He was calling all the shots.

She did wonder how Johnny was planning to keep Hayley out of sight. His business, his family, his life was in Chicago. And Hayley's face had been all over the news.

He had to have stashed her somewhere outside of the city. Maybe it was close enough to where he could visit her but far enough away that no one would put the two of them together.

Someone in his family could be watching her—like his mother. She'd always adored Johnny. He was her oldest son, and he could do no wrong.

Tapping her fingers restlessly on the table, she thought about her next move.

The answer was right in front of her—Sierra. It was possible Tracy had spoken to Sierra, too, or would be speaking to her. But she might be farther down the list. And Bree might have a better chance of getting information from Sierra than Tracy would. Not that Sierra had ever been a fan, but they did come from the same place. She had to give it a shot.

Getting up from the table, she walked over to the balcony door and opened it.

The weather was gray and cold, and the clouds sweeping over the city were foreboding—perhaps a portent of what was to come.

She shivered, but she was ready to fight back, whatever it took.

"I don't think this is a good idea," Nathan said as he drove Bree across town to the Bella Beauty Salon run by Sierra Littman.

"I'm not going to be in any danger at the salon," she said. "And I can't just do nothing. Sierra is a former friend. Maybe I can turn her to our side."

"How are you going to do that? The girl has always been mad for Johnny. And she might have liked you before you hooked up with Johnny, but after that she hated you. Why would she tell you anything now?"

"Because the last thing Sierra wants in Johnny's life is the child he had with his ex-girlfriend. If I can convince her that helping me get Hayley back will return her life to normal with Johnny, I think she might be willing to help."

He had to admit it wasn't a completely bad strategy. "Sierra was always very selfish."

"Exactly. And I doubt she wants to be a stepmom, not

judging by the lifestyle photos she posted online."

"But you're overlooking the fact that Sierra is controlled by Johnny and she might be more scared of him than she is concerned about being a stepmother to your daughter."

"I don't think Johnny hurts the women in his life. He never lifted a hand to me."

"You were scared of him when you left, Bree."

"That's because I was starting to see what he did to other people. I was overhearing odd conversations. The police seemed to be very interested in Johnny's actions. I was questioned several times about several incidents, including that one with Stix. I knew I had to get out of the relationship, but it still took me almost too long to get up the nerve to go. You know when I actually made the decision to leave?"

"I know when, but I don't know why."

"My jeans wouldn't snap."

He raised an eyebrow. "Okay. I was not expecting you to say that."

"I knew I was starting to show. Johnny was going to notice. He was already asking me why I'd stopped modeling when I was getting so many calls after my photo was in the paper. It was just a matter of time before he would know I was pregnant. That's the day I called you to help me get out of town."

"I'm glad you finally did make the decision, even if it was just due to the snap on your jeans. As for Johnny's potential for violence, I certainly saw the raging, willing-to-kill side of his personality after you left, and I suspect that's grown stronger in the last decade. I think Sierra will be scared of going against him. He has a lot of power over her. I'm sure he bought her the salon she's running."

"Well, I won't know until I talk to her, until I get a read on the situation." She paused, glancing over at him. "You need to stay outside, Nathan. Sierra hated you even more than she hated me. I don't think double-teaming her is a good idea."

"I hate for you to be alone with her."

"You don't think I can handle a hundred-pound hair stylist?" she asked dryly. "Believe me, I have taken down men much bigger, much stronger, and definitely more dangerous than her."

"She might have security at the salon."

"I doubt Johnny's bodyguards are hanging around the salon, at least not during the day. They might drive her and pick her up, but I think she'll be on her own."

"If she's there."

"It's Saturday, a busy day in the business. I have a good shot. So, you'll stay in the truck this time?"

"I'll consider it," he reluctantly agreed, putting his attention back on the road. "He didn't want to let Bree out of his sight for a second, but Sierra would probably react negatively to his presence, so he'd go with Bree's plan.

A few moments later, he was able to find a parking spot a few doors down from the salon. From his vantage point, he could see the front door, and if Bree needed help, he could get there quickly.

"It's going to be fine," she reassured him.

"That's usually my line to you," he muttered, having a bad feeling about it all.

"And when you say it, I try to believe it. You should do the same."

"I'm working on it. Good luck, Bree."

"I'll be back soon." She got out of the truck and walked down the street.

He kept his gaze on her until she entered the salon, and then watched the door for several minutes after. He didn't see anyone follow her inside. Hopefully, she was right about the salon being a safe place for this very dangerous conversation.

But all he could do was wait.

—⋙⋘—

The salon was busy as Bree had expected, with eight stylists working on clients, and two people waiting in the reception area. She didn't flash her badge; she simply told the receptionist to tell Sierra that Bree wanted to speak to her.

She had a feeling that Sierra would be curious enough to find out what she wanted. Sierra had always had a fear of missing out on anything, so she'd always been eavesdropping, hanging on to conversations, trying to stay in good with anyone who might have something going on.

She straightened as she saw Sierra walk through the salon. She wore black jeans and a loose gray crop top that fell off one shoulder and revealed her flat abs. Her long hair was sleek and straight, her expression a mix of surprise, wariness, and dislike.

"So, it is you," she said. "I can't imagine what you're doing here."

"I need to talk to you. Do you have a minute?"

"I'm very busy."

"It won't take long. Is there some place we could speak in private?"

Sierra considered her question. "All right." She turned and walked away, and Bree quickly followed her.

They moved through the salon, into a back hallway, passing by the restrooms, a small kitchen and finally entering an office with a desk, a love seat, and a table upon which there were dozens of beauty product samples.

Sierra didn't sit down, just crossed her arms and waited. "Well?"

"Do you know why I'm in town?" she asked.

"Why would I know that?"

"I work for the FBI now." She saw surprise flash across Sierra's face. *That was interesting. Sierra didn't know about her job. Did that mean she also didn't know what Johnny was up to?* "I came to Chicago to look for a kidnapped child."

"What does that have to do with me?" Sierra asked.

"It has to do with Johnny. I understand you're with him now."

"I bet that kills you," Sierra drawled. "Once he dumped your ass, he came crawling to me, just like I always knew he would."

She ignored that comment. "Do you live together?"

"Of course, we live together. We're in love."

"But you're not married."

A hard light entered Sierra's eyes. "Not yet, but Johnny bought me this beautiful ring," she said, flashing the diamond-and-emerald ring on her right hand. "It's only a matter of time."

She had a feeling Sierra was trying to convince herself as much as she was trying to convince her. "You got what you always wanted."

"I did. And I make Johnny happy—happier than he ever was with you."

She licked her lips, debating how to make her play. "Are you going to have kids?"

"Why are you asking all these questions?"

"Because Johnny is in trouble, and I think your life is about to change in a way you never imagined. Did you know he spoke to the FBI last night?"

"He was at work last night. He didn't say anything about the FBI."

"He doesn't want you to know what he's doing, but you need to know."

"If you're trying to scare me, it's not going to work. Johnny can handle whatever trouble you're bringing. I'm not worried. He knows very important people. They will always help him."

"They won't be able to help him this time, and you should be worried. Johnny kidnapped a child."

Wariness entered her eyes. "That's ridiculous. He doesn't go after kids."

Meeting Sierra's gaze, Bree had the feeling the woman thought she was telling the truth. She remembered that feeling. She'd once been told that Johnny had assaulted and almost killed a man, and she'd said the exact same thing—that that was ridiculous. Frowning, she brought herself back to the present. "Sierra—"

"No. We're done talking. I shouldn't have even let you back here. Johnny wouldn't like it."

She could see that Sierra was quickly pulling away. Like a turtle, who'd suddenly been shocked by a bright light, she was tucking her head back inside of her shell.

"Wait," she said, as Sierra moved toward the door. "The child means something to Johnny."

Silence followed her words. Slowly, Sierra turned her head. "What do you mean?"

"The girl is Johnny's daughter."

Sierra couldn't stop the gasp that came from her lips. "You're lying. He doesn't have any kids. He and I are going to have children. I will be his baby mama. No one else."

"He might not have known about the child until recently. Have you heard him talking to anyone about getting someone to look after a kid, or going to meet someone outside the city? Does he have a safe house somewhere? A place no one else knows about?"

Sierra stared back at her. "Oh, my God," she said slowly. "It's yours, isn't it?"

"Yes."

"You and Johnny had a kid." She shook her head in confusion. "But that doesn't make sense. You left."

"I left because I was pregnant, and because I didn't want my child to be swept up into Johnny's world. I was young. I was scared. I couldn't take care of a baby at that point in my life, so I gave her up for adoption. I didn't know where she went or who adopted her. But then last Tuesday, someone kidnapped a little girl, and yesterday I found out that that girl is my daughter. She's also Johnny's daughter. And I think he took her. He has her somewhere, Sierra."

"He doesn't have a kid at our house."

"He'd put her somewhere else."

"You're making all this up. You're trying to put Johnny in prison for dumping you all those years ago. You hate him. This is all crazy."

Despite Sierra's words, Bree could see that the truth was

setting in. It also seemed apparent that Sierra was completely in the dark—unless she was the greatest actress in the world, and Bree didn't think that was the case.

Now that she had Sierra's attention, she had to get her on her side. "You want your life with Johnny to stay the same, right? You don't want my child around. You don't want to share Johnny with a ten-year-old girl. And you won't have to, if you help me find her. I can keep you out of it, Sierra. I will never tell Johnny whatever you share with me. I give you my absolute word on that."

"I could never trust you. You stole Johnny from me."

"Oh, come on," she said, exasperated in spite of her plan to remain calm. "I didn't do that, and you know it. Look, I don't care that you're with him now. I even hope that you're happy. I know life wasn't easy for you. We come from the same neighborhood." She let that sink in, then continued. "I just want this girl to be back with her adoptive family. Her name is Hayley. She has a loving mother and father and two siblings."

"You're going to take her back to them?" Sierra challenged. "Why wouldn't you keep her? Now that you know where she is."

"Because she has a better family than I could give her."

Sierra gave her a long look, then shook her head. "Well, I don't know where she is."

"Think, Sierra. You know where Johnny's houses are, right? She has to be somewhere safe."

"You'll put Johnny in jail."

"I won't," she lied. "I just want my daughter back."

"Johnny must hate you," Sierra said. "You stole his child, his blood. He's going to kill you."

"Even if that wouldn't bother you, I don't think you want to raise the child he had with me, do you? I'm offering you a way to keep the life you have. It's a good deal."

"I don't know..."

A knock came at the door, and they both jumped. A young woman poked her head in. "Sierra, I need you to check

Deb's color. She's freaking out that it has been in too long."

"Okay. I'll be right there." Sierra turned back to her. "I have to take care of this."

"I'll wait for you."

Sierra's lips tightened, but she hurried out of the room. Bree just hoped that when she came back, Sierra would make the right decision for all of them.

Seventeen

It was taking Bree a long time, Nathan thought, impatiently tapping his fingers on the steering wheel. *Maybe that was a good sign.*

It might mean that Bree and Sierra were actually having a productive conversation. He knew Bree could be persuasive, and he also knew that however much Sierra had envied Bree, she'd also looked up to her back in the day. Perhaps that would come into play now.

His phone rang. It was Adrienne—again. She'd called him several times yesterday, and he'd never returned her call. He wasn't being fair to her, and that had to stop.

Taking a deep breath, he picked up, knowing that he was about to have a very difficult conversation, and one he should have had before last night.

"Where have you been, Nathan?" Adrienne demanded. "I've been calling and texting you for days."

Had it only been days? It felt like years had passed since he'd last seen her.

"I know. I've been really busy."

"Doing what? I went by your job site yesterday. Joe said he hadn't seen you, and he didn't know where you were. I felt marginally better that I wasn't the only one you were ghosting, but what's going on?"

"I told you that my friend's child was the little girl who

was kidnapped last week. I've been helping out on the case."

"You've been helping out? How? You're not a cop."

"That's true, but I'm trying to be a good friend."

"Maybe you should think about being a good boyfriend," she said tartly, then immediately backtracked. "I'm sorry. I shouldn't have said that. I just miss you. I really wanted to introduce you to my friend, Kari, and it just feels like something is off with us, Nathan."

He felt a wave of guilt for letting things go so far with Bree without talking to Adrienne first. "Something is off," he admitted. "We need to talk in person."

"What are you doing right now?"

"Actually, I'm still helping out on the case, so tomorrow would be better."

Silence followed his words. "You want to break up with me, don't you?"

"We should have a conversation face-to-face."

"So you can tell me it's over? Just say it now. Why wait?"

"Because I don't want to hurt you."

"I'm a big girl. Just tell me what happened. I thought things were going well. I know it's still pretty new, but we've been getting along. We've been having fun. What changed?"

He could hear the surprise and pain in her voice, and it bothered him that he was responsible for that. They had been doing well before Bree had come back into his life. But in retrospect, his version of "well" with Adrienne was nothing close to what he felt with Bree.

And even if Bree left him again, which was probably going to happen, Adrienne wasn't the right person for him. He knew that now. He had to be with someone he really connected with, someone he could talk to about anything and everything, and Adrienne wasn't that person. She was great; she just wasn't great for him.

"Nathan," she pressed. "Just talk to me."

"You deserve someone who really loves you, Adrienne."

"And you don't?"

"I care about you—"

"Oh, please, caring is an insulting word in this context."

"I'm not trying to insult you. It's complicated."

"It's not complicated, Nathan. At the end of the day, you either want to be with someone or you don't."

She made a good point. "I am sorry. I should have said something sooner."

"I'm sorry, too. Good-bye, Nathan."

"Good-bye."

He felt both relieved that the relationship was over and angry with himself for letting it go on as long as it had. He'd thought it was enough that they had fun together, and maybe it would grow into something, but if it didn't, it didn't. That's why he'd never opened up with Adrienne. Instinctively, he'd known it wasn't going to last. It wasn't that he hadn't trusted her; it was that he hadn't cared enough.

He hadn't cared about anyone the way he cared about Bree. She'd taken his heart a long, long time ago.

For so many years, he'd hidden his feelings away, but last night, he'd laid himself bare. He'd opened up and made himself vulnerable. In doing so, he'd woken himself up from the numb fog he'd put his heart and his emotions into when she got on that bus eleven years ago. Now, he was living again. He was feeling things. *He was in love.*

He sucked in a breath at that thought.

Bree could very, very easily break his heart again. But he wasn't going to regret taking the risk. This time he'd left everything on the field. If he lost, it wouldn't be because he hadn't tried. Because he hadn't told her how he felt. It was up to her now.

Tapping his fingers against the steering wheel again, he checked his watch. It had been almost thirty minutes since Bree had left.

A bad feeling shot through him. That was way too long.

Jumping out of the truck, he ran down the street and into the salon, raising a lot of questioning looks by his sudden appearance. His gaze swept the room, but he didn't see Sierra or Bree.

"Can I help you?" the receptionist asked.

"Where's Sierra?"

"She's in the back. Do you have an appointment?"

"No, but she'll want to see me," he said, striding through the salon.

Sierra was standing by a back door that led into a parking lot.

"Sierra," he said sharply.

She whirled around at his approach, her gaze widening. "Nathan Bishop? What are you doing here?"

"I'm looking for Bree."

"Well, that hasn't changed, has it? You were always looking for Bree."

"Where is she?" he demanded. He pushed open a nearby door and found himself looking at an empty office.

"Is everything all right, Sierra?" the receptionist asked, coming down the hall, her phone in hand, ready to dial 911.

"It's fine," Sierra said shortly. "Go back to the desk."

"Where is Bree?" he repeated, his hands knotting into fists to prevent himself from shaking the truth out of Sierra.

"I don't know. She was waiting for me in the office. I had to fix someone's color, and when I came back, she was gone, and this door was open. I assume she left."

He didn't assume that at all. "You're lying. Someone took her. Who? Johnny?"

"Johnny would not take Bree back in a million years. He has me now."

"But Bree had his baby, and you know that. What did you do? Did you tell her where Johnny is? Did you call Johnny?"

"I didn't tell her anything, and I didn't call Johnny. I also don't know anything about this girl that Johnny supposedly took. He's been with me every day, every night, the past week. I think you're both lying. And I want you out of my salon."

"Not until you tell me where she is."

"I have no idea."

"She wouldn't go out the back door when I was waiting in the front."

"Don't you ever get tired of waiting for Bree?"

"No, I don't. I love her. I always have."

"You think that's a surprise to me?" she asked harshly. "But she doesn't love you. And she never has. If she's with you, it's because she needs something. She always used you, and you always came running."

"Johnny went running to her, too. You had to wait until Bree was gone before you could get him. But you're going to lose him, Sierra. Because he's in deep shit. He kidnapped a kid. He's going down for that, and you're going to go with him, if you don't help me. Tell me where Johnny is."

"If you go looking for Johnny, he'll kill you this time. He won't let you make it to the hospital."

"You knew what he did to me?" he asked, shocked by her words.

"Yes. I was the one who called the fire department. I told them the old school was on fire. I figured they'd send a truck to check it out."

"That was you?" he asked in astonishment, remembering the sirens that had made Johnny leave him with breath still left in his body.

"Yes. Because believe it or not I didn't want him to kill you."

Sierra had saved his life and risked her own at the same time. "Why would you have done that for me?"

"I honestly don't know. Luckily, Johnny never found out."

He gave her a long stare. "Thank you."

She shifted her feet and gave a shrug.

He glanced beyond Sierra, seeing something glittering in the sunlight beyond the door. He walked outside to get it. It was Bree's phone. There was no way she'd left of her own free will. She'd ditched it on purpose, so he would know she was in trouble. He looked back at Sierra. "Someone grabbed her."

"I don't know who."

"You have an idea. Help me, Sierra. You're not like Johnny. You don't want Bree to die. She was your friend once."

"I can't remember that."

"Yes, you can. We were all the same, Sierra. We were all wounded, struggling to survive. We helped each other. And Bree helped you."

"That was a long time ago."

"You remember."

"I'm with Johnny now," she said, a note of worry in her voice. "I love him. He loves me."

"Then save him from himself."

Her lips drew into a taut line. "If he ever finds out..."

"He won't."

"He might. He had to have had people following Bree, because I didn't call him. I didn't call anyone."

If that were true, then maybe he was putting Sierra's life in danger. "I'll tell him I was following Bree. I saw her get grabbed. Your name won't come up."

She stared back at him. "Howie's Automotive on Hudson. Johnny has an office on the second floor. There's a fire escape on the side of the building. It goes into the storage room. There will be a guard in the hallway."

He was surprised at the level of detail in her answer. But then Sierra had always noted everything when it came to Johnny. "Thanks."

"I'm not helping you, Nathan. If Johnny sees you, he'll kill you. I'm probably sending you to your death. Are you willing to die for Bree? Because that's what it's going to take to save her."

He saw the cold truth in her eyes. He also knew the answer to that question. "Yes, I am." He paused. "Don't go home tonight, Sierra. Stay with a friend."

"Now you're worried about me?"

"I'm worried about everyone."

"Johnny would never hurt me."

"Don't bet your life on that."

Bree winced as the car she was in hit a pothole. She couldn't see anything with the hood that had been thrown over her head and tied around her neck so tight she could barely breathe. A zip tie had also fastened her hands behind her back.

She'd only seen one of the men who'd grabbed her out of Sierra's office, but there were at least two. They hadn't said anything to her; they'd just thrown her into a car and taken off.

Sierra must have called in Johnny's guards. Which meant they were taking her to Johnny.

Her heart raced at the thought of seeing him again. By now he knew she'd stolen his child, his blood, his heir. She'd told Nathan that Johnny had never gotten physical with her, and that had been the truth, but she knew now there was violence in Johnny's soul. What he'd done to Nathan after she left—what he'd probably done to a lot of other people— showed who he really was. And she'd hurt him in a way that no one else had. There was a good chance he was going to kill her. She'd known going to Sierra was a risk, but for a moment there, she'd really thought that Sierra might help her.

She'd been wrong.

Nathan had been right. He'd told her she was taking a huge risk.

It was one she'd thought she'd had to take, but now a terrible despair ran through her. If she'd blown this, Hayley might never be found.

She tried to reassure herself that no matter what happened to her, Nathan would keep looking. He'd make sure the agency continued to go after Johnny. He'd find her daughter.

Her heart filled with so much pain she almost couldn't

handle it. She wanted to see Hayley in person. She wanted to look into her daughter's eyes. She'd been denied that opportunity when Hayley was born, but she wanted it now, wanted it with a fierce sense of desperation.

The car came to an abrupt stop and she hit the side of the door with her shoulder. A moment later, that same door opened, and she was hauled out, a gun pressing into her back, as a low voice ordered her to move.

A man had a tight grip on her arm, so there was no chance of escape, not that she could go anywhere in her current state. She didn't think she was outside. They must have pulled into a garage. She smelled gasoline, and the floor was hard, probably concrete.

"Up," the man said. "Stairs."

She stumbled up the steps as he dragged her along. In the distance, she could hear a clanging—metal on metal. She heard the roar of an engine.

Was she in an auto shop?

But why were there stairs?

She tried to make a mental note of everything. When they reached the landing, they turned to the right. The light brightened behind her hood. There was daylight coming in from somewhere. A door opened.

She was shoved inside another room. This room felt darker.

Someone undid the tie around her hood, and it was yanked off her head.

She blinked in the shadowy room, trying to see who was there. A door closed behind her.

The man sitting behind a desk got up and came around, stopping in front of her. He had brown hair and dark-brown eyes and a ruthless, hateful look on his face.

Johnny!

"Bree," he murmured. "As pretty as ever." He set the gun in his hand down on the desk, but close enough to reach if he needed it.

"Johnny," she said, a lump growing in her throat.

Eleven years had passed since she'd run for her life, but now it felt like yesterday.

Johnny had aged, but unlike Nathan, he hadn't gotten more attractive with time. She'd once thought of Johnny as darkly handsome. Now, his thick hair had thinned, receding off his square forehead. There were numerous lines around his eyes and mouth—hard, bitter, angry lines. There were scars on his cheek, his jaw, and a long one down his neck.

There was no hint of the boy who had been funny and charming. That kid had completely disappeared. Johnny had become a man—a man who had clearly lived a life of violence, and she was even more glad she'd taken Hayley out of his reach.

She looked over her shoulder. Whoever had brought her here was gone. She was fine with that. One less person to take down. Although, taking Johnny down with her hands tied behind her back was probably optimistic.

"It's just us," Johnny said, drawing her gaze back to his.

Despite the situation, she refused to be intimidated by him. Straightening her shoulders, lifting her chin, she said, "Were you following me?"

"I didn't have to. After my conversation with the FBI last night, I figured you'd go find Sierra."

"If you wanted to see me, you didn't need to kidnap me. You could have just called—like you've been doing all along—and told me where to go."

His gaze narrowed. "I haven't been calling you."

"Oh, come on. Isn't the game over now? You're here. I'm here. Tell me what you want."

"I want to know where our daughter is."

Her jaw slackened in shock at his words. "You know where she is. You have her."

What kind of sick game was he playing with her?

"I don't have her," he said harshly. "I didn't even know about her until yesterday when the feds showed up, telling me the daughter I had with you was missing. They accused me of kidnapping her. Are you setting me up, Bree?"

"Setting you up? No. You're the one who took Hayley and lured me to Chicago by pretending to be the White Rose Kidnapper. You sent Calvin Baker to shake down Hayley's adoptive father for ransom. And then you killed Cal."

The expression in Johnny's gaze grew more incredulous with each word.

"I have no idea what you're talking about," he said. "I didn't kidnap anyone. I've never heard of this White Rose Kidnapper. And I haven't seen Baker in years."

A tiny seed of doubt took root in her mind. *Why was he lying? What did he have to gain by trying to maintain the pretense?*

"Do you think I'm just going to go away if you deny it?" she asked. "Because I can assure you that won't happen. I'm a federal agent, Johnny. I'm not the shy, insecure girl I used to be."

"I can see that." He gave her a long, harsh stare. "You're FBI now, and you want to take me down, so you made up this story about a kid. But you wouldn't have left town, pregnant with my child. You wouldn't have stolen her from me. You loved me."

The anger in his eyes burned through her. "I did love you then. But I loved my daughter more."

"There really was a child?"

"You know there was. You took her," she said again. "Did Detective Benedict help you? Is he involved in this, too? Did he get you my phone number? Did he help you dig up my past? I know you had to have had help from someone in law enforcement."

"Benedict?" he echoed. "I haven't talked to him in years."

"He was your father's friend."

"Not mine. I have my own allies in the CPD."

"Someone helped you."

"No one helped me, because I didn't do anything." He paused. "Why didn't you tell me you were pregnant?"

"I was scared."

"I never hurt you. I treated you like gold. I gave you

everything you could want. I was your knight in shining armor. That's what you used to tell me."

She had told him that. But those had been the words of a teenage girl, who'd thought Johnny was the answer to her sad, hard life. "You didn't hurt me, but you hurt other people."

"Not women—or children."

She couldn't help noticing he'd left men out of his answer. "I was a young, stupid girl when we were together. I was naïve to think you could be better than your parents, your brothers. I thought you had more good in you than you did. But I gradually came to see the truth. You were going down a dangerous, terrifying path, and I couldn't go with you. I didn't want my baby to live your life, to be in your family, to have bodyguards, to be constantly questioned by the police just because of her last name."

"My life is great. I run a lucrative business. I take incredible vacations. I have more money than you could dream of."

"Blood money. You run a criminal enterprise."

He shrugged. "I'm a businessman and a capitalist. Let's get back to you. You stole my child from me. I was her father. I had a right to see her, to raise her. It wasn't your decision."

"I made it my decision," she said forcefully. "And, to be honest, I wasn't just protecting her from you but also from me. I didn't want her to live my life, either. I wanted her to have two parents who were in love with each other, who adored her, and who could give her a safe, happy life."

"We were in love with each other."

"Infatuated, maybe, but it wasn't love. Because we didn't know what love was."

"You can't deny what we had."

"I was desperate for someone to love me, to protect me, so I saw in you what I wanted to see."

"Nathan helped you leave. He knew where you went, didn't he?"

She didn't answer, not wanting to bring Nathan into it.

"I almost killed him, you know," Johnny said in a conversational tone.

She shook her head. "Nathan was your friend once."

"Was he?" Johnny asked scornfully. "He'd been trying to get me away from you since we first met. And he finally did it. My only satisfaction was that you left him, too. That's the only reason I let him live."

"See, right there, you just showed me who you really are. You almost killed Nathan, and you act like it's no big deal. Whatever good I saw in you was just in my imagination. And none of this even matters because all that's important right now is our daughter." It killed her to include him in the relationship with Hayley, but it was looking more and more like he hadn't taken Hayley. And if he hadn't, she was going to need his help.

"Our daughter," he echoed, as if he was still getting used to that thought. He folded his arms across his chest as he perched on the front edge of his desk. "Did you name her Hayley?"

"No. I didn't name her. I didn't hold her. I didn't even see her eyes. They took her away right after she was born. I thought it would be easier if I didn't bond with her, but it wasn't." A torrent of emotion rose within her. "Sending her away broke my heart. I gave away a piece of myself."

"And you gave away a piece of me," he said sharply. "How could you deprive me of my own child? What gave you the right?"

"I just wanted what was best for her. And it was a good decision. Hayley has a great life now. You should see her bedroom. It's like a princess lives there. She has books and games and stuffed animals. She has a brother and a sister, grandparents."

"She would have had all that with me."

"Maybe you would have given her those things. But she would have also grown up with guns, with thugs, with drug deals and gamblers and addicts. She would have never been free. She would have always been looking over her shoulder, wondering if someone her father had crossed would come after her. I didn't want that life for her. You told me once that you sometimes wished you'd been born into another family. Maybe you don't remember that now. But I do."

Johnny's dark eyes glittered with surprising emotion. "I remember."

As they stared at each other, it felt like the anger shifted, eased. *Was it possible the good part of Johnny was still inside this hard, ruthless criminal?*

She had to appeal to that side. "Look, you can hate me for what I did. You can hurt me. I don't care. I just need to find Hayley."

"I don't have her, Bree."

"Come into the light. Let me see your eyes."

He straightened and moved away from the desk, stopping a foot away from her. Their gazes met for a long tense moment. So many emotions ran through her. He had lied to her before. But he wasn't lying now.

"Oh, God," she whispered. "You're telling the truth. But if you don't have her, who does?"

"I don't know."

She wanted to ask him to help her, but if Johnny found Hayley, he would never give her back.

On the other hand, what choice did she have? If anyone could find the kidnapper, it was probably him.

A loud crash came from the hallway. A shout. Then a grunt and a heavy thud.

Johnny started for the desk, for the gun, but he didn't get there.

The door burst open, and her heart jumped into her throat as Nathan barreled into the room, tackling Johnny to the ground.

Eighteen

—➤➤⧏⧏⧏—

Bree stared in shock as Nathan and Johnny fought with each other, fists flying, bodies rolling around on the ground. She wanted to help Nathan, but she couldn't do much with her hands behind her back. While she suspected Nathan had taken out whatever guards were in the hall, there would be more men coming. Johnny always had plenty of backup.

She moved toward the desk, thinking if she could find something to cut the ties, she could free her hands and get Johnny's gun, which was still on the desk. Or at the very least, she could put his gun out of reach, so he couldn't use it on Nathan.

But she'd barely taken a step when two men rushed into the room, pulling Nathan and Johnny apart.

One of them shoved Nathan up against the wall, while the other slugged him in the face.

"Stop," she cried. "Stop."

But they weren't stopping; they were going after Nathan, and he was no match for two of them. Blood was coming out of his nose, and he grunted as one of the men slammed him in the gut.

Johnny got to his feet, blood dripping down his face as well, murderous intent in his eyes.

"Make them stop, Johnny," she begged.

"Why would I do that?" he yelled.

"Because this isn't about him; it's about our daughter."
She stepped in front of him, putting herself between him and
Nathan. "We need to find Hayley, and we're wasting time."

"He went after me," Johnny argued, his gaze raging. "No
one goes after me."

"He thought you had Hayley. But you don't. Someone
else does. Please! Nathan can help us."

She could see the battle going on in Johnny's gaze, but
finally, he put up a hand.

"Stop," he said sharply.

Nathan slid down the wall as the two men backed off.
She didn't know how badly he was hurt, and she wanted to
run to him, but she didn't want to infuriate Johnny any
further.

Nathan struggled to get up, but his right eye was
swelling, and blood was still coming out of his nose.

"You always needed others to do your dirty work,
Johnny," Nathan said, obviously not worried about infuriating
Johnny. "Now, you stoop to kidnapping kids."

It was her turn to talk Nathan down. "Stop it, Nathan.
Johnny doesn't have Hayley."

Nathan gave her a look of utter disbelief. "He's lying. He
always lied to you, and you always believed him. You're
doing it again."

"He's not lying—not this time."

"He's playing you."

"I never played her," Johnny interrupted.

"You dragged her down in the mud with you," Nathan
returned.

"And you couldn't stand that she picked me and not you."

"This isn't getting us anywhere," she said, cutting into
their argument. "We need to bring a little girl home. Can we
just focus on that?" She only gave them a second to think
about it, and then she plowed ahead, turning to Johnny.
"Calvin Baker made a ransom demand from Hayley's father
yesterday. They met at the silos. I shot him in the shoulder.
Someone else made the kill shot from a sniper position. They

had to be a really good shot. They shut Calvin up before he could be interrogated. You say he's not working for you. But you can find out who he was working for, can't you? Because whoever that is has our daughter."

"I could ask some questions."

"Then do it. I don't believe this is just about me anymore," she added. "This is about revenge, and I think it's on both of us."

Johnny's hard gaze met hers. "Stay here." He took his gun off the desk and waved his men out of the room, shutting the door behind him.

After Johnny left, she ran to Nathan's side, wishing she could throw her arms around him. "I'm so sorry. We need to get you to a hospital."

"Forget about me. I'm fine."

"You're not fine."

"Doesn't matter. Do you really believe him, Bree?"

She looked into his eyes, needing him to see past his anger for Johnny. "I do. He didn't know anything until yesterday when he was questioned by the FBI. But before he comes back, I need to get my hands free. Can you help me?"

"Of course." Nathan got to his feet and ransacked the desk, pulling out a pair of scissors and cutting through the tie binding her wrists.

She shook out her hands in relief.

Nathan met her gaze. "Johnny's men kidnapped you. They tied you up and brought you here, and you want to trust him?"

"I don't have a choice. We need to fight fire with fire, and Johnny can find out who Baker was working for."

"You're making a deal with the devil."

"I know. If Johnny helps me find Hayley, he might try to take her."

"He *will* take her—it's not a question of *might*."

"Then we'll fight to get her free of him, but at least she'll be alive, and that's what's most important right now." She paused. "Do you know where we are?"

"Auto shop on Hudson," he said tersely. "I guess this is one of his businesses now."

"How did you find me?"

"Sierra told me where she thought you would be."

"She helped you? That's shocking."

"And maybe also a little too easy. Perhaps she thought Johnny would kill us, and she could get rid of us both at once." He pulled out her phone and handed it to her. "I found this in the parking lot."

"I wanted you to know I hadn't run out on you. I knew you'd come looking for me."

"I should have gone into the salon with you."

"Let's not look back." She put her phone in her pocket and glanced toward the closed door. "Where do you think Johnny went? Why did he just disappear like that?"

"Beats me," he said, wiping the blood off his face with the back of his sleeve.

"We need to get you out of here," she said decisively. "Johnny might go after you again."

"Or I'll go after him," he said darkly.

Her phone buzzed, drawing her attention away from him. *A text message.*

Her heart stopped as she opened the message and saw a photo of a little girl tied to a chair, tape over her mouth, terror in her eyes, and the word *daughter* scrawled across it. "Oh, God." She felt sick to her stomach.

Nathan took the phone out of her hand and enlarged the picture while she fought to keep the bile from rising in her throat.

A few deep breaths put her back into control. "Any clue to where she is?" she asked.

"I think she's at Howard School."

"Is that place still around?"

"Yes. Like so many other abandoned buildings in that neighborhood."

Howard had once been an elementary school, about a mile from their high school. It had been condemned a long time ago after toxic spills from a nearby factory had infused the soil.

"Every few years, the city tries to sell it to someone," Nathan added. "But its location in a run-down industrial area and a low-income neighborhood has made developers uneasy that the area can ever be revitalized." He paused. "It's another place from our past."

She met his gaze. "We all used to go there in high school. We got into a lot of trouble there."

"It's also where Johnny beat the crap out of me."

"No," she breathed.

"Yes. He did a lot of beatings there—like the one Stix went to prison for."

"The kid from Northwestern."

"The one you gave Johnny an alibi for."

"The night of the fashion show," she murmured. "Oh, my God—the newspaper photo was from that show. I didn't put it together. I should have figured that out sooner."

"This is about that night," Nathan agreed.

"Revenge," she breathed. "Against both Johnny and me."

"Which means that it's either Stix or the kid from Northwestern behind this."

He'd no sooner finished speaking when another text came in. They read it together: *Come alone. If you're not here in fifteen minutes, she's dead.*

"Let's go," Nathan said.

As they ran toward the door, gun shots echoed from the shop below, followed by shouts and more firepower.

"What the hell is that?" she asked, as Nathan managed to break open the door.

"No idea," he yelled. "But there's a fire escape off the storage room. It's how I got up here."

She ran down the hall, staying close to Nathan. More shots were fired. It sounded like they were coming from an automatic weapon.

Nathan grabbed her hand and pulled her into a small room, then pushed her toward the window. She climbed over the sill and made her way down the fire escape as fast as possible.

When they reached the ground, they took off running, dashing between buildings and down alleys to where Nathan had hidden his truck. It sounded like a war back at the auto shop, and she didn't know what to think about that. But thankfully, they were out. Now they just had to save Hayley.

Nathan gunned the engine, as they took off. She looked in the side view mirror for any sign of a tail, but there wasn't one.

"If Johnny doesn't survive whatever is going on back there, he won't be able to help us," she said.

"Maybe that's the point."

Her phone buzzed again, and she saw another text coming in. This time it was a video message. Hayley was facing the camera and no longer tied to the chair. She looked right into the camera and said, "Mommy, please come and get me. I'm waiting. Hurry."

It was the first time she'd ever heard her daughter's voice and tears streamed out of her eyes. She played the message again, her heart twisting in agony. "I know she's not talking to me; she's talking to Lindsay, to her mother, but it still hurts."

Nathan put his hand on her leg. "Hang in there, Bree. We're going to get her."

"I know I'm going to see Hayley; I just don't know if I'm going to be able to rescue her," she said, overwhelming fear running through her. "I'm afraid whoever has her is going to kill us all."

"We won't let him. As I recall, there are at least three entrances to the school and a lot of broken windows. There will be multiple ways to get in and out."

"I'm sure there will be multiple guards watching those doors and windows, too. It's not going to be easy."

"We've never had easy. We've always beaten the odds."

She met his gaze. "You're right. We've been through a lot together."

"And we'll do this together, too."

"I have to go in alone, Nathan."

"I understand that. But I will not be far behind. You saw what happened to Mark yesterday when he went by himself. He'd be dead if it wasn't for you."

"I've been thinking about that." She opened a new text on her phone and typed in a lengthy message.

"Who are you writing?"

"Agent Tracy Cox, my Chicago nemesis, but also a good agent. I want you to send this as soon as I get out of the car. I want the kidnapper to think he's getting his way at first, so you have to keep out of sight. I'm sure he knows by now that you're working with me."

"I can stay hidden."

"I'll probably have a ten-minute head start before the agents show up. Hopefully, I won't need them. But if I do, I have to trust they'll come in the right way."

He pulled the truck around a corner and turned off the engine. The school was still out of sight, but she knew exactly where it was. These were the streets of her youth: the dark, barren, depressing, run-down neighborhood which she'd somehow managed to survive once. She had to make it twice.

She looked over at Nathan. "This is it."

"Be careful, Bree. I don't want to lose you."

"I don't want to lose you, either." She gently touched the side of his bruised face. "Don't be a crazy-ass hero."

"Don't worry about me. Go get your daughter."

She leaned over and gave him a kiss, then got out of the truck and ran down the street.

--->>><<<---

Nathan watched Bree leave with tremendous misgivings, but he reminded himself that she was trained for situations like these. She'd just never had her daughter's life at stake before. But she would keep it together. She was smart, tough, and determined.

And he would be right behind her.

He sent her text to the FBI and then got out of the truck. He went in the opposite direction from where Bree had gone. Fortunately, there weren't many people out. A lot of the buildings in this area had been destroyed by a fire several years ago, and others were either out of business or closed on the weekend.

Howard School was three blocks away and located next to the river. It should have been a picturesque location, but it wasn't, and on this gray, gloomy day, he felt nothing but foreboding.

The school had been one of their favorite places to get into trouble or shelter them from the snow or get drunk on a hot summer night. The police and the city would periodically try to lock the building down, keep people out, but it never lasted long.

The truth was that no one cared about this part of the city; they never had. Maybe one day the whole area would be redeveloped, but that was a long way away. For now, the abandoned buildings, many filled with dangerous asbestos and inhabited by rats, would continue to be a blight on the city.

It wasn't a coincidence that Hayley was here. The school was where Johnny had conducted business. It could be Stix behind the plan, or the kid Johnny had almost killed for stealing his drug business. It could even be Sierra. She'd told him earlier that she'd saved him by calling in the fire department. She'd known where Johnny was then.

Maybe Sierra was behind the whole thing, he suddenly wondered. What if she'd found out Bree had had a kid with Johnny? What if she'd wanted to torture her former rival? What if she'd wanted to get rid of the one person who could take Johnny away from her—his daughter Hayley?

The way the kidnapper had played on Bree's emotions seemed almost feminine in nature, not that he wanted to discredit women, but another woman might certainly know that Bree's most vulnerable point would be the loss of her child. And Sierra had known Bree when she was in her teens.

She'd probably known about the shelter. She'd definitely known about the fashion show, because she'd been jealous of Bree's photo in the paper.

But would Sierra really go against the man she'd loved for years? The man who had probably financed her salon and was letting her live the life she always wanted?

Frustrated, he decided to put the guessing aside. He was probably going to find out soon enough. What he needed to worry about was how to enter the school without being seen and how he was going to save Bree and Hayley.

As he neared the building, he kept a wary eye on the windows and doors facing him.

All was quiet. He couldn't see anyone moving behind the broken windows.

The building backed right up to the water, just a narrow cement path between the structure and a low retaining wall.

He hid behind the adjacent building, waiting and watching for a long minute. There were no guards outside, but who knew how many people were waiting inside?

Time to find out.

He didn't head to one of the doors, instead aiming for a window on the ground floor. There were plenty of those around, and he didn't think they could guard all of them. Hopefully, he was picking the right one.

Nineteen

$\longrightarrow \Longrightarrow \twoheadleftarrow \longleftarrow$

Bree walked past the large sign that said No Entry and warned of legal prosecution for trespassers, a sign she'd ignored many times before.

The lock and chain on the front door of the school had been sawed off. It didn't look to be a particularly old lock, maybe that had been recent, but when she entered the building, a nasty stench made her gag. Rats scurried away as she stepped over broken bottles, discarded needles, and other garbage.

She moved into the hallway and looked both ways. There were three classrooms on the left plus the principal's office and three classrooms on the right. In front of her was the multi-purpose auditorium. There were stairs at both ends of the hallway, leading up to the second floor, where six more classrooms could be found as well as restrooms.

She'd been in every single one of those rooms at one time or another. She'd even climbed out onto the flat-top roof that overlooked the river. She could do this. She could find her daughter.

Pausing, she listened for some sign of life.

Why was it so quiet?

She could hear her heart pounding and felt like a sitting duck. A shooter could come out of any of the classrooms or the offices or the auditorium, and she would have no escape.

But she didn't think she was going to die that fast.

The game was coming to a climax, and she could do nothing but play along.

The sound of crying made her pulse race. It sounded like it was coming from the auditorium.

She ran forward, pushing through the large door at the back of the room. The rows of seats had long since been taken away, and huge chunks of the ceiling now covered the floor. There was more garbage in this room, and it was cold and dark with barely any light coming from the boarded-up windows.

Squinting in the darkness, she stepped over more trash, making her way to the stage. The curtain was drawn.

That seemed a portent of the show to come.

Licking her lips, fear ravaging her insides, she heard a child's sobbing get louder. The thought of Hayley being kept in this hellhole turned some of her fear into anger.

She walked faster.

She went up the stairs on the right.

The curtain suddenly opened.

A bright light hit the stage and there was Hayley sitting in the middle of the floor, arms around her knees, rocking back and forth, crying her little heart out.

She ran toward her, dropping to her knees, knowing that they were both spotlighted for whoever was watching, but she didn't care.

"It's going to be okay, Hayley." She wrapped her arms around the little girl—*around her daughter*. She could hardly believe she was holding her. "I'm here. I've got you."

"I want my mommy," Hayley said, looking into her eyes.

The simple phrase broke her heart. "I'm going to take you to her."

"She's not dead? They said she was dead. And my daddy, too."

"Your family is fine," she reassured her, mentally taking note that Hayley had used the word *they*. "Who brought you here?"

"A tall man and a short man," she said with another sob. "They smell bad."

"Do you know where they went?" She looked around, but with the light on, she could barely see anything.

The light suddenly went off. She blinked in the darkness, and jumped to her feet, pulling Hayley up with her, putting her body in front of her daughter's as a man appeared in front of her. He was definitely the tall man, well over six foot seven, and when he came out of the shadows, he had a gun trained on her.

Her heart leapt again as all the clues fell into place. "Stix," she murmured. "Stan Tix."

"I'm glad to see you haven't forgotten me, Bree Larson— or I guess it's Adams now. You left this shit-filled city and made a new life for yourself. Some of us didn't get to do that."

"You did all this for revenge against me and Johnny?"

"Surprised? Did you really think I'd ever forget the two people who ruined my life? I was on my way to a pro basketball career. I was going to be rich, famous—I was going to have everything. But I lost it all, because of Johnny, and because of you."

"You did it to yourself. I didn't do anything."

"You lied to the cops to protect Johnny. You backed up his story. You told them Johnny couldn't possibly have assaulted that kid, that he was a good guy."

"I didn't say any of that. I just said he was at the fashion show. He was in the audience. I didn't know anything."

"He wasn't in the audience. He was here, beating up a college kid for trying to take over his drug turf. I arrived just in time to save that kid from dying, and I ended up with blood on my hands. But it was the knife in the back that took me down, the one placed there by Johnny, and left there by you."

"That kid said two guys beat him up. You were one of them. He identified you. There was DNA evidence."

"I didn't do the beating. The second man was Baker— Johnny's right-hand man. And the kid saw me when I was trying to help him. But he had serious head injuries. He couldn't remember when I'd entered the room."

Was that true?

Frowning, she thought about the other part of his statement. "You said Baker was there, too."

"He was."

"But he has been working with you. He's part of this kidnapping. He made the ransom call. Why wouldn't you hate him, too?" she asked in confusion.

"I did hate him. So, I used him. Now he's dead."

"You were at the silos. You shot him."

"I was done with him. And I didn't need him talking to you."

"You could have taken me out at the silos."

"That wouldn't have been nearly as much fun."

As he shifted his weight, the light glinted off the big ring on his hand—the World Series Cubs ring.

"You took Hayley out of the auditorium," she said. "How did you get her to go with you?"

"She wanted to come with me. I had her bunny," he replied.

She put her hand on Hayley's arm, feeling the little girl's body shaking as she clung to Bree's waist. "I can't believe you kidnapped an innocent child to get back at Johnny and me. She's not part of this. You want me; I'm here. Let Hayley walk out."

"Oh, I don't think she's going anywhere, not until we have a happy family reunion."

"Johnny isn't coming."

"I think he is."

"Look, I don't know anything about that night, Stix. I didn't set you up. I didn't know what happened."

"Pretty girls never know anything about what their bad boyfriends are doing," he said, a bitter note in his voice. "Well, my pretty girl left me. She had a baby with someone else. She got married and forgot all about me."

"I'm sorry. But I still don't understand why you went to

such elaborate lengths to mess with me. Why did you send me all over the city? You sent that girl—Emma—to talk to me on the train. And now I guess the photo at the shelter makes sense, because that was the night all this happened. But it's so complicated. How long have you been planning your revenge?"

"Since the day I went to prison."

She shook her head, seeing the crazy anger in his eyes. He was obsessed, fanatical; he would not be talked out of anything, but she still felt like she had to try. "Is Emma all right?"

"Who the hell is Emma?"

"The little girl on the train. Now you're confused?" *Was he completely out of his mind?* "Why focus on me? Johnny was the one who really hurt you."

"I know exactly what's happening. And don't worry, Johnny is part of this. He should be here any second. My men will make sure of that. You see, I've put together my own army. I found a lot of good soldiers in prison. They taught me how to fight someone like Johnny, and how to win."

He'd no sooner finished speaking when the doors to the auditorium opened, and Johnny was shoved toward the stage by another man with a gun. Johnny looked worse than he had after his fight with Nathan. His clothes were ripped, and he was barely able to walk.

As he got closer, she saw that his leg was bleeding, and someone had tied a rag around it. He'd been shot. The warfare at the automotive shop must have come from Stix and his associates.

Hayley cried louder as the men drew closer.

Johnny gave her what felt like a reassuring look, but she wasn't comforted. He could barely walk. *What the hell kind of help was he going to be?* And he appeared to be alone.

Obviously, Stix had taken out Johnny's men.

Unless one or two of them had survived and would come after their boss?

She hoped that was a possibility.

Even without them, Nathan was around somewhere, and FBI agents were on their way. She just had to keep everyone alive in the meantime.

The only good thing about this nightmare was that Stix wanted to savor his moment of revenge, of triumph. He didn't want them to die too fast. He wanted them to understand that he was in charge now, that they would die at his hands.

"Watch the front," Stix told his associate. "Where's Rico?"

"Out back," the man said, letting go of Johnny as left.

She was happy to see him go; it definitely improved her odds, but Stix still had the only gun, and with Hayley hanging on to her for dear life, she couldn't take him down with any sudden moves.

"How did you know about my baby?" she asked, hoping Hayley wasn't paying attention to the conversation, but she seemed too frightened to be taking much in.

"A friend clued me in," Stix said.

"A friend? Does he have a name?" she asked sharply.

"I know who he is. You don't need to know," Stix replied. His gaze hardened on Johnny. "You got nothing to say, Johnny boy? Look who's in charge now?"

Johnny spit on the floor in response.

Anger stiffened Stix's spine, and he seemed to get even taller. "I'll do the talking then. You sent me to prison for what you did. You took away my life, the family I was supposed to have, and now you're going to lose yours."

"Bree is not my family," Johnny said harshly. "I don't give a damn about her anymore."

She believed Johnny, but Stix didn't.

"You don't love Sierra," Stix said. "You're just using her, the way you use everyone. Bree is the only one you cared about, and even if you hate her for what she did to you, you still want her." He paused, giving Bree an evil smile. "I actually admire the guts it took for you to walk away."

"Then let me go. Let Hayley go."

"Unfortunately, there's always collateral damage." He

turned back to Johnny. "I know what you care about, and that's blood—family. Well, your blood is right here on this stage. And I'll be doing her a favor by not letting her grow up with you."

Bree sucked in a breath at Stix's twisted words.

Johnny didn't rise to Stix's bait. He just stared back at his one-time friend with burning hatred in his eyes.

No one was backing down. But she needed to find a way to defuse the situation.

"Do whatever you want to me and Johnny," she said, bringing Stix's attention back to her. "Hayley is not part of this. She wasn't even born when you went to prison."

"I don't think so." Stix raised his gun and pointed it at her. "In fact, I think she goes first, and you two will watch."

"You don't want to do that," she argued. "You just told me you were innocent of your crime, and that you tried to save the kid Johnny almost killed. You don't want to hurt this child."

"I've changed. Prison will do that."

He had changed and the gentle giant she had once known was nowhere to be found. He was going to kill them all. She had no doubt about it.

Johnny must have made the same assumption, because he suddenly moved, throwing his body in front of hers as Stix fired his weapon. The bullet ripped through Johnny's chest.

Hayley screamed.

She ducked down, wrapping Hayley up in her arms, praying the next bullet would hit her and not her child.

But before Stix could fire again, a crashing noise above the stage distracted him. He looked up, and then a body came down from the rafters, knocking Stix off his feet.

Nathan!

The gun flew out of Stix's hand, sliding across the stage as Nathan attacked him.

She pushed Hayley to the side and grabbed Stix's gun off the floor.

She was just in time as the man who'd brought Johnny in

earlier came rushing toward the stage. She fired, hitting him square in the chest. He fell to the floor. She turned her gun toward Stix, but he and Nathan were so entangled, she couldn't risk hurting Nathan.

Hayley was screaming, and her maternal instincts were firing on all cylinders. She needed to get her daughter off the stage and safely away.

"Give me the gun. Get her out of here," Johnny told her, his face a picture of contorted agony as he sat up, blood coming from his chest and his leg.

She had no time to dither, tossing the gun to Johnny, then grabbing Hayley and running toward the stairs.

As another blast rocked the auditorium, she prayed that Johnny had not shot Nathan.

Not knowing how many men they might have to get through to get out of the school, she decided to go up to the roof. Hopefully, they could find a place to hide until more help arrived.

When they got on the roof, the dark day gave them some shadows, but they still needed to find cover. The roof was patchy in places, and she had to be careful where they stepped, so they didn't fall through.

Large heating ducts rose up like stalwarts along one side of the roof, but they were too thin to hide behind. Then she spied a big heating unit about four feet wide by six feet long and it was next to a raised portion of the roof. They might be out of sight there. She moved quickly across the roof. "Climb in, Hayley," she said, pushing the little girl behind the unit.

"Don't go," Hayley cried, clinging to her hand. "I'm scared."

"I'm not going anywhere," she said, sliding in next to her. As Hayley's fingers tightened around hers, she felt a crazy sense of familiarity. She'd never held her baby's hand until now, but it felt so absolutely right, and the connection between them was powerfully strong.

She would save her daughter, or she would die trying.

—➤➤◄◄—

Nathan had taken out two of Stix's men on his way into the school, but he'd had the element of surprise. Now he was going toe-to-toe with a man who had six inches and forty pounds on him. Not only that, Stix was fighting like a yard dog who'd been chained up too long. There was a starving hunger in him, a powerful need for the revenge he'd been seeking for more than a decade.

Thankfully, Johnny had shot another one of Stix's men, who had come into the room after Bree and Hayley left. He just needed to take Stix down, give Bree time to escape.

His fist connected with Stix's jaw, and as Stix's eyes bugged out, he thought he might have gotten the advantage.

But then Stix seemed to gather superhuman strength from somewhere, throwing his entire body weight at him.

He felt the edge of the stage underneath his foot and then he went flying. He landed hard on his back, his head bouncing off the floor, something sharp cutting his back. He saw stars and felt a rocketing wave of pain rip through him as a curtain of darkness began to descend.

He couldn't let that curtain hit the ground. He couldn't lose consciousness. Bree needed him.

He fought through the haze threatening to take him under and somehow found a way to get back on his feet. But Stix was gone. Two of his associates were dead on the floor, and Johnny was barely moving.

He struggled to get himself up the stairs to the stage. Johnny was barely breathing, gasping in the last few seconds of his life. There was too much damage, too much blood.

"Roof," Johnny bit out, clutching his bloody chest, as he looked at him. "Save Bree," he bit out. "And my daughter." He struggled for breath. "Tell Bree...I finally did one good thing. Hope it's enough." Johnny's eyes closed as he uttered his last breath.

Nathan didn't have time to think about what Johnny's death meant. All he could focus on was getting to Bree. He grabbed the gun that had just fallen from Johnny's hand and ran toward the stairs, hoping Stix had gone in the opposite direction.

—➤➤◄◄—

"The tall man is back," Hayley whispered, her eyes widening again.

Bree's gut tightened as Stix came out on the roof, and a terrible fear for Nathan washed through her. *If Stix was up here, then Nathan...*

But she couldn't think about that now. She couldn't let Stix get to Hayley. And it wouldn't take long for him to find them. She was going to have to find a way to turn the tables.

"Stay here," she whispered.

"Don't leave me," Hayley pleaded.

"I'll be back soon. You have to be very, very quiet. Okay?"

Hayley's bottom lip trembled, and her eyes filled with tears. "I want to go home."

"It's almost over. I won't let anything happen to you. Just don't move."

Hayley nodded her head.

She crept out from behind the heater. She moved away from Hayley as quietly as she could, hoping that if Stix heard her, he'd see only her and not Hayley.

Stix was definitely enraged, pacing along the river-side of the roof, probably looking for a way down. Maybe he didn't know they'd come up here. Or maybe he just hadn't seen the heating unit yet.

He was such a big man. She didn't know if she could physically take him down, but she had to try. Right now, he hadn't seen her. She could catch him off guard.

As he moved closer to the edge, she saw her opportunity. If she could grab onto the heating duct at the same time she kicked her feet out, she might be able to knock him off without taking herself over the side at the same time.

She'd only have one chance. If it didn't work, she'd be dead. And Hayley would die, too.

That wasn't going to happen.

Commit, she told herself.

She could do this. She could do this for her daughter and for Nathan and even for Johnny, who had somehow, incredulously, taken a bullet for her.

Taking a deep breath, she gathered herself together and then ran full speed ahead. Two feet before she got to Stix, she grabbed the pole and then swung her body into midair, her feet hitting him dead in the chest as he turned around.

The force knocked him backward.

He tried to grab on to her legs.

His hand caught her foot for a brief second.

She kicked him away, holding onto the duct with all her might, and hoping it wouldn't break.

Stix waved his arms in the air, flailing, searching for something to save him.

But there was nothing for him to grab on to.

He let out a roar of anger and fear, shock widening his eyes, as he fell backward over the side of the building.

Heart pounding, she let go of the duct and walked over to the edge, seeing Stix's body floating face-down in the dark river.

The door to the roof opened behind her, and she whirled around, her hands automatically fisting as she prepared to do battle again.

But it was Nathan who stepped on to the roof, a gun in his hand.

She'd never been so happy to see him in her life.

He ran forward and swept her up into his arms, hugging her tight. But he didn't hang on long. "Stix," he bit out. "Where?"

"Down there," she said, tipping her head.

He looked over the side and then back at her. "How did you manage that?"

"You wouldn't believe it if I told you."

"You are one serious badass, Bree."

"Just a mother fighting for her kid." She paused. "Johnny?"

He shook his head.

She nodded, not really sure how she felt about Johnny's death.

"Everyone else is down or took off," he added. "I think we're okay."

"Good." As she finished speaking, she saw vehicles heading toward the school. Help had arrived. "Do you still have my phone?"

"Right here," he said, handing it to her.

She punched in Tracy's number. "I've got Hayley. She's safe. We're on the roof with Nathan. I don't know who else is still alive downstairs, but be careful coming in."

She ended the call as Tracy said they'd be right there. Then she ran across the roof and squatted down next to the heating unit. She held out her hand. "It's over, baby. The bad men are gone."

Hayley crawled out and wrapped her arms around Bree's neck. "I'm going to see my mommy now?" she asked.

"Really, really soon." She hugged the little girl as tightly as she could, closing her eyes, memorizing the moment, because she knew it would probably be the last time she ever held her daughter.

A few minutes later, the roof was swarming with police and FBI. She set Hayley on her feet and then stood up, but Hayley still held on to her arm, as if she couldn't trust whatever was coming next.

Tracy came over to her, and Bree couldn't really imagine what she was going to say—probably that she was done being an agent. But the words that came out of Tracy's mouth shocked her.

"Nice work, Agent Adams."

Bree met her gaze, knowing that while Tracy might be a territorial hard-ass, she'd also wanted to save Hayley. "Thanks."

Tracy gave Hayley a smile. "I'm Agent Cox. I'm going to take you to your parents."

"No. She's going to take me," Hayley said, clinging to Bree's arm. "She promised."

"I did promise."

"Okay," Tracy said. "That's fine. Her parents are at the hospital. There's an ambulance downstairs. They can check Hayley out on the way."

"I know it's against protocol for me to go with her—"

"But you should go with her," Tracy said, meeting her gaze.

"Thank you."

"You did it all yourself. I think we both knew you would."

As Tracy stepped away to speak to ASAIC Hobbs, Bree looked at Nathan. "I need to stay with Hayley."

"Of course. I'll meet you at the hospital."

"You should get checked out, too. You don't look so good."

He smiled through his bloody bruises. "Really? Because I never felt better in my life."

She had so many things she wanted to say to him, but first she had to return her daughter to the family who loved her.

Twenty

⟶⟩⟩⟨⟨⟵

On the way to the hospital, the female paramedic checked Hayley out with a careful, reassuring smile, as Bree held Hayley's hand. It didn't appear that Hayley had been physically injured during her time in captivity. She had some bruises, but she told Bree that the tall man had taken her to a house, and a woman had brought her food and given her a book to read.

Hayley didn't know what the woman's name was. She described her as having dark hair and eyes but couldn't provide any more detail. She said the woman had told her that she'd be okay if she did what she was told. She also said no one had hit her or hurt her in any way, for which Bree was immensely grateful.

The emotional trauma of the kidnapping and the captivity would be very difficult for Hayley to deal with, but at least she wouldn't have to suffer through memories of physical or sexual abuse.

Apparently, Stix had been willing to kill Hayley, but only because she was Johnny's blood and her daughter, the two people he'd blamed for the destruction of his life, not because he just wanted to hurt a kid.

She still had so many questions, but for now the only thing that mattered was that Hayley was safe.

When they arrived at the hospital, they were escorted up

to the fifth floor, bypassing the ER since Hayley was not in physical peril. What she needed most was to see her parents, and they were waiting in Mark's hospital room.

It wasn't until they entered the room, and Hayley saw her mother sitting on the bed next to her father, that she let go of Bree's hand and ran into her mother's arms.

Lindsay and Hayley cried together at their reunion, while tears dripped down Mark's face as he leaned over to put his hand on his daughter's head.

She'd seen reunions like this before, parents overjoyed at the return of their beloved child, but this one hit home. *This was her child, her daughter.* She wanted to be part of the circle, but she couldn't be.

An arm came around her shoulder, and she looked up into Nathan's warm, compassionate gaze. He was probably the only one who knew exactly how she was feeling.

"She's going to be okay," she told him. "Stix didn't hurt her."

"I'm glad." He paused. "Are you really not going to tell her you're her mother?"

"How can I? She thought she lost her family, and now she has them back. Look how happy she is—how happy they are."

"She has a right to know who her mother is."

"When she's ready to know, that's when they'll tell her."

"You're letting them call the shots?"

"She's their daughter." As she said the words, she realized how true they were. "I gave birth to her, but they've raised her and loved her for the past ten years. Who's to say they don't have more right to her than I do?"

"You sound like a mother, Bree."

"I want to make the choice that's right for her and not the choice that's right for me."

"Maybe one day it could be right for both of you."

"One day," she echoed, turning her gaze back to the Jansens.

Lindsay helped Hayley onto the bed, so she could hug

her father. Then she turned and looked at Bree, enormous gratitude in her eyes, as she mouthed the words, "Thank you."

She nodded, her eyes blurring with tears, watching as Lindsay wrapped her arms around both her daughter and her husband. She knew she should step outside, but it was so difficult to leave knowing that she might never see Hayley again.

Finally, she forced herself to move. They stepped into the hallway, and she shut the door to Mark's room, wanting to give the family a few minutes of privacy.

The corridor was already filling with police and agents, and the media would be swarming in front of the hospital. Thankfully, this story had a happy ending.

Tracy moved over to join them. "We have a lot of dead bodies and a lot of questions," she said. "We're going to need you both to come into the office."

"Nathan needs to see a doctor," she said quickly.

"I'm fine, Bree," he said.

"You're not fine. You could have a broken rib or a concussion."

"I've arranged for Mr. Bishop to be seen in the ER," Tracy replied, motioning a nurse forward. "Nurse Collins will escort you down there. When you're done, an agent will bring you to the office."

"I really don't need a doctor," Nathan complained.

She gave him a smile. "Just get yourself checked out."

"All right. But I am fine."

"I hope so."

As Nathan left, Tracy gave her an assessing look. "Is something going on with you two? I thought you were just childhood friends."

"It goes deeper than that," she admitted. "Nathan and I have been through a lot together, not just this week, but at other times in our lives."

"He knew your deep, dark secret."

"One of a very small number of people. He's the one who helped me get out of Chicago."

"He seems like a good man."

"The best. I wouldn't have made it through this without him."

"Maybe you'll want to transfer to Chicago."

"I'm sure your team would love that."

Tracy smiled. "I must admit I didn't want you here."

"Really. I'm surprised to hear you say that," she said dryly.

"I admit that I can get a little territorial. And we have a past. When you showed up, I knew what would happen. You would become the center of everything, and that's exactly the way it went down."

"That wasn't what I was expecting. I really thought I would just be consulting on a case."

"I never thought that. You're too independent, too damned smart, and too good at your job to just sit on the sidelines."

"Wait—you're complimenting me?"

Tracy shrugged. "I'm just stating the facts. I don't like the drama that follows you around. And I still think you act on emotion far too often, but you're also very intuitive and good at reading situations."

"Thank you. You're a good agent, too. We might approach things differently, but we usually end up at the same place. I wish you didn't see us as competitors."

"I'm starting to realize that's a weakness of mine."

She was surprised at Tracy's words. "We can both be good agents."

"Yes. I suppose we can."

"That is if I keep my job after all this."

"I suspect you'll find a way," she said with a knowing gleam in her eyes. "So, tell me what went down at the school. Who was behind all of this?"

"Stan Tix."

"The deceased individual we found in the river?"

"Yes. We called him Stix because he was so tall. He was a red-hot basketball player in college and was going to go pro, but instead he went to prison for a violent assault that he claims my ex-boyfriend Johnny committed. Stix also blamed me for his prison sentence, because I was Johnny's alibi."

"Did you lie for your boyfriend?"

"I didn't think I did. I was modeling in a fashion show that night. I saw Johnny before I went backstage and then after the show, about two hours later. I told the police I was sure he'd been at the show the whole night. But according to Stix, Johnny and Calvin Baker were at Howard School beating up a rival drug dealer while I was walking the runway. Stix said he tried to stop it, and that's why his DNA and fingerprints were found at the scene. He went to prison for ten years. During that time, he plotted ways to get back at us."

"But why was he working with Baker, if Baker was part of it?"

"He said he was using him. And when he was done, he shot him."

"That's cold."

"He was clearly out of his mind with plans of revenge." She paused. "I still don't know how Stix found out about the baby I gave up for adoption, or how he knew so much about my past. He said something about someone telling him, but he didn't give me a name." She thought about that for a second. "Maybe it was Charles Benedict."

"You said last night you had concerns about the detective, but that's still a big leap."

"Maybe not. Benedict worked for Johnny's father when I got pregnant. Maybe he figured out that I left Johnny because of that. I need to talk to him."

"I'm sure you'll get that chance. Did Hayley say anything to you on your way over here?"

"She told me that there was a woman taking care of her at a house. They didn't take her to Howard School until earlier today. Thankfully, she wasn't hurt."

"She's lucky. She seems quite attached to you. Did you tell her who you really are?"

"No, and I'm not going to. The Jansens are her parents, and I'm going to let them decide if and when they want to share that information."

"That decision must be killing you."

"It's rough, but I always wanted her to be safe and happy, and now she truly can be. There's no threat left to her. The Jansens are great parents. They love Hayley, and she loves them." She gave a helpless shrug. "That's why I gave her up—so she could have that kind of family. I'm not going to take it away now." She cleared her throat. "Anyway, we can go over all this."

"Oh, we definitely will," Tracy promised.

"I did want to ask you if you've heard what's going on in New York. Dan told me earlier that the real White Rose Kidnapper struck again."

"Yes. But we actually got good news from your team an hour ago. They caught the kidnapper and saved the child."

"Oh, my God, that's amazing. How did they do it so fast?"

"The kidnapper was in a rush this time, angry that someone was impersonating him here in Chicago. He made mistakes he hadn't made before, and your team was able to track him down."

She could hardly believe the man they'd been tracking for three months had been found so quickly. "Who is he?"

"He's a forty-two-year-old delivery driver for a flower shop in Williamsburg, New York. His mother left him with his abusive father when he was thirteen. But she took his eleven-year-old sister with her. Apparently, he hated his mother for leaving him behind and hated his sister for having the life he wanted. Those emotions formed the foundation of his desire to target girls of that age. He wanted to be famous. He wanted people to know him, to be afraid of him. He quite liked the name the media had given him, and he didn't like news of a copycat."

"So, this case actually helped solve the other one. I'm glad some good came out of it."

"We should get down to the office."

She had a feeling she was headed for a very long night. But it didn't matter. She'd tell them whatever they wanted to know. There were no more secrets to keep.

—————

Nathan opened his apartment door for Bree a little after nine p.m. After four hours of questioning, both individually and together, they'd finally been allowed to leave.

They'd taken a cab to his apartment after leaving the FBI office. His truck was still at the hospital, but he'd get that tomorrow. Right now, he just wanted to hold Bree, and as soon as he closed the apartment door, that's exactly what he did.

She wrapped her arms around his waist and rested her head on his shoulder. Her silky hair brushed his chin, and he held her tight, grateful that Hayley was safe and that they were both still alive. The day could have ended so much differently.

"It feels like a decade has passed since we had breakfast here together," she told him, lifting her head.

He smiled. "I think we still have some Chinese food from last night, if you're hungry."

"Tracy got me a salad earlier. But if you're hungry—"

"No, the agent interviewing me also got me some food."

"I'm glad. That was a hellishly long session."

"There was a lot to explain. Speaking of explaining...I heard some of what Stix was saying to you on the stage, but not everything. I know he was out for revenge, but there's a part of this whole thing that just doesn't really make sense."

"Which part?"

Seeing the new tension in her expression, he was sorry he'd brought it up. "Never mind. It doesn't matter."

"You're talking about the way Stix orchestrated my trip through time—Emma coming up to me on the train, the flyer for the shelter, the photo for the fashion show. Although, the photo makes more sense now, because that was the night Stix was charged for attempted murder, and I gave Johnny an alibi."

"But all of that—the threatening calls from the kidnapper with the altered voice—was that Stix? Or was it Calvin?" Nathan asked.

"I don't know."

"And why all the attention on you? Why wasn't Stix gaslighting Johnny?"

"I wish I could have asked him all that. I still don't know who told him I had a kid. He mentioned some mysterious friend. And how did he find Hayley? I'm hoping we'll get more information as we investigate his life since he got out of prison. There's a woman somewhere who took care of Hayley. Maybe she'll know something."

"I hope so, but it's over, and that's what is important. Stix was obviously sick in the head—kidnapping a little girl, hiding her away, pretending to impersonate some other serial kidnapper, staging that whole scene at the school. You can't make logic out of crazy."

"No, but I wish I could." She moved her hands from around his back and cupped his face. "Your beautiful face is so bruised. It almost hurts me to look at you. I know you're in pain."

"Hey, the other guys I fought are dead, so I'm doing okay. I'm just sorry Stix ever got up to the roof. The man was strong. He threw me over the stage. Want to tell me how you pushed him over the edge?"

"I waited until he was standing right by one of those tall heating ducts. I ran forward, grabbed the duct, kicked up my legs in my best martial arts move and connected with his chest. I knew I needed to hang on to something, or I'd go into the river with him. He tried to grab my foot, but I kicked him again, and down he went, flailing his arms like a desperate bird."

He shook his head in amazement. "And to think I ever worried that you couldn't take care of yourself."

"You did take care of me today, Nathan. You came after me when Johnny's men grabbed me and took me to the shop. You jumped down from the beam over the stage like some superhero and tackled a man with a gun, giving me a chance to escape."

"Johnny put himself in front of a bullet for you," he couldn't help saying, even though the last thing he'd ever imagined himself doing was praising Johnny.

"I was shocked he did that. I guess his instinct to protect his daughter was stronger than his instinct to protect himself."

"Or it was his instinct to protect you."

She shrugged. "We'll never know."

"I heard his last words, Bree."

Her eyes widened. "What did he say?"

"He said to tell you that he finally did one good thing. He hoped it was enough."

Moisture filled her eyes, and he didn't know how he felt about her sadness for a man who had been his rival, his enemy—a man who had almost killed him once. But he couldn't look away. He couldn't ignore her feelings, whatever they were.

She blinked back the tears. "I'm not crying because I'm sad that he's dead."

"You're not? It kind of looks like you are."

"I'm sad because I wish he could have found that goodness in himself a long time ago. What a wasted life."

"You always saw the good in him."

"No, I didn't; I just wanted to see it. It was never really there. It was only in my head."

"Well, today it was there."

"I'm grateful he saved me, and he saved Hayley. But I'm not going to mourn him. He lived a life in a violent world, and he contributed to that violence. He hurt a lot of people, including you, most of all you," she said, running her hand down his cheek. "I have put you through so much, Nathan. I don't know why you're still with me."

He smiled as he rested his hands on her waist and drew

her close. "You know why. I love you, Bree. I've been in love with you since I was thirteen years old. I think it happened the first time I saw you. You've always been the one for me, even when you weren't. I know it wasn't the same for you. I know you've loved other people."

"I'm sure you have, too, Nathan."

"I've cared about the women I've been with, but honestly Bree when you showed back up in my life, you made a mockery of all those feelings. I was just kidding myself thinking I felt anything close to what I felt for you with any of the women in my life."

"What about Adrienne?"

"I talked to her while you were in the salon. I told her it was over."

"Really?"

"She said she was surprised. But I'm not sure that's true. Even before you came back, Adrienne and I weren't quite in sync. We didn't have enough ease with each other to share our secrets."

"Or hatred of Brussels sprouts."

"You're going to make me eat some, aren't you?"

"I am," she said with a laugh. "But not tonight."

"Thank God—a reprieve." He leaned over and kissed her, because it had just been too long since he'd tasted her lips. He felt an overwhelming rush of desire, of love, of thankfulness that she was alive and safe and with him.

And then her phone buzzed.

As he let her go, he said, "I'm beginning to hate that thing."

She checked her phone. "It's from my friend, Parisa. Nothing important. She just wanted to let me know she's around to help if I need her."

"She's a little late."

"I could have asked sooner, but I had you."

"You're always going to have me."

A shadow crossed her face, and she pulled away, walking over to the windows. As he moved to join her, she turned around.

"Nathan, I love you, too."

"Why am I hearing a *but*?"

"This city…" She let the words hang. "Chicago is your home. It's where your family is. But I don't know if it's where I want to be. The past is no longer haunting me. Johnny is dead. Stix is dead. Hopefully, there isn't anyone else here who hates me."

"So you could come back. It seemed like the Chicago agents were treating you with more respect tonight."

"I did make my peace with Tracy. But there's something else."

He read the truth in her eyes. "Hayley."

She nodded. "I don't know if I could live here and not want to see her all the time. I just think it would be too hard."

"Maybe you could see her—be a part of her life. Mark and Lindsay are reasonable people. And after you saved their daughter, I think they feel damned grateful to you."

"That's probably all true. But I need to let them tell Hayley when it's right for her and for their family. That might not be for a long while."

He felt a heaviness settling over his heart, the same despair he'd felt when she'd gotten on the bus eleven years ago, and he'd wondered if he'd ever see her again. For days afterward, he'd been mired in pain—a pain that had gone far deeper than his physical wounds. Was he really going to let her walk away again?

"I can leave Chicago, Bree."

"But you love it here."

"I love you more. I can be a contractor anywhere. I do have to finish the house I'm working on, but after that, I can free myself up." As he was spoke, he was actually starting to like the idea. "It's not like I've never thought of leaving before."

"There's still Josie and Grace. You family is here."

"They have Kyle. And he might actually appreciate not having Josie's big brother looking over his shoulder."

"He might need you looking over his shoulder."

"I can still do that. And I can still see my sister and my niece. There are plenty of flights to Chicago from all over the world. I've never lived in New York. It might be fun."

"I can't believe you'd move for me," she said in wonder. "I feel selfish."

"No. You're not being selfish; you're being honest. I think it would be difficult for you to be here with Hayley nearby, at least for the foreseeable future. I still hope that will change, because I think you'd both be better off if you were in each other's lives. But everything is fresh and raw and needs time to settle out."

"I can work out of other cities besides New York," she said. "I went there because I had a mentor there, but he died last summer, and while I love my team, I could do something else somewhere else. Maybe we start over someplace new."

"I like the sound of that. We could always go west, find a house by the beach."

"With a view of a beautiful harbor and lots of sailboats," she said.

"When we dreamed that as kids, I always saw you in the picture."

"I saw you, too. I actually saw you on a surfboard."

He grinned. "I have never been on a surfboard."

"You'd look so good on one. I can see you now in a pair of sexy board shorts." She took her hands in his, her expression turning serious. "I do love you, Nathan. I loved you when I was a scared girl and you were my sweet, protective friend. I loved you when I was a reckless, rebellious teenager making stupid decisions and not sure how to handle the weird feelings I sometimes got when I was around you."

"You did not."

"I did. I just didn't realize it. And then I stupidly chose to get involved with a mobster." She gave him a helpless smile. "But I loved you when you helped me get away, when you kept my secret, when you supported my choice." She took a breath, gazing deep into his eyes. "Most importantly, I love you now. I love who I am with you. I love how we are together. It feels so honest. I feel so connected to you. I can't imagine even going back to New York for one day without you."

His heart swelled as he read the absolute truth in her eyes. "I feel the same way. We know each other's hearts. So, let's find a way to be together."

"Okay, let's do it."

"*It* as in..."

She laughed. "Yes, but maybe not tonight. You should sleep. You're so bruised; you must be in pain."

"The only thing I feel right now is happy. I will sleep later—after I show you how much I love you."

"You already did that a thousand times over today. So, let me show you." She gave him a tender kiss and led him into the bedroom.

Twenty-One

➤➤✦◄◄◄

Happiness was pretty simple, Bree thought, as she and Nathan ate breakfast late Monday morning. They'd had a wonderful Sunday—making love, sleeping, talking, and watching a stupidly funny movie at one point, because they just needed to laugh. They didn't talk about anything that had happened, giving themselves a twenty-four-hour hiatus on all dark and serious subjects. But that hiatus was coming to an end.

The call from Nathan's doorman confirmed that Agent Tracy Cox was on her way up.

Bree got to her feet, taking their empty plates to the sink.

"Does it feel like bad news if she's coming here to talk to you?" Nathan asked.

"It doesn't feel like good news. But I guess we'll find out."

Nathan moved down the hall to open the door.

"Sorry to bother you," Tracy said. "But I wanted to touch base before you go back to New York. Or are you going back to New York?" she asked, her speculative gaze encompassing both of them.

Bree smiled at Nathan, then looked back at Tracy. "My long-term plans are up in the air, but I will be heading back to New York in a few days. I just need to catch my breath."

"That's completely understandable."

"So, what have you learned?" she asked.

"We found the woman who was taking care of Hayley. It was Stanley Tix's older sister, Carla. She said her brother rented her a house in Lake Geneva, Wisconsin for two weeks and told her he needed her to take care of a little girl who was in trouble. He claimed that Johnny was going to kill the child if Stan didn't hide her away, and that Johnny had already killed the girl's parents. Carla didn't have internet or cable at the house, so she claims she was unaware that the girl she was taking care of had been kidnapped."

"And local newspapers in Wisconsin might not have covered the kidnapping," Bree said. "He was smart to take her out of Illinois."

"Carla is still facing serious charges, but on first glance, it doesn't appear she did anything except take care of Hayley."

"I'm glad there was someone there to do that. What about the girl on the train? Emma and her sister, Tasha? Any word on who they were tied to?"

"Yes. Tasha is an actress. She and her sister, Emma, were standing in line at an open-call audition when a man approached them. He gave them $5000 cash to stay in the shelter for two nights and then hang in a car with him one day. She said they were outside the FBI office and they watched you walk to the train. Emma and her sister followed, Emma talked to you, then went to the café where she met up with Tasha. They left the flyer at the café and the photo in the shelter."

"Such an elaborate scheme," she murmured.

"Very complicated," Tracy agreed. "Not something most people would think of."

"I didn't know Stix was that clever," Nathan put in.

"The girls must have been able to give a description of their contact," Bree suggested.

"Yes, and we have a sketch of him." Tracy reached into her bag and pulled out a piece of paper. "Do you recognize him? He's apparently on the shorter side—five-five, Tasha thought. He's probably late twenties, brown hair, beard, bad skin."

Bree stared at the photo, but the face didn't seem at all familiar. "I don't know this guy."

She glanced at Nathan.

He shook his head. "I don't, either."

"That's too bad," Tracy said. "We don't have anything else to go on. He paid the girls in cash. He didn't tell them his name. They said they were in a gray car, but they didn't know the make or the license plate. The man didn't speak much beyond giving them instructions of what to do."

"I'm sure he was a minor level player," Bree commented, handing Tracy the sketch.

"That would be my guess," Tracy agreed. "We'll pass this on to organized crime. As they go through the members associated with Johnny and/or Stanley Tix, they may be able to identify him."

"I'd sure like to tie him up as a loose end. Stix did tell me that someone fed him the information about Hayley's birth and adoption, and I still don't know who that is."

"Neither do we, but I can tell you this—someone provided Stix with a great deal of information about you, not just about Hayley's birth. We found pages from your FBI file at the house in Wisconsin."

Her jaw dropped in shock. "What?"

"All the details from the investigations you've been conducting since you got to New York, reports and reviews dating back to your training at Quantico. We also found personal handwritten notes that refer to the adoption agency used by the Jansens and the name of a woman—Diane Miller. I'm assuming that's the same Diane you told us about, the one who had set you up in Detroit"

"Her last name was Brady when I knew her."

"They both could be aliases."

"What does this mean?" Nathan interrupted. "Are you saying that Stix had help from someone in the FBI? Who else could get an FBI file?"

"It sure looks that way," Tracy said. "And there's something else. Detective Charles Benedict was found dead of an overdose in his home last night."

Bree had almost thought she'd lost the ability to be shocked, but the hits just kept on coming. "Suicide?"

"It looks that way. He left a note saying he was sorry he'd crossed a line he shouldn't have crossed. We're not sure what it means yet, but it appears you were right about him being involved in some way."

"That's all the note said? Nothing more specific?" she asked.

"Unfortunately not. The police are investigating as well. We'll also look into any connections Benedict might have had with anyone in the bureau, in case he was the one who provided that FBI file to Mr. Tix." Tracy took a breath. "On a positive note, Hayley is safe. Johnny and a half-dozen men who worked for his criminal enterprise are dead. Stix and his associates are also dead. So, the streets are going to be safer for a lot of people."

"What about Sierra?" Nathan asked.

"She's not talking," Tracy replied. "But it doesn't appear she knows much of anything. I think that's it." She paused. "If we need more information from either of you, I'm sure someone will be in touch."

"Someone?" Bree asked curiously. "Not you?"

"I'm going to be on vacation the next week or so."

"Really? Where are you going?"

Tracy flushed. "I hear there's a lovely beach in Ecuador." She smiled. "You're going to see Diego."

"If he's in the area, I might look him up."

"Tell him I said hello."

"I don't know if it's a good idea," Tracy said, uncertainty in her gaze. "I haven't seen him in years."

And suddenly Bree wondered if this was really why Tracy had made the trip over to Nathan's apartment to brief them.

"I hadn't seen Nathan in eleven years. Sometimes time

doesn't matter."

"We'll see. I'm not quite the romantic you are."

"Bree is not romantic," Nathan said with a laugh. "I am the romantic one."

"Hey," she said, giving him a playful punch on the arm. "How can you say that?"

"Because it's true. You might be one badass, superwoman, FBI agent, but sentimental romantic stuff—that is not your thing. But I don't care, because I just need you, not the romance."

"Well, maybe I'll surprise you," she told him, knowing once again he was right about her.

Tracy smiled as she got to her feet. "I'm glad you two found each other again. And I'm glad you and I got to work together again, Bree. Good luck with whatever comes next."

"You, too," she said.

"I'll let myself out," Tracy added, nodding to Nathan.

As the door shut behind Tracy, Nathan said, "What do you think about all that? Was Detective Benedict Stix's connection? Or is there someone else we need to worry about?"

"I'm not sure. I'm unsettled by the fact that my FBI file was in the house in Wisconsin, but with Stix and Benedict both dead, I think we're okay. Stix was really the only one with motive. He could have paid someone to give him that file. Perhaps Detective Benedict used his agency connections to get it. The FBI and the police will probably dig up more information over the next few months."

"Months? I'd like the answers now."

"And here I thought I was the impatient one." She moved closer to him, wrapping her arms around his neck. "I think we're good, Nathan."

"We're very good," he said, giving her a kiss. "I just wish we could start the rest of our lives right now. But you have to go back to New York."

"And you need to finish your house. We'll be responsible people and take care of our obligations, and then we'll be free to do whatever we want to do."

"As long as we do it together, I'm happy." He gave her a wicked smile. "I am, however, feeling a little weak. I don't know if I'm completely healed from my injuries. I think I should go back to bed, and you should go with me."

"That sounds like a plan."

Epilogue

~~➤➤❮❮➤~~

Six weeks later

Bree landed at Chicago O'Hare a little before four and grabbed a cab to get into town. She had a six-hour layover in Chicago, which gave her just enough time to attend one very special birthday party before she and Nathan got another plane to Los Angeles. The next chapter in their lives was about to begin. She could hardly wait.

The last month and a half had been incredibly busy. She'd had to finish up the current work on her plate, which had been made easier by the arrest of the White Rose Kidnapper, thereby closing the biggest case she'd been working on. That man would be going to jail for the rest of his life.

In addition, she'd kept in touch with the Chicago team, who had wrapped up Hayley's kidnapping case. It appeared that Detective Benedict had been working with Stix, as the police had found evidence of several calls and a money transfer between them. She still didn't know how Benedict had gotten her FBI file, or figured out that Hayley was her child, but she was satisfied that the key players were dead.

Her last lingering concern had been that Johnny's family would try to lay claim to Hayley, but apparently Johnny had not had time to tell anyone in his family that Hayley was his daughter, and the FBI and police had kept that information out of the press, maintaining that Hayley's copycat kidnapping had been used to lure Bree to Chicago where Stix could get revenge on her and Johnny, the two people he believed had destroyed his life.

The only other person in Johnny's circle who knew differently was Sierra, but she'd kept her mouth shut, preferring to enjoy the money and the deed to her salon that Johnny had left her in his will.

Feeling confident that Hayley was out of danger, she'd moved forward with her own plans, calling contacts and scouring available jobs with the FBI office in Los Angeles, finally landing one in White-Collar Crime. Going after individuals and companies involved in financial and corporate fraud would be a nice change from the sadness that had often come with the CARD team. While she was very proud of the work she had done, she was ready to live a life that was not quite so dark, but she could still put criminals out of business.

She tapped her fingers impatiently on her thighs as the taxi took her to Lincoln Park. She thought about that morning almost seven weeks ago when she'd come to Chicago to find Hayley.

She'd found her daughter, her love, her life…and to think how afraid she'd been to return. Sometimes confronting the past was a good thing.

Finally, the cab pulled up in front of Hayley's house. There were no news vans out front, just two large bouquets of balloons on either side of the walkway. And coming down the street was Nathan. He must have been waiting for her.

She jumped out of the cab and threw herself into his arms.

They'd talked every day of the last six weeks, sometimes more than once, and they'd done a bunch of video chats, but now she was holding him, kissing him, sharing the love and the passion that had only grown deeper with absence. It was difficult to tear herself away, but she managed to do so with a breathless laugh.

"We better keep this PG-rated," she said. "We're on the sidewalk."

"I don't care," he said with a grin. "I've missed you, Bree."

"I've missed you, too." She kissed him again. "I'm so excited to start our life together. No regrets about leaving Chicago?"

"Not even a small one. I'm ready to go. Are you?"

"As soon as we do this," she said, feeling nervous for another reason.

She hadn't seen or spoken to Hayley or the Jansens since she'd dropped Hayley off at the hospital after the confrontation with Stix, but a week earlier, she'd received an invitation to Hayley's birthday party. It had obviously been written by Hayley, but there had been a small handwritten note attached from Lindsay, saying she hoped she could make it.

She knew from Nathan that Mark and Lindsay had not told Hayley that she was adopted yet. They felt it was too soon after the kidnapping, and they were following Hayley's therapist's advice to let things be for a while. They were, however, very much open to sharing Hayley's life with Bree and welcoming her into the house as a friend, if that worked for her.

"Am I doing the right thing?" she asked Nathan.

"If it's what you want, then you're doing the right thing."

She frowned. "That's not exactly the reassurance I was looking for."

"I think it would be great for Hayley to have you in her life, in whatever capacity you and her parents are willing to accept. I just don't know what it's going to do to you to be with her and not be able to tell her you're her birth mother. I don't want to see you sad or hurting. If this is going to be too difficult, we'll just drop that present on the porch," he said, motioning to the brightly-wrapped gift in her hand. "And head to the airport."

"It is going to be hard, but I want to do it. And you know what makes it a little easier?"

"What's that?"

"It's not Hayley's real birthday. That won't be for five days."

"That's right. The birth certificate was altered. Someone is going to have to fix that some time."

"Some time, but not now. Not while Hayley is still fragile."

"She's doing good. I've seen her once or twice. She's bouncing back. It will take time, but I think she'll be able to put all this behind her."

"I'm sure she's confused about what it was all about. Stix talked about her being my daughter when we were on the stage, but she was crying so loudly, I didn't know if she heard or not. I hoped she hadn't."

"She doesn't appear to have said anything about that."

"That's good."

He took her hand. "Let's go."

The front door was open, so they walked inside. The living room hallway, living room, and dining room were decorated with streamers and filled with kids and adults. A buffet had been spread out on the dining room table. A huge vanilla-iced birthday cake decorated with pink and purple bunnies sat on a side table. It was sure to be a hit with all the kids.

She searched the crowd for Hayley and felt a rush of love and happiness when her little girl came running down the hall. Hayley wore a pretty blue dress, her long brown hair flowing out behind her, her brown eyes glittering with happiness.

"You came," Hayley said with delight, as she held out her arms.

Bree swept her into a hug, so happy at Hayley's reaction. There was no shyness, no restraint, no lingering fear or sadness. When she let her go, she said, "Happy Birthday."

"I'm so glad you're here," Hayley said, hanging on to Bree's hand. "I want you to meet my parents and my friends and see my room."

"I want to do all of that," she said with a laugh.

"Come upstairs first," Hayley said.

She glanced back at Nathan. He gave her a smile and a nod of encouragement. "Go. I'll be right here. And take your time."

She would definitely take all the time that she was given, and she would cherish every second.

—➤➤◀◀—

"That goofy smile on your face must mean that Bree is somewhere nearby," Josie said, giving Nathan a nudge in the ribs with her elbow.

"She went upstairs with Hayley to see her room."

"Hayley is thrilled that Bree said she'd come to her party. She's been talking on and on about Bree to Grace. She's almost as taken with Bree as you are."

He grinned. "Bree is very loveable."

"Oh, I know. I always liked her. I just didn't always like the way she treated you."

"All that is in the past, Josie."

"I still don't know everything that happened."

"And you don't need to know," he said quickly. While he felt slightly guilty that he hadn't told Josie that Bree was Hayley's mother, he had to respect Bree's decision to keep the secret until the Jansens decided the truth should come out. "All that's important is what's coming next. I hope you and Grace and Kyle will consider doing Christmas in California this year. We'd like to host."

"Let's see…sunny, seventy-degree days in Santa Monica, or wind chill of minus eight in Chicago? It's a tough call. Yes, of course, we'll be there. I'm going to book tickets next week. And Kyle is going to make sure he gets the time off. After everything that happened with Hayley, I think he has started to realize the importance of spending time with your family when you can."

"I'm glad."

"And I'm glad you're with Bree. She's the love of your life. She always has been."

"Yes, she has," he admitted.

"While I'll miss you, I think starting over in California is going to be good for you. And you won't have to worry about snow; you can build houses all year round."

"I'm looking forward to the change. But I'm going to miss you and Grace—and Kyle," he added belatedly.

She laughed at that. "I know you and Kyle don't see eye-to-eye, but I love you both."

"I'm still going to keep my eye on you," he promised.

"I have no doubt." Her gaze turned serious. "But to be honest, Nathan, I have let you consider me your responsibility for far too long. I needed you when I was a kid. You got me through life. You saved me more than once. But I'm okay now. I probably should have said that a long time ago. I'm doing good, and I'm not in danger of going backward. I've got my life together. I'm not interested in drugs or alcohol or any of the vices I got swept up into. You don't have to worry about me anymore. Just be happy. It's your turn." She gave him a hug and blinked away some tears. "This sucks. I really hate good-byes."

"It's not good-bye. We're going to see each other at Christmas."

"I know. It won't be same, but it will be fine. And maybe one day you can give Grace a cousin."

"You're getting a little ahead of yourself."

"As if you haven't thought about having a little girl who looks just like Bree," she teased. "But a son would be good, too. I know Bree has a career, but maybe one day."

"Definitely one day," he promised.

—◆◆—

Bree smiled as she sat on the end of Hayley's bed and watched her daughter name off every one of the stuffed animals in her collection.

She'd never been able to hang on to her toys as a child. And she'd stopped naming anything, because as soon as she did, it was almost guaranteed to disappear. But Hayley didn't live with that uncertainty. And even though she'd been through a horrible ordeal, she seemed to now trust again in the safety of her life.

She was so glad to see that. She hated to think that her child would be forever scarred by someone wanting revenge on her and Johnny.

"Mommy got me a new bunny," Hayley said, taking a very white, very fluffy bunny from the center of her bed. "I left the other one at the house by the lake. But I like this one better."

"I love all your animals and your room. It's so pretty. I wish I would have had a room like this when I was growing up."

"Sometimes I get scared in the dark," Hayley said suddenly, her gaze turning serious. "Sometimes, Mommy sleeps with me. I think she gets scared, too."

"I understand. But you don't have to be afraid anymore. You're safe now."

"I wish you could stay here. Mommy says you don't live in Chicago."

"No, I don't," she said, a lump growing in her throat. "But I'll come and visit you whenever I can. And you can write me if you want."

"Will you write me back? I like to get email. I like to get real letters, too. Which do you like?"

"I like them both. And I will definitely write you back. I will always be available if you need me, Hayley. You can write me or call me. I'll make sure you always have my phone number."

"Mommy says you're like my guardian angel."

"I like the sound of that," she said with a smile. "Too bad

I don't have any wings."

Hayley giggled. "Then you could fly."

"That would be fun." She looked up as Lindsay came into the room with a tentative expression on her face.

"I hope I'm not interrupting," Lindsay said. "It's time to open your presents, Hayley."

"Yay!" Hayley clapped her hands with delight.

"Why don't you go downstairs and help Grandma put them in a pile for you?" Lindsay suggested. "Bree and I will be right down."

"Okay."

As Hayley ran from the room, Bree got to her feet. "I appreciate you inviting me."

"Hayley really wanted you to come. She's been talking about you nonstop since you left." She paused. "I wanted you to come, too. I never had a chance to really say thank you."

"You wrote me a nice note."

"It didn't begin to express what I was feeling. You saved Hayley's life. Nathan told me what you did—how you shielded her body with your own. You risked your life. So did Nathan. And Mark and I are forever grateful."

"I'm just sorry Hayley was ever in danger and that it was because of me."

"It was because of a crazy person. You told me not to blame myself for Hayley's abduction. I have to return the favor. It's not your fault what happened. And having learned a bit about Hayley's biological father, I can understand why you felt the need to give up your child and disappear. I worry a little still that someone in his family might try to claim her, but as the weeks pass, I feel a bit more secure that that won't happen."

"I don't think you have to worry about it. The Hawkes are busy fighting over who is going to take over for Johnny. Their world is far from here. And Hayley isn't a part of it."

"I'm glad about that."

"Johnny did take a bullet for Hayley," Bree couldn't help pointing out. "I won't try to tell you he was a good person, because he obviously was not, but when I knew him as a young man, he wasn't nearly as evil or as cold as he grew up to be. In the end, he died for his child, and that's something. I hope that when Hayley is older, when she wants or needs more information, she can take that one piece of him and hold it close." She took a breath. "I never knew who my father was. I'd like to think he would have taken a bullet for me, but probably not."

"You had a very rough life, didn't you? Nathan has told us a little about your past. I didn't realize he'd had such difficult life, either."

"Well, all that seems like a long time ago now."

"You're an amazing person, Bree. I feel a little guilty that Hayley doesn't know who you really are to her, but I can tell you that she already loves you."

"I love her, too. She said that I could be her guardian angel, and I think I would like that."

"Really?" Lindsay asked uncertainly. "You're still okay with us waiting to tell her the truth?"

"I trust you and Mark. You have been magnificent parents to my daughter. I want Hayley to know when you want her to know, when it's the right time." She fought her way through a sudden rush of tears, wanting to say what she needed to say. "I wanted Hayley to have a great mother, someone she could always count on, and you are that person, Lindsay. I didn't have a mom like you when I was growing up, and it's a gift, a very special gift."

Lindsay dabbed at her eyes. "That's a very sweet thing to say."

"It's the truth."

"Mark and I have been talking to my parents about moving out of Chicago. We're thinking about going to Austin. My aunt lives there, and Mark has job opportunities. We wouldn't mind putting some distance between ourselves and everything that happened here."

"That makes sense."

"But we would definitely still keep in touch with you."

"I hope so. I told Hayley I would always be available if she needs me."

"I'm sure she appreciated that," Lindsay said. "So, you and Nathan are going to be Californians…"

"Yes. We always dreamed about the beach when we were kids. We decided it was time to make the dream happen."

"Nathan said he always loved you, but it was never right…until now."

"He's a good man. And I am very lucky to have found him again."

"Well, we better go downstairs and watch Hayley open her presents."

"That sounds good to me." She followed Lindsay downstairs. Hayley was sitting in a big chair with the birthday party guests packed into the living room, the kids sitting on the floor, the parents perched on every available piece of furniture.

Nathan was standing in the entryway. He put his arm around her as Lindsay moved into the room to sit next to Hayley.

"How did it go?" he asked quietly.

She gazed into his eyes. "Really, really well. This party, this loving crowd, this beautiful family—it's the kind of life we always dreamed about, Nathan, and my daughter is living it. That's something great."

"Yes, it is."

"I'm so glad I came." She leaned her head against his chest, feeling more happiness than she'd ever imagined possible.

The next day, Bree woke up in Manhattan Beach. After a long flight the night before, they'd landed just before midnight and had taken a cab to the small house they'd rented for a month while they looked around for a more permanent location. Too exhausted to explore, they'd tumbled into bed and into sleep.

But now the sun was shining through the curtains and she was eager to take a better look around her new home. Nathan was already out of bed, so he'd obviously gotten a head start on her.

She washed up, threw on leggings, a workout top, and a pair of flip-flops and headed down the hall.

She could see Nathan standing outside on the deck. She grabbed a cup of coffee on her way out to join him. Setting her mug on the wide rail, she gave him a happy smile. "We finally have our view."

"Yes, we do. What do you think?"

"It's perfect."

"They were standing on the second floor of their rental house, and the deck overlooked the strand, a wide pavement for biking, jogging and strolling that ran for several miles, alongside the beaches of Manhattan, Hermosa, and Redondo. It was a great place for people watching. And on the other side of the strand was a wide swath of sand leading out to the Pacific Ocean.

"It's just like your poster," Nathan said. "The one you put up in your room so many years ago. Endless blue sky, the Pacific ocean, and even one sailboat."

"I can't believe how lucky we are to be here."

"I don't think luck had much to do with it. We both worked hard to get here."

"And we're here. We're holding the dream in our hands."

"Well, not quite," he said, taking her hands in his. "Now, we are."

She gazed into his beautiful brown eyes and felt an enormous wave of love. "Have I told you lately that I love you?"

"I think it's been at least a few hours."

"Well, I do."

"I love you, too." He gave her a tender kiss. "We could go back to bed."

"That sounds tempting, but I was thinking we should explore. It's such a beautiful day. Let's take a walk, find a market, pick up some food. I'm going to cook for you tonight."

"Hold on—you're going to cook?"

"Yes, and you know what's on the menu?" she said with a playful smile.

He groaned. "No way. Not our first night in California."

"Californians love Brussels sprouts. And you are going to love mine. You'll try one, right?"

"Have I ever been able to deny you anything?"

"Actually, I think you have said no a few times."

He laughed. "Let's not talk about that. Shall we go? I am kind of hungry now, and before we think about dinner, I'd like to grab some breakfast. It looks like there's a beachside café down there." He pointed to where a group of people were waiting outside, menus in hand.

"Let's do it."

Nathan grabbed their house keys and they walked downstairs and around to the strand. There were a ton of people out, which probably wasn't surprising on a Saturday morning. What was surprising was that it was almost Thanksgiving and it was already seventy degrees.

"I think I'm going to like this weather," Nathan said, putting his arm around her shoulders.

"It's so warm. I can't believe it. I'm surprised you didn't go for a run this morning."

"I might go later. It will certainly be different being able to run outside during the winter."

"I don't think they have winter here." She paused as they neared the restaurant. "It looks crowded."

"I'll go inside and put our name in and grab some menus."

"Sounds good," she said, not wanting to fight through the line.

Nathan came back a moment later and handed her a menu. "Twenty minutes for a table, they said."

"That's fine. Let's sit over there." She started to move across the pavement when a man on a skateboard came around the corner, almost knocking her down.

Nathan quickly pulled her back against him.

The man gave her a quick look, and then continued on his way.

Her heart was suddenly beating fast, and it had nothing to do with almost being knocked over.

"Are you okay?" Nathan asked with concern.

"That—that was Wyatt," she said.

"Who's Wyatt?"

"One of my friends from Quantico."

Nathan gave her a doubtful look. "The scruffy guy on the board with a thick beard and the baseball cap is a federal agent?"

"One who often works undercover." She looked down the path, but Wyatt had disappeared.

Had it been him?

It had certainly looked like him. But why wouldn't he have said hello, instead of the quick stare, and the even faster takeoff?

"Maybe I'm wrong. I'm probably wrong," she said.

"You want to go after him?"

"No. I want to have breakfast with you. I want to focus on us. If it was Wyatt, and he needs to talk to me, he'll get in touch. Until then, I'm not going to worry about it."

They crossed over to a low cement wall and sat down. After a brief perusal of the menus, they set them to the side, put their arms around each other and took in the beautiful view.

"I'm going to make you happy, Bree," Nathan promised, turning his head to look at her. "No more loneliness for you. I'm going to stick so close, you'll get sick of me."

"I don't think that's possible. I'm going to make you happy, too. And I was thinking maybe one day..." She was afraid to finish the thought.

"What?" he asked curiously.

"Nothing. It's too soon."

"What's too soon? You know you can't keep secrets from me. Tell me what you want."

"I want us to have a family. I'd like to have a child with you, Nathan."

"I'd like that, too."

"I'm not ready quite yet," she added. "There's a scared, cynical part of me that's a little afraid to trust in all this perfection. I'm afraid to jinx it by planning for the future. That's usually when things go wrong."

"Nothing will go wrong," he promised. "Look around you—we've got nothing but blue skies."

"Storms always come."

"If they come, we'll just ride them out. We'll hold each other and let the thunder roll over us."

She smiled into his eyes, knowing she could trust this man to stick with her no matter what came their way, and she would stick with him. "Yes, we will," she said, and then she leaned in and gave him a kiss. "I think I've changed my mind about breakfast."

He laughed. "Me, too. Race you back?"

"You're on."

THE END

Want more
OFF THE GRID: FBI Series?

Available in 2018
Desperate Play (#3)

Available in 2019
Elusive Promise (#4)
Dangerous Choice (#5)

Continue reading for an excerpt from
Barbara Freethy's NYT Bestselling Book

SILENT RUN

Excerpt from
SILENT RUN

—➤ ➽ ⫷ ⪡—

A woman wakes in a hospital bed with no idea of who she is. Her memory is gone, her baby missing. All she has is the gripping certainty that she is in mortal danger. Then a handsome, angry stranger barges in and makes a terrible accusation. He was her lover--and her child's father--until she disappeared seven months ago.

Jake Sanders swore he'd never forgive Sarah Tucker, but he isn't about to let her get away again--especially not with his daughter still missing. If he has any chance of recovering his baby, he must help the woman who betrayed him retrieve the pieces of her shattered memory--without letting his feelings get in the way.

Haunted by troubling flashes of memory, Sarah begins to realize she's lived a life of lies. But what is the truth? And where is her baby?

Prologue

Large raindrops streamed against her windshield as she sped along the dark, narrow highway north of Los Angeles. She'd been traveling for over an hour along the wild and beautiful Pacific coastline. She'd passed the busy beach cities of Venice and Santa Monica, the celebrity-studded hills of Malibu and Santa Barbara. Thank God it was a big state. She could start over again, find a safe place to stay, but she had to get there first.

The pair of headlights in her rearview mirror drew closer with each passing mile. Her nerves began to tighten, and goose bumps rose along her arms and the back of her neck. She'd been running too long not to recognize danger. But where had the car come from? She'd been so sure that no one had followed her out of LA. After sixty miles of constantly checking her rearview mirror she'd begun to relax, but now the fear came rushing back.

It was too dark to see the car behind her, but there was something about the speed with which it was approaching that made her nervous. She pressed her foot down harder on the gas, clinging to the wheel as gale-force winds blowing in off the ocean rocketed through the car, making the driving even more treacherous.

A few miles later the road veered inland. She looked for

a place to exit. Finally she saw a sign for an upcoming turnoff heading into the Santa Ynez Mountains. Maybe with a few twists and turns she could lose the car on her tail, and if her imagination were simply playing tricks on her, the car behind her would just continue down the road.

The exit came up fast. She took the turn on two wheels. Five minutes later the pair of headlights was once again directly behind her. There was no mistake: He was coming after her.

She had to get away from him. Adrenaline raced through her bloodstream, giving her courage and strength. She was so tired of running for her life, but she couldn't quit now. She'd probably made a huge mistake leaving the main highway. There was no traffic on this two-lane road. If he caught her now there would be no one to come to her rescue.

The gap between their cars lessened. He was so close she could see the silhouette of a man in her rearview mirror. He was bearing down on her.

She took the next turn too sharply, her tires sliding on the slick, wet pavement.

Sudden lights coming from the opposite direction blinded her. She hit the brakes hard. The car skidded out of control. She flew across the road, crashed through a wooden barrier, and hurtled down a steep embankment. Rocks splintered the windshield as she threw up her hands in protest and prayer.

When the impact finally came it was crushing, the pain intense. It was too much. All she wanted to do was to sink into oblivion. It was over. She was finished.

But some voice deep inside her screamed at her to stay awake, because if she wasn't dead yet, she soon would be.

Chapter One

The blackness in her mind began to lessen. There was a light behind her eyelids that beckoned and called to her. She was afraid to answer that call, terrified to open her eyes. Maybe it was the white light people talked about, the one to follow when you were dead. But she wasn't dead, was she?

It was just a nightmare, she told herself. She was dreaming; she'd wake up in a minute. But something was wrong. Her bed didn't feel right. The mattress was hard beneath her back. There were odd bells going off in her head. She smelled antiseptic and chlorine bleach. A siren wailed in the distance. Someone was talking to her, a man.

Her stomach clenched with inexplicable fear as she felt a strong hand on her shoulder. Her eyes flew open, and she blinked rapidly, the scene before her confusing.

She wasn't home in her bedroom, as she'd expected. A man in a long white coat stood next to the bed. He appeared to be in his fifties, with salt-and-pepper hair, dark eyes, and a serious expression. He held a clipboard in one hand. A stethoscope hung around his neck, and a pair of glasses rested on his long, narrow nose. Next to him stood a short, plump brunette dressed in blue scrubs, offering a compassionate, encouraging smile that seemed to match the name on her name tag, Rosie.

What was going on? Where was she?

"You're awake," the doctor said, a brisk note in his voice, a gleam of satisfaction in his eyes. "That's good. We were getting concerned about you. You've been unconscious for hours."

Unconscious? She gazed down the length of her body, suddenly aware of the thin blue gown, the hospital identification band on her wrist, the IV strapped to her left arm. And pain—there was pain... in her head, her right wrist, and her knees. Her right cheek throbbed. She raised a hand to her temple and was surprised to encounter a bandage. What on earth had happened to her?

"You were in an automobile accident last night," the doctor told her. "You have some injuries, but you're going to be all right. You're at St. Mary's Hospital just outside of Los Olivos in Santa Barbara County. I'm Dr. Carmichael. Do you understand what I'm saying?"

She shook her head, his brisk words jumbling up in her brain, making little to no sense. "Am I dreaming?" she whispered.

"You're not dreaming, but you do have a head injury. It's not unusual to be confused," the doctor replied. He offered her a small, practiced smile that was edged with impatience. "Now, do you feel up to a few questions? Why don't we start with your name?"

She opened her mouth to reply, thinking that was an easy question, until nothing came to mind. Her brain was blank. What was her name? She had to have one. Everyone did. What on earth was wrong with her? She gave a helpless shake of her head. "I'm... I'm not sure," she murmured, shocked by the realization.

The doctor frowned, his gaze narrowing on her face. "You don't remember your name? What about your address, or where you're from?"

She bit down on her bottom lip, straining to think of the right answers. Numbers danced in her head, but no streets, no cities, no states. A wave of terror rushed through her. She had to be dreaming—lost in a nightmare. She wanted to run, to scream, to wake herself up, but she couldn't do any of those things.

"You don't know, do you?" the nurse interjected.

"I... I should know. Why don't I know? What's wrong with me? Why can't I remember my name, where I'm from? What's going on?" Her voice rose with each desperate question.

"Your brain suffered a traumatic injury," Dr. Carmichael explained. "It may take some time for you to feel completely back to normal. It's probably nothing to worry about. You just need to rest, let the swelling go down."

His words were meant to be reassuring, but anxiety ran like fire through her veins. She struggled to remember something about herself. Glancing down at her hands, she saw the light pink, somewhat chipped polish on her fingernails and wondered how it could be that her own fingers didn't look familiar to her. She wore no rings, no jewelry, not even a watch. Her skin was pale, her arms thin. But she had no idea what her face looked like.

"A mirror," she said abruptly. "Could someone get me a mirror?"

Dr. Carmichael and Rosie exchanged a brief glance, and then he nodded to the nurse, who quickly left the room. "You need to try to stay calm," he said as he jotted something down on his clipboard. "Getting upset won't do you any good."

"I don't know my name. I don't know what I look like." Hysteria bubbled in her throat, and panic made her want to jump out of bed and run... but to where, she had no idea. She tried to breathe through the rush of adrenaline. If this were a nightmare, eventually she'd wake up. If it wasn't... well, then she'd have to figure out what to do next. In the meantime she had to calm down. She had to think.

The doctor said she'd had an accident. Like the car crash in her dream? Was it possible that had been real and not a dream?

Glancing toward the clock, she saw that it was seven thirty. At least she knew how to read the time. "Is it night or morning?" Her gaze traveled to the window, but the heavy blue curtain was drawn, making it impossible for her to see outside.

"It's morning," the doctor replied. "You were brought in around nine o'clock last night."

Almost ten hours ago. So much time had passed. "Do you know what happened to me?"

"I'm afraid I don't know the details, but from what I understand, you were in a serious car accident."

Before she could ask another question, the nurse returned to the room and handed her a small compact mirror.

She opened the compact with shaky fingers, almost afraid of what she would see. She stared at her face for a long minute. Her eyes were light blue, framed by thick black lashes. Her hair was a dull dark brown, long, tangled, and curly, dropping past her shoulders. There were dark circles under her eyes, as well as purple bruises that were accentuated by the pallor of her skin. A white bandage was taped across her temple. Multiple tiny cuts covered her cheekbones. Her face was thin, drawn. She looked like a ghost. Even her eyes were haunted by shadows.

"Oh, God," she whispered, feeling as if she were looking at a complete stranger. Who was she?

"The cuts will heal," the nurse said. "Don't worry. You'll have your pretty face back before you know it."

It wasn't the bruises on her face that filled her heart with terror; it was the fact that she didn't recognize anything about herself. She felt absolutely no connection to the woman in the mirror. She slammed the compact shut, afraid to look any longer. Her pulse raced, and her heart beat in triple time as the reality of her situation sank in. She felt completely vulnerable, and she wanted to run and hide until she figured everything out. She would have jumped out of bed if Dr.

Carmichael hadn't put his hand on her shoulder, perhaps sensing her desperation.

"You're going to be all right," he said firmly, meeting her gaze. "The answers will come. Don't push too hard. Just rest and let your body recuperate from the trauma."

"What if the answers don't come?" she whispered. "What if I'm like this forever?"

He frowned, unable to hide the concern in his eyes. "Let's take it one step at a time. There's a deputy from the sheriff's office down the hall. He'd like to speak to you."

A police officer wanted to talk to her? That didn't sound good. She swallowed back another lump of fear. "Why? Why does he want to talk to me?"

"Something to do with your accident. I'll let him know you're awake."

As the doctor left the room, Rosie stepped forward. "Can I get you anything—water, juice, an extra blanket? The mornings are still so cold. I can't wait until April. I don't know about you, but I'm tired of the rain. I'm ready for the sun to come out."

That meant it was March, the end of a long, cold winter, spring on the nearby horizon. Images ran through her mind of windy afternoons, flowers beginning to bloom, someone flying a kite, a beautiful red-and-gold kite that tangled in the branches of a tall tree. The laughter of a young girl filled her head—was it her laughter or someone else's? She saw two other girls and a boy running across the grass. She wanted to catch up to them, but they were too far away, and then they were gone, leaving her with nothing but a disturbing sense of loss and a thick curtain of blackness in her head.

Why couldn't she remember? Why had her brain locked her out of her own life?

"What day is it?" she asked, determined to gather as many details as she possibly could.

"It's Thursday, March twenty-second," Rosie replied with another sympathetic smile.

"Thursday," she murmured, feeling relieved to have a new fact to file away, even if it was something as inconsequential as the day of the week.

"Try not to worry. You'll be back to normal before you know it," Rosie added.

"I don't even know what normal is. Where are my things?" she asked abruptly, looking for more answers. Maybe if she had something of her own to hold in her hand, everything would come back to her.

Rosie tipped her head toward a neat pile of clothes on a nearby chair. "That's what you were wearing when they brought you in. You didn't have a purse with you, nor were you wearing any jewelry."

"Could you hand me my clothes, please? "

"Sure. They're a bit bloodied," Rosie said, as she gathered up the clothes and laid them on the bed. "I'll check on you in a while. Just push the call button if you need anything."

She stared at the pair of blue jeans, which were ripped at the knees, the light blue camisole top, the navy sweater, and the gray jacket dotted with dark spots of blood or dirt, she wasn't sure which. Glancing across the room she saw a pair of Nike tennis shoes on the floor. They looked worn-out, as if she'd done a lot of running in them.

Another memory flashed in her brain. She could almost feel herself running, the wind in her hair, her heart pounding, the breath tight in her chest. But she wasn't out for a jog. She wasn't dressed right. She was wearing a heavy coat, a dress, and high stiletto heels. She tried to hang on to the image floating vaguely in her head, but it disappeared as quickly as it had come. She supposed she should feel grateful she'd remembered something, but the teasing bit only frustrated her more.

She dug her hands into the pockets of her jeans and jacket, searching for some clue as to who she was, but there was nothing there. She was about to put the jacket aside when she noticed an odd lump in the inner back lining. She ran her fingers across the material, surprised to find a flap covering a hidden zipper. She pulled on the zipper and felt inside, shocked when she pulled out a wad of twenty-dollar bills. There had to be at least fifteen hundred dollars. Why on earth had she stashed so much cash in her jacket? Obviously she'd taken great care to hide it, as someone would have had to examine the jacket carefully in order to find the money. Whoever had undressed her had not discovered the cash.

A knock came at her door, and she hurriedly stuffed the money back into her jacket and set it on the end of her bed just seconds before a uniformed police officer entered the room. Her pulse jumped at the sight of him, and it wasn't with relief but with fear. Her instincts were screaming at her to be cautious, that he could be trouble.

The officer was on the stocky side, with a military haircut, and appeared to be in his mid-forties. His forehead was lined, his skin a ruddy red and weatherbeaten, his gaze extremely serious.

"I'm Tom Manning," he said briskly. "I'm a deputy with the county sheriff's department. I'm investigating your car accident."

"Okay," she said warily. "I should tell you that I don't remember what happened. In fact, I don't remember anything about myself."

"Yeah, the doc says you have some kind of amnesia."

His words were filled with suspicion, and skepticism ran through his dark eyes. Why was he suspicious? What reason could she possibly have for pretending not to remember? Had something bad occurred during the accident? Had she done something wrong? Had someone else been hurt? Her stomach turned over at the thought.

"Can you tell me what happened?" she said, almost afraid to ask.

"Your car went off the side of the road in the Santa Ynez Mountains, not far from San Marcos Pass. You plunged down a steep embankment and landed in a ravine about two hundred yards from the road. Fortunately, you ran into a tree."

"Fortunately?" she echoed.

"Otherwise you would have ended up in a boulder-filled, high-running creek," he told her. "The front end of your Honda Civic was smashed, and the windshield was shattered."

Which explained the cuts and bruises on her face.

"You're a very lucky woman," the deputy added.

"Who found me?" she asked.

"A witness saw your car go over the side and called nine-one-one. Does any of this sound familiar?"

The part about going off the side of the road sounded a lot like the dream she'd been having. "I'm not sure."

"Were you alone in the car?"

His question surprised her. "I think so." She thought back to her dream. Had she been alone in the car? She didn't remember anyone else. "If I wasn't alone, wouldn't that other person be here at the hospital?" she asked.

"The back door of your car was open. There was a child's car seat strapped in the middle of the backseat, a bottle half-filled with milk, and this shoe." Officer Manning held up a clear plastic bag through which she could see a shoe so small it would fit into the palm of her hand. Her heart began to race. She had the sudden urge to call for a time-out, to make him leave before he said something else, something terrifying, something to do with that shoe. "Oh, God. Stop. I can't do this."

"I'm sorry, but I need to know. Do you have a baby?" he asked. "Was your child with you in the car?"

END OF EXCERPT

About The Author

Barbara Freethy is a #1 New York Times Bestselling Author of 66 novels ranging from contemporary romance to romantic suspense and women's fiction. Traditionally published for many years, Barbara opened her own publishing company in 2011 and has since sold over 7 million books! Twenty of her titles have appeared on the New York Times and USA Today Bestseller Lists.

Known for her emotional and compelling stories of love, family, mystery and romance, Barbara enjoys writing about ordinary people caught up in extraordinary adventures. Barbara's books have won numerous awards. She is a six-time finalist for the RITA for best contemporary romance from Romance Writers of America and a two-time winner for DANIEL'S GIFT and THE WAY BACK HOME.

Barbara has lived all over the state of California and currently resides in Northern California where she draws much of her inspiration from the beautiful bay area.

For a complete listing of books, as well as excerpts and contests, and to connect with Barbara:

Visit Barbara's Website:
www.barbarafreethy.com

Join Barbara on Facebook:
www.facebook.com/barbarafreethybooks

Follow Barbara on Twitter:
www.twitter.com/barbarafreethy